DOCTOR WHO

HOPE

MARK CLAPHAM

GW00670916

B B C

Published by BBC Worldwide Ltd
Woodlands, 80 Wood Lane
London W12 0TT

First published 2002
Copyright © Mark Clapham 2002
The moral right of the author has been asserted

Original series broadcast on the BBC
Format © BBC 1963
Doctor Who and TARDIS are trademarks of the BBC

ISBN 0 563 53846 5
Imaging by Black Sheep, copyright © BBC 2002

Printed and bound in Great Britain by Mackays of
Chatham
Cover printed by Belmont Press Ltd, Northampton

Dedicated to the co-authors who got me where I am today:
Lance Parkin, Simon Bucher-Jones and Jonathan de Burgh
Miller.

Prologue
Don't Forget to Catch Me

Cool water rippled in the afternoon sun, coursing over the two ramps of shiny black rock. The water flowed smoothly down the polished twin surfaces, the only obstacle in its constant descent the maple-leaf motifs carved into the rock, emblems of the country whose soldiers the memorial commemorated.

'"In two world wars, one million Canadians came to Britain and joined the fight for freedom",' said Dave Young, reading from the engraved disc on the ground nearby. '"From danger shared our friendship prospered."'

'It's beautiful,' said Anji Kapoor. She stepped up behind Dave and gave him a hug, standing on tiptoe to kiss the back of his neck. 'And you always read so nicely.' Dave was an actor, his speaking voice one of his great assets.

'Thanks,' said Dave, gently turning in her arms and snaking his own arms around her waist. He held her close, kissed her on the lips, then pulled back.

'Come on,' he said, thinking of the ageing Canadian tourists nearby. 'I don't think this is appropriate behaviour for a war memorial.'

Green Park in the summer was full of tourists, yellow backpacks and clicking cameras everywhere. From where Anji and Dave sat, in the shade of an ancient tree, they could see summer-school students clambering over the nearby Victoria Monument, while others peered through the railings around Buckingham Palace. So much activity, so much eagerness to *see* and to *do*. It was days like this Anji felt lucky to live in London, to be able to live with its sights and sounds, get to know them in her own time rather than rush around the place on a tour bus. To find a tall tree in the heart of the city, and sit beneath it in the arms of her boyfriend.

'When I'm dead and gone,' said Anji jokingly, pointing to the monument, 'will you have a tacky gold statue put up in my memory?'

Dave shivered, even though it was a warm day. Anji felt him hold her slightly tighter. 'Don't joke about that. I'm not letting you die any time soon.'

'Sorry,' Anji said quietly. 'I haven't got you down, have I?' She tugged his sleeve affectionately.

'Nah,' said Dave hesitantly. 'It's just I don't like thinking about it. Neither of us is going to live forever.' He wrapped his arm around her, kissing the back of her neck.

She wriggled in his grasp, turning around to face him. His expression seemed haunted, far removed from the usual carefree Dave.

'Hey,' Anji said firmly, giving him a chastening slap on the shoulder. 'This is silly. It's not like either of us is going to drop dead tomorrow.'

Dave looked about to protest, but she froze him in a glare of certainty, and he backed down before he had begun.

'Yeah, I suppose you're right,' he said.

'Of course I'm right,' she replied, getting to her feet. 'Now come on.' She tugged his arm, pulling him to his feet. 'An ice cream will cheer you up.'

'Can I have a flake?' he asked, a wry smile returning.

'If you're good,' she replied slyly, kissing him on the cheek.

Bleak thought dispelled, Anji and Dave wandered arm-in-arm through the sun-drenched day.

Part One
Headhunt

Chapter One
Out of the Box

That last card might as well have been from the tarot pack, thought Kyrro as he was hastily ejected from the Silver Palace. A low four, when he needed at least a seven. The card should have had 'Death' written across it, an etching of the grim reaper looking out from it, that would have been appropriate for the gravity of the situation. Kyrro's credit limit was up, his account at the Palace dry until he could prove himself solvent once more. The croupier had looked up from the card with an expression close to pity, clearly knowing Kyrro was a dead man walking. Out of luck, out of cash, and soon after out in the cold. Kyrro had protested slightly, but the head of security, Myra-whatever, only needed to suggest that Kyrro take up his grievance with the Palace's owner for him to shut up and accept his expulsion.

Kyrro slid his breath filter over his mouth and nose. He may be broke but he at least had a couple of the basics covered. Breather, decent clothes, a place to stay – even if that place was on the other side of Hope, requiring an unenviable night-time walk. At least he had those few things, more than the real derelicts, the 'swingers' who lived between the city's stilts, hanging from girders and living on scraps, their unprotected lungs raw from the fumes rising from the waters beneath. At least Kyrro had some dignity left, some small way to go before he sank to the level of those poor wretches.

The caustic smog and the effects of alcohol were blurring Kyrro's vision, so he was especially careful as he stumbled down the rusty metal steps to the lower levels, the dim glow from tenement windows lighting his way as the steps weaved around the towers. The steps led to a walkway towards the edge of the city, hidden in the lower levels with only the flare of the occasional gaslight to illuminate the concourse. The boards creaked as Kyrro walked, peering downwards to make sure there weren't any missing slats. If he fell now, down into the toxic soup below, there would be no witnesses, no evidence of his passing. Kyrro knew he was going to die one day. He just couldn't stand the idea of going unnoticed.

A vicious sea breeze stung Kyrro's eyes as he reached the edge, where a pierledge would lead him around to his lodgings in one of the bloated habi-clusters that clung to the edge of the town. At least this area was better lit, the watchtowers dotted around Hope's 'coastline' casting a fierce sodium glare over everything around them. Kyrro could hear the raucous conversation of militia members patrolling the upper levels, close enough to be audible but too far up for Kyrro to make out any words.

And then there was something else, another sound somewhere nearby. Kyrro stopped dead in his tracks – if it were the creaking of a girder about to snap, or the bubbling prelude to a gas explosion, he would need to get away fast. He listened carefully, backing away slightly as he realised there was a scratchy, scrabbling noise coming from somewhere nearby, somewhere just ahead and slightly below where he was. It was only when the hand gripped the railing and the white figure dragged itself over on to the path that Kyrro realised what that implied. And by then he was already running.

In the spaces between space itself, in the timeless region outside time, a blue box spins through the void. Both creature and machine, yet strangely neither, this blue box is a TARDIS, a travelling machine skimming across the surface of space-time, occasionally dipping below the surface to spend a while in the murky depths of reality, where days pass in order and the laws of science stay constant. This TARDIS disguises itself as a police box, an old communications device from a planet called Earth, a thing of wood and blue paint with a flashing light on top. Inside, the TARDIS – which, what with the rules of physics having no bearing outside conventional space-time, is bigger inside than out – adopts a different guise, that of a technological marvel, gleaming white futurism decorated in a refined Victorian manner.

In the ship's console room, its apparent centre, stands the ship's captain, a man called the Doctor who is more of a 'man' than he once was. While once two hearts pumped within the Doctor's chest, now only a single pulse beats beneath his ribs. Fortunately for the Doctor, his second heart allows him to survive the death of the first. Less fortunately, much of what separated him from the common humans around him seems to have gone with his now cold heart. Though he would never admit it, considering himself something of a libertarian, he has always felt like a lord, walking amongst lesser beings for a hundred years. Now he is just another man. His appearance belies this humbled status – an aristocratic figure with a noble bearing, sharp blue eyes and flowing chestnut curls, the Doctor wears finely pressed clothes as he stands at the TARDIS's central console, deep in thought. As he thinks, he rubs his newly shaven chin, unconsciously searching for his recently departed beard.

Fitz Kreiner is a different matter. He lies on a sofa near where the Doctor stands, and he has never been bothered by being considered a lesser man, or even less than a man. While he occasionally embraces the extraordinary, Fitz's lanky stature and shabby dress sense show him to be a twentieth-century everyman. While the Doctor prowls the console, determined to control where the TARDIS may land next, Fitz is accustomed to travel. He appreciates the journey, wherever it may take him.

Away from the console room, down twisting white corridors, are a number of rooms, and in one of these the TARDIS's other passenger stirs in her sleep, pushing towards wakefulness.

Anji Kapoor woke up slowly, her conscious mind gradually lifting itself out of that dark, warm place inside her head where dreams took place, and letting her senses take in her environment. Anji tentatively stuck her head out from under the covers, eyes and ears open. There was a soft machine hum in the background, and glowing circles embedded in the walls around her. She was in the TARDIS. Home. What a relief.

She grinned sleepily at the thought that the TARDIS was now her home, her idea of familiarity, of safety and comfort. The whole idea was ludicrous. The TARDIS was, after all, an alien time machine; dozens of glowing white, futuristic rooms packed into a little blue telephone box. Not what she'd ever imagined as her dream home. But, compared to all the places she'd been of late, this alien call box was home. Or at least a better, safer place to wake up than a storm-lashed wasteland in the path of a city-machine, or in the attic room where an Ogre's mother had made dresses for several ugly sisters, or any of the other places she had woken up in the past few months.

Anji wondered how long she had slept. There was no day and night in the TARDIS, no windows for the sun to shine through. It could be whatever time Anji wanted it to be.

Anji decided that whatever time it was, it probably wasn't time to get up. Besides, she knew that a vital skill for getting through periods of intense exertion was being able to totally relax when the opportunity arose. When under pressure at work, she'd always found the time for a long hot bath in the evening, usually on a Thursday night when Dave was busy wading through his comics.

Dave. The thought of him made Anji tense with guilt, as if she wasn't allowed to be content without him. It had only been a matter of months since her boyfriend had died, the man she had lived with for years. Surely, lying in a warm bed, she should still feel the absence of him, still be painfully aware that he wasn't there beside her? But, of all the things she had considered possible as she awoke, Anji had never believed Dave was there with her.

She had become used to waking up alone. It didn't upset her any more, and this realisation in itself was enough to bring on a twinge of grief and guilt, a guilt only increased by her full awareness that the end of her mourning, the fact that she had moved on and into a new phase, was a perfectly healthy thing for her.

8

In some stupid, irrational way she just couldn't help feeling that Dave deserved better than for her to get over his death like this. But what more could she do? Taken away from home, thrown into danger wherever she went. Life in the TARDIS hardly lent itself to periods of contemplation.

It was unhealthy to lie around letting matters such as these fester in an unoccupied mind, thought Anji. Like it or not, it was time to get up and get on with things. She threw back the covers and, casting unproductive thoughts aside, rose from her bed to start the day.

Whatever time of day it actually was.

Kyrro had barely seen whatever had come over the rails. The fog had stung his eyes, the breeze from the toxic sea had only made it worse... all he saw was some kind of pallid, insect-like thing, black bug eyes staring out as it dropped on to all fours on the pathway. And then the flash of something bright, something polished. Something sharp.

Kyrro ran, and with a slight gasp of relief realised he was heading towards the nearest watchtower. He'd never been a big supporter of the militia, but Kyrro hoped they didn't know that. Forcing his burning lungs to take in a deep breath as he ran, Kyrro released the icy, fetid air as a long cry for help. He hoped someone was listening.

Anji found the Doctor in the console room, and instantly felt a tension. Not just in the way the TARDIS's pilot was bent over the central console, punching buttons and sliding levers, but a tremor in the air, like a vibration from nearby machines. The light from the ceiling flickered slightly, as if the ship's power was being diverted. Ripples of raw energy shuddered through the crystalline shapes within the console's central column. The TARDIS was straining, being pushed to its limits.

'Good morning Anji,' said the Doctor, not looking up. He was perfectly polite, but there was an edge to his voice, a note of obsession. His curly hair seemed messier than normal, his sleeves rolled up and his waistcoat crumpled. Whatever the Doctor was working on, he was taking it seriously. 'Why don't you fix yourself some breakfast? Fitz might even help, if you can get him off that sofa.'

'Hey,' said Fitz Kreiner, from his position draped across the sofa between two of the room's alcoves, a leather-bound book open on his knees. 'If it's toast you're after, then my bread-loading skills are at your disposal. Just say the word.'

'That's OK, tiger,' said Anji, tapping Fitz on the shoulder. 'I'll get by without you. But thanks for the offer.'

Fitz grinned, returning his attention to his book. 'Any time.'

As Anji fixed herself some food in the kitchen area, she watched the two men in the console room. The Doctor and Fitz had a lot in common – some shared history, a tendency to be anti-authoritarian at best and downright obstinate at worst – but they were also so far apart. Fitz, in spite of all his big talk and outright lies, was one of the most 'real', most human people Anji had ever met. He could try and be the man of mystery all he wanted, but there was something about Fitz's scruffy leather coat and unshaven appearance that could never be anything other than down to earth. Over the last few months she had realised she could rely on Fitz, on his good nature and humanity. The Doctor, on the other hand, was very much something else. Anji watched him muttering to himself as he operated the TARDIS controls, talking to the machine as if engaged in a motivational exercise rather than a technical operation. What was he thinking? Anji knew by now that she couldn't second guess, she simply wasn't the right species to read the Doctor's body language or relate to his mindset. She was never going to guess what he was up to – time technology hardly being her strong point – so she might as well ask.

'So, what are you doing?'

The Doctor's head darted up at Anji's query, a look of confusion passing over his features, as if he wasn't sure what to say. Was he worrying about how to explain something so complex, or unsure of what to tell her? He seemed almost embarrassed.

'I'm seeing how far the TARDIS will go,' he said, slightly coyly. 'Pushing into the future, seeing how long we can go in one trip. It's about time the old girl had her abilities stretched a bit. I want to see how far she can go.'

In the time she had been with the Doctor, Anji had never quite managed to understand his relationship with the TARDIS. The TARDIS was a machine, and yet the relationship was very personal. Perhaps it was the very fragility inherent in flying a box through the cold expanses of time and space that made it vital for the Doctor to believe in the TARDIS as something more, the intensity of the journey that made a vehicle into both a home and a friend. How much better to think that one's survival rests in the hands of a friend, a sentient being, than life and death depending on the cold workings of circuits and engines? Either way, Anji knew how much the Doctor valued the TARDIS, how desperately he protected it from outside influence and how jealously he protected its secrets. This exercise, this marathon journey into the far future, was some kind of test of fealty, as if the Doctor were willing the TARDIS to go further, to push on, to show how far she would go just for him.

'How far into the future are we going?' asked Fitz, strolling over to the Doctor's side.

'As far as we can,' said the Doctor.

Anji wondered how far would be too far.

For some people an office is just a place of work, a functional area separate from the rest of their lives. For others it is a home away from home, desk littered with family photographs, personal items lining the shelves, certificates and suchlike on the wall. For other, even more desperate cases the office can become their primary home, gaining the constant, lived in quality of an adolescent's bedroom, a place where life is lived constantly, where the evidence of eating and sleeping is as prevalent as the work being done.

The office of Powlin, Chief of the Hope City Militia, defiantly fitted into the latter category. High up in one of the coastal watchtowers, accessible from a winding stairwell, it was a small, functional room buried in paper, crime scene images covering all available surfaces. High on the wall a narrow window looked out over the bleak sea, while a dull light bulb hung from the ceiling. Powlin currently had his feet up on the desk, but he wasn't sitting at it. He was slumped, lightly sleeping, in a low, battered chair in the corner of the room, a case file open on his knee. The office chair that nominally belonged with his desk sat, unused and unloved, in a corner, a pile of books and dirty laundry dumped on top of it.

Suddenly, the intercom on the wall burst into life, and Powlin was awake. The voices of militiamen on duty echoed across the comms system, discussing some kind of emergency. A man was in distress nearby, screaming murder, and officers were on the way to investigate.

And Powlin just *knew* this was the break he was after. He was out of the door in seconds, pulling his heavy coat on as he went. He caught a glimpse of himself on the way out. Yellowing skin, heavily lined. A face sagging under the weight of responsibility.

Perhaps tonight his main responsibility would be resolved, and a little of that weight would lift. Maybe.

Anji saw the confusion pass over the Doctor's face as he tried to adjust one of the controls.

'What's wrong?' she asked.

'It's stuck,' said the Doctor simply. His confusion began to turn to panic, his voice slightly desperate. He tried another switch. 'This one too.' He tried another couple of switches. 'They're all locking. I've been pushing her too hard.'

'What do we do?' asked Fitz, staring at the controls. Anji doubted whether he knew what any of them meant, even though he'd been travelling with the Doctor for longer than she had.

'We need to shut down, gradually materialise,' said the Doctor, hands racing across the console. 'Quickly enough to stop us breaking up, gradually enough to not rip ourselves apart in the force of our sudden halt.' He gritted his teeth. 'Tricky, tricky,

tricky.' He gradually pulled one the levers that materialised the TARDIS at its destination. Anji could see the tension in his arm as he moved the lever steadily but firmly. 'Gently does it, no sudden halt. We just stop.'

From deep within the TARDIS there came the mechanical, roaring sound that indicated the ship was about to appear somewhere new. Anji was sure the sound had a strained, slightly worn tone to it. Beneath her hand, the console began to shake. She gripped the edge, unsure whether she was trying to steady herself or the ship around her.

Kyrro was nearly at the watchtower, he knew it. He could hear the footsteps of his pursuer behind him, but he was sure he could also hear movement ahead. The militia would rescue him, surely? It was their job to protect the citizens of Hope, after all.

Kyrro only remembered what a cold night it was when he ran on to the patch of ice. Then one foot was sliding forward, and his other leg was dragging behind. He tried to break his fall, allow himself to stumble back on to his feet, but instead he just cracked his elbow as he hit the ground. Kyrro tried to push himself up but, as he tried to rise up on bloodied knees and elbows, something landed on his back, pressing Kyrro's face down on to the icy ground. He felt the air being pushed out of his lungs by the pressure, the ice burning his cheek, a pain in his twisted arm.

Then he felt another kind of pain, as something hot and sharp pierced the back of his neck, cutting straight through the top of Kyrro's spine.

'Stupid,' said the Doctor, eyes closed, fingers drumming the console. 'I was stupid, pushing too far. Luckily the old girl got us out of it.' He opened his eyes, prowled around the console, examining the now dormant controls. The background noise had faded to a dull hum, and the lights had dimmed slightly. Anji thought the TARDIS seemed unusually subdued, but at least they had managed to arrive somewhere.

'Are we safe?' asked Anji.

'Oh yes,' said the Doctor, flicking the scanner control. The screen fizzed into life, displaying an image of a thick yellow mist, a shiny surface stretching out into the distance. 'We've arrived intact, no thanks to me.'

'Looks cheery,' said Fitz, looking at the hostile place on the screen and obviously ignoring the Doctor's self pity. 'Tell you what, why don't we leave?'

The Doctor sighed. 'Unfortunately, the TARDIS will require a little time to recalibrate after her exertions.' He tapped the console thoughtfully. 'I suggest we leave her to recover for a while. The atmosphere out there seems to have sufficient oxygen levels for your purposes... and quite a few other things, by the looks of it. Here, you'll need these.' He disappeared into the lab area, and returned holding a couple of small gold discs. Anji recognised them as being from the equipment of the humans they had met on the fairy-tale planet, presumably some obscure bits of space colonist equipment.

'I've been analysing these, and they seem to provide some measure of protection against adverse environmental conditions,' said the Doctor. 'As long as you each keep one on your person, they'll extend a microscopic filtration layer that will reprocess any impurities in the atmosphere. But be careful; they won't make you immortal and they have their limits – swallow a cup full of cyanide and you'll still die.' He passed Anji and Fitz a disc each, then went to get his coat. 'Oh, and it might be best to wrap up warm,' he added. 'It's cold out.'

Powlin overtook the militiamen who were on their way to investigate the disturbance. He heard them swear as they felt obliged to increase their speed to keep up with him. There was an old system of chains linking the upper and lower sections, and Powlin grabbed one side, hooking his foot into a link. His weight pulled that side of the chain, gravity causing it to carry him down to where he needed to be at a manageable speed. Powlin jumped off halfway down, landing on a pipe that ran down to the outer pathway. He landed on that path with a skid, quickly adjusting his balance so as not to topple over the railings.

He allowed himself a couple of seconds to get his bearings. Ahead in the fog, he could just make out a hunched figure. There were no sounds of screams, or any other human noise. Powlin drew his gun, raising it as he steadily walked forward.

At the sound of his approach the figure stood up, turning towards Powlin. And as the militia officer saw what had previously been obscured, the bloodied figure lying across the pathway, he knew his instincts had been correct.

'Stop right there,' he shouted, barely having time to take in the blank, black eyes and pallid complexion of the creature in front of him. If he backed away, Powlin would shoot him down, and to the thing's left was a sheer wall of rusting steel.

Powlin tried to focus on the figure in the gloom. What the hell was it?

And then the creature did something that Powlin hadn't even considered as an option. It jumped over the ledge.

Shocked at this suicidal action, Powlin looked over the railing, expecting the sound of a body hitting the poisonous waters. Powlin had seen people fall in before, and mentally winced as he waited for the screaming to start as skin burned and acid chewed through flesh.

Instead he heard a crack, the sound of one solid mass hitting another.

It was one of the bleakest places Anji had ever seen. The TARDIS stood out as a glowing mass of blue compared to the endless fog stretching out around them. It was night-time, and their torches cut through the fog to show… ice. Fog and ice, her two least favourite types of weather. Anji wasn't pleased. It was worse than walking to the station on a winter morning, and there wasn't even any hope of a cappuccino at the other end.

'Watch your step,' said the Doctor redundantly, gingerly pacing around ahead. Anji noticed that he had made sure to protect himself from the elements. Perhaps he was feeling the environment more than he used to, an aftereffect of his recent illness. He seemed somewhat despondent, probably kicking himself for pushing the TARDIS too far. As she watched he unconsciously rubbed his chest with one hand, waving the torch around with the other.

'Whoa!' said Anji as she slipped on the icy ground. 'I can see what you mean. This ice is really bad.' It was also bitterly cold – no wonder there was ice everywhere. Anji pulled her scarf tighter around her neck, shoving her hands deeper into the pockets of her long cashmere coat.

'Let's head this way,' said the Doctor, pointing at a dark mass looming up out of the fog ahead. It seemed to be a mass of buildings, lights flickering in the darkness. Anji was sure she could detect industrial noises at the edge of her hearing.

'Looks interesting,' said Anji noncommittally. From this distance it could be a castle or a tower block, a village or a palace. At least the ground might be salted.

Regretfully leaving the warmth and safety of the TARDIS behind, Anji and Fitz gingerly followed the Doctor across the ice.

They had barely walked ten paces when, from somewhere ahead, there came shouts, and the sound of something hitting the ground from a great height.

Powlin fumbled through his pockets, searching for his multi-vision goggles. He found them in the depths of one of his coat's inner pockets, under a mass of paper scraps. These possibly vital reminders of important case information went flying into the night as Powlin desperately pulled out the goggles and strapped them to his head. Gun in one hand, the other hand adjusting the goggles' control switches, he leaned over the railings. Thermal scan revealed what had happened; the surface of the sea had frozen over in the extreme cold. It was an infrequent event, but not unknown; the water and the heavier toxic elements would separate, the clean water freezing and the polluted gunk trapped beneath. The ice was actually quite valuable – a rare clean source of water.

The killer had clearly landed on the ice, but a quick sweep

failed to reveal him. Perhaps his heat signature was shielded. Powlin flicked a switch, overlaying motion detection over the thermal scan. Something very fast was running across the ice towards… three slow-moving heat signatures?

Powlin didn't have time to worry about that. He raised his gun, thumbing the pad next to the trigger, selecting explosive shells and heads-up link-up. The goggles allowed him to lock on to the running figure, and he unleashed a volley of shots, miniature heat signatures streaking across his field of vision.

What a nice, friendly place, thought Fitz as he threw himself to the cold ground. Five minutes since they arrived, and someone was shooting at them. Shrapnel flew as whatever was being thrown at them hit the ground, exploding and sending ice fragments flying. Fitz looked up, only to see a white blur jump over him, running away from whoever was firing, towards the TARDIS.

The ground began to shake – or was it just concussion? Fitz couldn't tell. The firing had temporarily stopped, but Fitz's ears were still ringing.

'Oh dear,' said the Doctor, lying on his back where an explosion had thrown him. 'I think we may have made a dangerous misinterpretation.'

'What are you talking about?' shouted Anji from nearby.

'I don't think we're on solid ground here,' said the Doctor, scrambling to his feet on the slippery surface.

Fitz could feel the ground – if ground it was – shaking beneath him. As if something was pressing up from beneath the surface. Fitz had the sneaking suspicion it wasn't a very big mole.

Powlin couldn't lock on to anything now. His target had disappeared into a greater blur of motion, as something large cut through the ice in the distance. Tremors were moving across the entire area, and the heat signatures were totally obscured by the fallout from his own explosive shells. Feeling dizzy just looking at the chaotic mass of signals, Powlin tore off his goggles. What the hell was going on out there?

* * *

Gas seeped out of the crack as it developed, liquid spraying out. A droplet hit Fitz on the back of his bare hand, and he yelped as the vile liquid burned his skin, flesh sizzling. He backed away.

'Watch out, that stuff is lethal!' he shouted to his companions, pulling out a hanky and wrapping it around his hand. Probably not the most hygienic dressing, but it would have to do.

'Something's coming,' said the Doctor, over the roar as further cracks developed in the ice around them. 'We're on some kind of lake, and something's breaking through the ice.'

'Can we get to the TARDIS?' asked Anji, jumping off a section of ice that was slowly sinking under her weight, detached from the rest by the increasing cracks.

The Doctor shook his head. 'No, we're cut off. He pointed in the direction they had previously been walking towards, the dark mass in the distance looming ahead. 'We need to get to solid ground before the ice breaks up totally.'

As if to illustrate his point, a crack developed between his feet, the two sections of ice sheet pulling apart. Even the Doctor covered his nose and mouth with his cravat as noxious gases bubbled out from the liquid beneath.

'Run,' shouted the Doctor. 'We haven't got long.'

They ran, skidding and pitching on the uneven, slippery surface. Cracks shot across the ice, and Fitz saw Anji nearly slip into a chasm that opened up before her, jumping across on to a wobbling, uneven section of ice before the Doctor helped her to safer ground. Fitz himself had to duck out of the way as a geyser spurted between the cracks nearby, acid raining down around him. Fitz felt something sting the back of his neck, but managed to protect his face and eyes. He could swear that, somewhere behind them, he could hear the grinding of metal tearing through the ice, but didn't have any inclination to go back and find out what was going on. Survival was the only thing on his mind.

'Look!' bellowed the Doctor from nearby as Fitz barely kept his footing, a gulf of liquid bubbling up next to him, chunks of ice drifting away. The ice was breaking up with terrifying speed, and soon there would be nowhere safe to stand, nowhere to run. Tearing his eyes off the ground, Fitz looked ahead at what the Doctor wanted him to see. They were heading towards a mass of girders, some kind of structure stretching into the fog to both their left and right, tall enough to disappear into the mist twenty feet or so from what Fitz supposed must be 'sea level'. The struts of this giant, pierlike building were large, but not beyond climbing. As they cleared the final few feet, Fitz had to jump as the ice gave way beneath him, throwing himself forward on to he nearest girder and hanging on for his life.

He looked to his right, and saw the Doctor helping Anji up. As Anji caught her breath, Fitz saw the Doctor looking out to sea. Somewhere out there, Fitz realised, the TARDIS was sinking to the bottom of the sea, however-many-feet of polluted liquid stopping them from retrieving their ship, their way out of this horrible place. But for the Doctor it was a far greater loss. The TARDIS was his home, the centre of his existence. Without it he was lost, in body and spirit.

'Will the TARDIS survive sinking into that stuff?' asked Anji, between breaths.

'Yeah,' said Fitz. 'The problem is getting it back.' He turned to the Doctor. 'But we will. We'll get her back.' He pulled himself up into a more comfortable position. 'There's signs of life here, someone ran past us. This must be some kind of building. All we need to do is find someone with… a submarine.'

'Fitz,' said Anji harshly. 'They *shot* at us. I don't think they're likely to lend us any naval vehicles.'

'No,' said the Doctor firmly. 'Fitz is right, we have no choice but to try. Someone here must have the equipment we need to retrieve the TARDIS.' He looked around the structure they were perched in. 'This place didn't build itself.'

'So,' asked Anji. 'Where do we go from here?'

All three of them gradually looked up at the body of the structure they were on. There didn't seem to be any option.

'We go up,' said Fitz.

Chapter Two
The Only Way is Up

Anji had rock-climbed in the past, back when she was a teenager. She had even done a bit of climbing at the gym, clambering up the odd artificial rock face they had for such exercises. But climbing the struts and girders wasn't like that at all. There was no safety rope, no one had been over the territory to check whether it was safe, or indeed climbable at all. She slipped a couple of times, trying to keep a grip on the oily girders, but Fitz or the Doctor were always there to steady her, to stop her from falling into the hostile waters below. When she reached the top they helped push her over on to the ledge – and from the other direction, strong hands pulled her up.

In spite of her limbs begging her just to relax, to rest on the platform after her ordeal on the ice and the long climb after that, she forced herself to roll into a crouch and face the residents of wherever she was, ready to flee.

The row of gun barrels she faced were an incentive not to make any sudden moves. The men holding the guns didn't seem too friendly, wrapped as they were in heavy clothing, swaddled up with goggles covering their eyes. Anji should, she thought, have tried to give them a winning smile or engage in some witty banter. Instead she looked at the gun barrels blankly, gawping at them.

Behind her she could hear the Doctor and Fitz being dragged up on to the ledge – although a walkway was probably more accurate. Still crouching down, she looked at the well-worn panels, seemingly of different materials and ages, that were patched together to make up the path they were on. What sort of place was this?

'Thank you,' said the Doctor. 'It's not too pleasant down there.' Seemingly ignoring the guns pointed at them, he helped Anji to her feet. 'I'm the Doctor, this is Anji and the gentleman over there is Fitz. We had a little trouble on the ice.'

'I'm not surprised.' This new voice was cultured and morose, with a slightly lilting accent. It came from a man in late middle age, thin with sagging, depressed features. Unlike the others he was only wearing a coat rather than layers, although he appeared to have dressed in a hurry. One other thing sprang to Anji's attention – this newcomer didn't have a single hair on him, as far as she could see. Not even eyebrows.

'That sea could burn the skin off your body in seconds if you were to fall in,' said the man. 'What were you doing down there?'

The question was phrased innocently enough, but the edge to the man's tone – and the evil-looking weaponry brandished by his associates – added a certain tension to the conversation.

'Our ship landed on the ice,' said the Doctor simply. 'We were walking towards here, when shots were fired. The ice began to break up. Our ship was lost, and we ran here. You wouldn't know who fired at us, would you?'

'Ah,' said the man, putting on a slightly embarrassed expression. He pulled a hefty pistol from his coat, and waved it apologetically. 'That would have been me, I'm afraid. I was trying to apprehend a particularly dangerous criminal. You didn't happen to see where he went, did you?'

'Someone ran past us,' said Fitz. 'But I didn't get a good look. Why, what did this guy do?'

The morose-looking man nodded to his associates to back off. They lowered their weapons and moved out of Anji's field of vision. Behind them lay a dark heap, a body resting in a pool of its own blood. As Anji approached it, she had a terrible feeling. Her feeling was confirmed as she got a closer look and she instinctively backed away, the Doctor gripping her shoulders supportively as she backed into him. Fitz made a low noise of disgust as he got a good luck at the grisly sight.

'Decapitation,' said the Doctor coldly.

* * *

Powlin watched the three strangers' reactions to the headless cadaver with fascination; even by throwback standards their responses were unusual. The girl was shocked and distraught, as if unused to seeing such things, and made no attempt to disguise her distaste. The younger of the men was trying to appear relaxed, but was noticeably avoiding looking directly at the corpse. Most interesting of all was the older man, the Doctor. He was displaying a rich range of emotions, superficially consoling his associate while sneaking constant, fascinated glances at the corpse. His expression radiated a righteous sense of injustice at the murder, but beneath that, somewhere in his eyes, there seemed to be a flicker of passion, a delight in being presented with a dangerous, unpredictable situation, in being surrounded by lethal forces and having to negotiate his own way through such territory.

The Doctor's interest precluded any possible involvement in the crime. Here was a man who knew nothing about the situation, but desperately wanted to know more. Powlin could relate.

'These three are harmless,' Powlin told his militiamen. 'Get the victim back to the watchtower, I'll meet up with you later.' He turned to the Doctor and his associates. 'As for you, I'll need to know a bit more about who you are, and what you came to Hope for. My name's Powlin, and as head of the militia I enforce the law around here. So, let's start with the basics. Who are you people?'

'We're travellers,' said the Doctor. Powlin noted the Doctor's flimsy clothing, the fuzzy and soft coat, the silky waistcoat. Suicidal dress in these parts. 'And until we crashed on the ice we were just... travelling.'

Powlin found the idea of sailing across an acid sea for no apparent reason so incomprehensible that he could think of little to say in reply. These strangers, wherever they came from and whoever they were, didn't seem to have any relevance to the job in hand. While the Doctor might be an unknown quantity, aside from being throwbacks the other two seemed harmless, the short girl shrinking into her coat to escape the cold, the 'Fitz' person stamping his feet to keep warm. Lost in the cold, just like the rest of us, thought Powlin. He'd find out what he needed to know and send them on their way.

'So, can any of you three describe the man who ran past you?' he asked.

'White,' said Fitz. 'As in totally, bleached white. Really fast. Other than that...' He trailed off.

Powlin turned to the Doctor and Anji. 'Anything to add?'

The Doctor shook his head. 'I didn't see anyone. I was rather distracted by someone shooting at us.'

Powlin elected to ignore that. 'Well, if you think of anything else, report to your nearest watchtower. Otherwise... just stay out of trouble.'

And with that he turned and walked off.

As Powlin walked away, Anji nudged the Doctor with her elbow. He was gazing thoughtfully at the floor, where a rough outline showed where the body had fallen.

'Hmm?' asked the Doctor distractedly, locking eyes with her.

'We have no idea where we are,' whispered Anji urgently. 'And the only person we've spoken to is disappearing into the fog.'

The Doctor looked shocked. 'You're absolutely right! Come on Fitz, we've got to keep in contact.'

Anji kept close to the Doctor and Fitz as they marched along beside Powlin, badgering the sullen man with an endless stream of questions. Anji kept pace – a job in itself, what with her being a head shorter than any of the others – but didn't engage in conversation. Anji's uncomfortable thoughts earlier in the morning had left her a little out of sorts, and she preferred to observe her surroundings rather than speak to anyone. What with the running, and the guns, and the darkness, she hadn't really taken a good look around before. As she followed the others along the metal gantry, she looked around her at this strange city. There didn't seem to be much in the way of electric lighting, but blue gas flames acted as torches, burning from outlets in the walls.

Rubbish. The whole place seemed to be welded together from

bits of scrap metal and other detritus. To their right, a railing made from bits of old pipe and lengths of chain stopped them falling into the hostile sea. To their left, a sheer wall of metal, indented with what looked like the occasional airlock door. Scuffed paintwork made out crude letters in a language Anji didn't recognise, and she presumed this whole section of the city's edge was the bulkhead of a ship of some kind, presumably built into the city walls as fortification or flood barrier. Eventually, this hull curved and they found themselves at the bottom of a motley collection of rusty iron forming a stairwell. To their left a series of steps disappeared into the city.

'This is my watchtower,' said Powlin, pointing up. Anji cranked her neck back, and could just make out some kind of lighthouse towering above them, slitlike windows glowing into the night as the militia looked out over the sea. It resembled a post-industrial attempt at a medieval fortress tower.

'I hope I've been... of help,' said Powlin, as if unused to polite conversation. He made a vague attempt at a wave, then disappeared up the stairwell to the tower, footsteps clattering as he went.

'So, where now?' asked Anji.

'Well,' said the Doctor wryly. 'If you'd been listening to our friend Powlin, you'd know that this way –' he pointed to the steps leading into darkness – 'will take us straight to the centre of Hope. Apparently we should watch our backs, although I don't think any of us intended to let our guard down.'

Fitz frowned. 'I thought you'd be wanting to follow up on this murder. Grisly business, innocents in peril, that sort of thing.'

'I will, but later. Our immediate priority is retrieving the TARDIS. The thing about the dead is, they're never going anywhere in a hurry. The TARDIS, on the other hand – I don't feel comfortable leaving her there, at the bottom of the sea. She may not come to any harm, but...'

Fitz put a supportive hand on the Doctor's shoulder. 'We understand. TARDIS first. We can get around to anything else later.'

Together, they stepped into the darkness.

* * *

24

By the harsh light of liquid crystal they met, in a chamber devoted to the clean lines of machine-tooled perfection, each surface polished to revel in its glittering, inorganic quality. They had come to worship their goddess, to celebrate the binary world of mechanical logic, to live their digital dreams.

They are a brotherhood, although such organic concepts as family and fraternal feelings have been put behind them in their search for perfection, their constant upgrading. Gathered in their robes they chant hard integers, allowing their minds to relax into a dream-state of ones and zeroes. The founders of their faith live on somewhere in the outer universe, far away from Endpoint. The Perfected Ones themselves are long since dead, martyred in battle, reduced to the components on which the brotherhood model their own adaptations. But this brotherhood have one who makes their quest worthwhile, who holds out a light of hope for them. A virtual messiah, carved out of the air in pure, gleaming holographic form, a messenger from a better world of pure data.

As they chant they are gradually aware that she is among them, that their queen has a proclamation to make. In the centre of the room a face forms, feminine features pooling from liquid mercury, the soft curves of organic womanhood adapted into something more precise, a colder and more efficient vision of beauty. They are awestruck by the dark grates that are her eyes, the chiselled steel of her cheekbones, the plated slit in her perfect features that is her mouth. When that mouth deigns to speak, they all listen.

'The equations are all balanced,' their queen says. 'This is the optimum time to strike, to remove the aberration. It is time to terminate the abomination.'

The flickering blue flames of the gas torches lit their way as they followed the steps, and Anji took the opportunity to have a good look around. The path the steps took was supported by beams linked to buildings on either side, and somewhere below was the sea.

'Hope isn't an island,' said the Doctor, fascinated as he peered over the edge. 'The city is built on stilts, as there's no actual ground here for it to rest on. There are clearly a large number of main structures going down to the sea bed. Everything else is cantilevered in between. It's a miracle of crisis engineering.'

Anji had to admit she was impressed. The buildings either side of them resembled tenements, vast grey structures with pokey little windows and that swollen, looming quality that comes from buildings designed to cram as many people into as little space as possible. But they were impressively tall, many storeys high, and the way that bridges interconnected the various buildings while acting as support struts was equally ingenious. Anji was sure she occasionally heard the sound of people walking by overhead, but with the constant clattering of nearby machinery, the hum of power lines crisscrossing above her and the bubbling of the gas pipes, it was hard to be sure. Who did live here, anyway? She asked the Doctor what Powlin had told them.

'They call themselves Endpointers,' butted in Fitz enthusiastically. 'They're descended from a number of races, including humans. They think of us as throwbacks, apparently.'

'Throwbacks?' said Anji. It was a term little used where she came from, the sort of folk logic her grandparents' generation might have used.

'The hostile environment has made the Endpointers a breed apart,' said the Doctor, expanding on Fitz's ramblings. 'Stronger, more resistant to toxins and harsh weather. They don't have hair, their eyes are protected by an inner lid rather than eyelashes, their lungs are probably highly evolved. To them we seem like chimpanzees do to Homo sapiens. Ancestral features occasionally pop up in the Endpointer gene pool – a child with hair here, someone with blue skin picked up from a reptilian ancestor there. But actual, pureblood humans haven't been seen for centuries. Certainly, Powlin was quicker to presume we were genetic freaks than Homo sapiens.'

'I wonder what happened to all the people,' mused Fitz.

'Evolved into these ones, I should think,' said the Doctor, gently mocking what he clearly saw as an outmoded, human-centric view of history.'No species can last forever without evolving into something new. Not even yours, exceptionally tenacious though it may have been. Sooner or later the distance from Earth, from the environment humanity evolved to live in, genetic engineering and eventual intermingling of the gene pool with those of other species – these were bound to have the inevitable, cumulative effect of turning humanity into a completely different species.'

'Look on the bright side,' said Fitz. 'Humanity could have evolved into yicky insect creatures, something gross like that.'

'On the down side,' countered Anji, 'we're among people who regard us as their inbred yokel cousins.'

'Great,' said Fitz enthusiastically. 'It's been a while since I've played the banjo.' He whistled a twangy redneck tune while playing air-banjo.

Anji laughed. 'Still, I'd quite like to get out of here. Freezing to death in a polluted wasteland isn't my idea of fun.'

'It isn't just the city that's cold,' said the Doctor quietly. 'It isn't even just the planet. It's the universe as a whole. I pushed the TARDIS too far, well past the point when the finite amount of energy in the universe has become too dispersed, where existence itself is beginning to wind down and die out.' He pointed up at the sky – it was a purely dramatic gesture, as none of them could see anything but a persistent smog. 'Out there stars are dying, entropy is setting in. We shouldn't be here.'

Thanks for the cheery thought, Doctor, thought Anji. She felt even colder now, thinking of that increasingly lifeless universe. Only a short time ago she wouldn't have been concerned by the big picture like that, by distant star systems and faraway futures. Now she had only just begun to explore the universe, discovering places and times far away from twenty-first-century Earth. The universe seemed new to her, young and fresh. She didn't want to see it old and dying.

As they emerged from between the tenements Anji realised that the sloping path had gradually led them several storeys up, to a viewpoint that allowed them a broader view of Hope.

'People live here?' asked Fitz, amazed.

Anji could see what he meant. Hope was a shanty town of tremendous proportions, buildings leaning in on each other, towers and walkways welded on to the side of already haphazard-looking constructions, patchwork, uneven walls of different metals, bits of what looked like vehicles of some kind broken up and made part of the fabric. Smokestacks and wind turbines pierced the sky, ladders and bridges cut across everywhere. It was a maze built over a web built over anarchy. And, although it was the dead of night, Anji could see people moving around; walking over bridges, lowering themselves on ropes and chains, even swinging by in treacherous-looking cable cars.

'It's beautiful,' she said, almost to herself. 'In a really ugly way.'

'I agree,' said the Doctor, and Anji turned to see the new day reflected in his eyes, his old enthusiasm slightly restored. He was smiling, eyes narrowed as he looked out across the city. Perhaps he was thinking of the complexity of it all, thought Anji, thinking of the new places and people that could be hidden in such a city. The Doctor was nothing if not restless, eager for new experiences.

'What are we waiting for?' said Fitz. 'Let's find someone who can show us the best places around here.'

Fitz wasn't too impressed with Hope so far, although it showed signs of getting more exciting. The place was built out of rubbish, the mood pretty grim and the people little more than humans with funny skin and no hair. Or perhaps Fitz was just getting horribly blasé about the whole space-time-travel thing. As they walked out on to a disc-shaped platform suspended between four pylons, Fitz got the distinct feeling that things were about to get more interesting. They seemed to be entering some kind of market square, with dozens of shacklike stalls open for business. Food was being served from great vats, while mechanical components and weapons of all kinds were being sold, the only common factor being the rough condition of the items. Heat and light were provided by fires in squat metal dishes, and Fitz had to pat out his leather coat when a smouldering ember tried to set it alight.

Contrary to his expectation that everyone here would be the same, Fitz could already make out different social groups. At the bottom of the pile were those who seemed to lurk around the market for no commercial reason, and were probably here mainly for the heat, sneaking close to a fire whenever the opportunity arose. Their clothes were little more than rags, their mouths and noses protected by grubby cloths wrapped around their faces. At the other end of the scale there were some aristocratic types around, Fitz recognising their status by the brightly coloured and elaborate masks over their mouths and noses, their sharper clothes and relaxed posture. However, their social status clearly didn't offer much protection, as these toffs moved in packs for safety, and wore pistols visibly to discourage anyone thinking of relieving them of their wealth.

In between the lowlifes and the rich tourists there were the natural inhabitants of a place like this, practically clad in thick, protective clothing like the militiamen they had seen earlier. These were the men and women buying and selling, dealing from stalls and elsewhere, dragging anyone they could find into games of chance and inadvisable bets. Fitz was just getting worried about where all this social conflict could lead when a fight broke out nearby.

The argument seemed to be over some kind of gambling debt, and was between a tall man in expensive-looking purple overalls and a shorter, more muscular figure in more ragged attire. As is traditional in these circumstances the bustling crowds had formed a circle around the two men as they began to push each other back and forth, shouting increasingly desperate insults. In the crowd Fitz, the Doctor and Anji stuck close together, just in case the conflict spread.

The excitement of the crowd increased as the shorter man pulled a gun from his coat, placing it under the taller man's chin.

To Fitz's horror the Doctor broke away from them, pushing through the crowd to try and stop the inevitable, but he burst through the circle just too late. There was a sharp crack as the taller man became a head shorter, blood spraying out as the smouldering corpse collapsed to the ground.

'That wasn't –' shouted the Doctor, stopping short as the killer turned his weapon around towards him. Fitz's guts tightened as the Doctor and the killer stared each other down. Then the gun was lowered and the short man casually walked away, leaving the Doctor to be pushed aside by the crowd, eager to strip the corpse of any valuable belongings.

'This is a terrible place,' said the Doctor as Fitz and Anji caught up with him. Anger seemed to have rooted him to the spot, and Fitz didn't dare touch him, nervous of what might happen if he interfered. 'Murder is an acceptable street game, violence rules and no one dares challenge it. Civilisation is gone and savagery has taken its place.'

They watched silently as the now naked corpse was tipped over the railings by the mob. A cheer rippled through the crowd as the body fell, disappearing into the darkness below.

'Forget that other murder,' said the Doctor coldly. 'No one else seems to care. Let's get the TARDIS and leave. There's nothing for us here.'

'But surely we can do something?' said Anji. 'We could contact the militia.'

There was uproarious laughter at this, and the three travellers turned to see a small man standing behind a stall loaded with canisters, laughing shrilly within the depths of his voluminous grey coat. He was short, his dark, beady eyes were too close together for Fitz's liking and his smile was the wide smile of a predator about to bite something's head clean off. Presumably he was hairless – Fitz couldn't tell due to the man's huge balaclava.

'From out of town, are we?' asked the man, still giggling to himself. Considering they came from a different species, this seemed something of an understatement. Fitz suspected the guy was taking the piss. 'Militia, indeed. As if they give a toss about some scummer who can't pay his debts. And who can blame them, eh?' He paused briefly for a response which didn't come. 'Quite. Anyway, welcome to Pazon's Patch, and it's a grand local tradition for visitors to pay me large amounts of money on their arrival.'

'The only thing we're looking for is information,' said the Doctor, eyes narrowed, unimpressed by Pazon's flippant attitude towards what had just occurred.

'Information, I can do information,' said Pazon. 'But my main business is culinary. Perhaps I can interest you in some food and drink, and then we can talk about this information you're after.' Pazon leaned back into a classic negotiating posture, waiting for the Doctor to make him an offer.

'Sounds good,' said the Doctor through gritted teeth. 'What have you got?'

'On the food side we've got carbos and protes, vitcliks and some fresh stimulikes,' listed Pazon breathlessly.

'And drinks?' asked Fitz. The food hardly sounded exotic, more a list of mineral supplements. He hoped the beverages were more enticing.

'Depends on your budget,' said Pazon. 'I have sulph-shakes and caffy for those early morning cravings, and for the health-conscious, simple full and semi.'

'Skimmed?' asked Anji, clearly thinking that Pazon was referring to milk. Fitz had a horrible feeling that wasn't the case.

The stall owner seemed baffled. 'Recycled,' he said, as if to an exceptionally dumb child.

'Ah,' said Anji, clearly none the wiser. Then it sank in. 'Ah,' she repeated, a slight look of disgust on her face before she quickly repressed it. Fitz repressed a smirk in response.

'Don't have semi and full recyc where you come from?' said Pazon, his tiny eyes narrowing even further. 'You must be from way out. Salvation is it? Not from one of those church yachts that usually go around the poles, are you? Only you won't find many up for conversion around here.'

'No, no,' said the Doctor quickly. 'Nothing like that.'

The man slumped. 'Either way, you're not likely to be able to pay for anything, are you?'

'Depends,' said Anji. 'What system of exchange do you use here?'

Pazon pulled a grubby disk from a pocket, and showed it to Anji as if it were a magical item.

'This is a coin,' he said patiently. 'And you exchange it for goods and services. And, if there's any difference in value, they give you back some little coins in return.'

'Yes, thank you,' said the Doctor impatiently. 'We get the idea. Perhaps you could tell us where we can get some local currency. We have a particularly large job that needs doing, and we'll need funds.'

'Large job?' asked the man.

'We want to retrieve something of ours,' said the Doctor. 'It fell into the sea.'

Pazon blinked. 'That is a big job.' He whistled. 'Only one place you'll find the clout to get a job like that done. Same place you'll be able to hoc your exotic foreign goods for a line of credit. The Silver Palace.'

'Palace?' asked Fitz. 'You have royalty here?' Probably a King Rat, he thought to himself.

Pazon laughed, an unpleasantly low but reedy chuckle. 'Something like that. Follow the path to the right, you'll know when you get there. It's hard to miss.'

'Thank you,' said the Doctor. He nodded to Fitz and Anji, and they began to make their way in the direction indicated.

'Oh, and come back when you've got some money sorted,' shouted Pazon as they left.

'Cheeky little sod,' Fitz heard Anji mutter.

'Forget about it,' snapped the Doctor, and Fitz felt himself recoil, and saw Anji do the same. They exchanged glances; the Doctor had never seemed this brutal before.

'We find this Silver Palace, we get the TARDIS back, we leave,' said the Doctor. 'Everything else is a distraction.'

Fitz and Anji exchanged further glances as the Doctor strode off ahead of them, not even waiting to see them follow.

'It isn't good for him, this place,' said Anji. 'It isn't good for any of us. We need to get out while we can.'

The acolyte tries not to scream as one of the Brotherhood's surgeons works on him, burning into his arm to upgrade crude flesh with advanced weaponry. Screaming is an organic impulse, and all that is organic must be resisted, the acolyte knows this. But the pain digs deep as the surgeon connects his nerve-endings to circuitry, allowing this new weapon to be controlled by the primitive reflexes of the acolyte's petty organic form.

Soon a fiery, righteous light will emerge from that limb, as the acolyte assists in the slaughter of the abomination. The acolyte lets the pain wash over him, knowing that this upgrade will make him stronger, better. Soon they will attack the Silver Palace, and if anything gets between them and the abomination, then they too will die. This is not supposition, this is not faith, it is logic.

Nothing stands in the way of the Brotherhood and lives.

Chapter Three
A Fistful of Fingers

The Silver Palace was hard to miss, although Anji thought it was somewhat misnamed; it was more a fortress than a palace, a twisted mass of shining metal rising up from between the blocky tenements. Strings of electric lights illuminated the metal, while torches burned either side of the entrance. This stunning work of medieval futurist insanity was surrounded by a sheer drop, with only one slim metal bridge leading towards the building's entrance, a yawning archway that appeared like a grotesque mouth, the slitlike windows above resembling desperate, unfocused eyes. All the windows on the vast castle's outer walls seemed small, and Anji thought she could see the glint of weapons aimed out at a potentially hostile world.

'This is not good,' said Fitz, articulating Anji's exact thoughts.

'Oh, I'm sure it's not that bad inside,' said the Doctor uncertainly. 'They could have a crazy golf course in there for all we know.'

'Well they definitely have the space for one,' agreed Anji. 'This place is big.'

'They don't just have space, they have resources too,' added the Doctor. 'Look at all the electric lighting. I should imagine that very few could afford to expend that amount of energy in a place like Hope. This is definitely the place we want to be if we're going to find anyone to help us.'

They carefully crossed the bridge – which Anji suspected could retract into the palace, acting as an automated version of a drawbridge – and approached the archway. Two simian figures emerged from the shadows, holding long, rusty spears. A slight crackle at the end of each spear suggested they might do more than deliver a sharp prod. The guards themselves seemed to be from a slightly different sub-species to Pazon and Powlin. Although still hairless and humanoid they seemed over-developed, threateningly tall and rather wide with thick fingered, wide-spanned hands poking out from their scruffy robes. Their brows were thick and hung heavy over their dark, red little eyes.

'Good morning,' said the Doctor. 'We would like to come in, if we may.'

'Not regulars,' said one guard, his voice a deep rumble.

'New entrants require proof of liquidity,' said the other, his shoulders flexing with suspicion.

The Doctor frowned. 'I'm not sure quite what I have that might be of use to you.' He began to dig around in his pockets, and cupped the contents in front of him. Anji peered over at the tangled mess. She recognised a poodle's woollen bootie, and there were a couple of mismatched shoelaces, a few coins of various denominations, a battered supermarket reward card, what looked like a diamond engagement ring, a nugget of gold, a wrapped sweet, an old computer chip, a toy VW Beetle and, rather disgustingly, an old apple core.

The two guards hovered over the Doctor menacingly, and prodded the collection of valuables with interest.

'See anything that takes your fancy?' asked the Doctor hopefully.

One of the guards lifted the apple core by the stalk, staring at it thoughtfully.

'This is new,' he said. 'What is it?'

'It's an apple,' said the Doctor. 'A fruit.'

The other guard waved a flat metallic scanning device over the apple core, and it made a disgruntled beeping noise.

'Interesting,' said the second guard, examining the readings on the scanner. 'In exchange for this sample we offer you a preliminary credit rating of 750, with an accumulated credit extension of 10,000 in the case of profitable exploitation.'

'Does that mean we're allowed in?' asked Fitz uncertainly.

'I believe so,' said the Doctor, turning back to the guards. He idly stuffed his valuables back into his coat pockets. 'We accept the offer.'

The guards nodded, and while one disappeared into an alcove with the Doctor's apple core the other tapped on a keypad to open the door.

'These people must really like fruit,' whispered Fitz as they walked through the vast doors.

'I'm just glad they didn't take the reward card,' muttered the Doctor. 'There's six months' worth of points on there.'

Having let the three strangers into the Palace, the two doormen resumed their positions in the alcoves within the gateway, lances raised in case of attack. Born in the martial community of Victory, their dedication to their jobs involved maintaining a zenlike sense of stillness during inactive periods. Intelligent yet focused, watchful without being paranoid or twitchy, they were the ideal guards. Which made their failure to react to the group of hooded figures approaching them all the more unlikely. They did not respond in time to defend themselves and avoid the taser jolts that slammed into their bodies, disrupting their nervous systems and leaving them slumped against the walls. As the hooded figures gathered around the keypad, attaching the necessary equipment to hack the doorcode, the two doormen lay unmoving.

Powlin sat in his office, sipping red hot caffy from an old, chipped beaker. It was warm in the watchtower, but he could still feel the cold from outside, gripping him deep within. The caffy went some way towards remedying this, while also nudging his brain cells into life. Another victim, another body in cold storage in the depths of the watchtower. Powlin wouldn't bother attending the post mortem. He knew what the diagnosis would be. Cause of death was the decapitation itself, a procedure so quick and efficient that the victim was probably dead within seconds. One burst of pain as the weapon sliced through flesh and bone. The weapon in question was some form of cutting tool, probably with a micro-engineered blade judging by the clean nature of the wounds.

Not that this series of crimes had always been so clean. When the decapitations began, a couple of months before, the first few had varied in efficiency. One victim had his skull cleaved in half, straight down the middle, and Powlin still wasn't sure whether this was the work of the same killer or just part of Hope's everyday brutality. The militia was an organisation with limited influence, but these killings soon became unacceptable even by Hope's standards. They rapidly dropped into a pattern, and became professional, repetitive acts of butchery. Every two to three nights one or two victims would be found, usually around the edges of Hope, usually the kind of vagrants and lowlifes no one particularly cared about. No personal effects or valuables were ever taken, and the heads were never found.

Powlin sipped his caffy again, and flinched as it burned the surface of his tongue. Although tonight's killing had left him with no definite leads, his own role in events as the first living witness to one of the slayings provided fresh, albeit confusing, evidence. Powlin dug around in the papers next to his chair until he found some scrap paper, then began to crudely sketch the figure he had seen standing over the body. It had all been so indistinct, but he had made out a couple of features – round black eyes or eye sockets, a narrow muzzle-like face, the general pallid whiteness of the creature. Powlin looked at his primitive drawing. Although humanoid, what he had drawn didn't seem to resemble an Endpointer, certainly not any of the residents of Hope. The creature had fled across the ice, away from Hope. Could the city be facing a threat from outside? Powlin gripped the warm mug tighter. This was far worse than the savagery he was used to as Militia Chief. This was something other. Something alien.

Now this, Fitz thought, was more like it. Now he understood why the Silver Palace had such a grandiose name. While it resembled a fortress from the outside, the interior was pure casino, albeit a little rough around the edges. The room they entered was a wide, open space reminiscent of a warehouse, painted a rusty red. Down one side of the room ran an underlit bar, which seemed to be doing a busy trade. At the other end of the room was a stage, where a rather attractive young woman was singing, supported by an unenthusiastic backing band. The rest of the room was given over to various tables where people sat, played cards and engaged in other chaotic gambling pursuits. Staff in tight-fitting crimson uniforms were all over the place, working the tables either as croupiers or waiters. Their uniforms had nifty silver trim, and a logo which resembled an italicised dollar sign, a sloping 's' with a line through it. Fitz idly wondered what it meant. Whatever, the Silver Palace had drinks, gambling, table service; it was exactly the kind of seedy space dive Fitz liked to see.

Fitz turned to the Doctor and Anji. 'Time to see how far our credit stretches, don't you think?' He rubbed his hands together gleefully.

'Don't get carried away,' said the Doctor sternly. 'Remember, we're here to find someone who can retrieve the TARDIS, not bankrupt ourselves with huge gambling debts.'

Fitz gave the Doctor a mock salute. 'No problem. But, fiscal problems aside, I still think we should start our search at the bar.'

Miraso examined the sample with interest. It was definitely organic, probably some form of fruit. Black seeds were visible within the browning flesh. There were none of the telltale signs of a genetic forgery, a familiar species re-engineered to resemble something more exotic. Miraso knew those signs well – she had been a forger herself in the past, before her current employment at the Silver Palace. As deputy to the Palace's owner she tended to take first look at acquisitions such as the current sample, as well as overseeing the long term development of any breeding programmes initiated. Today though, her boss was having one of his periods of scrutinising every detail of the Palace's operation. These periods of micro-management came infrequently but suddenly, and the fear of sudden scrutiny was enough to keep the Palace free of any mismanagement, at any level. Even the lowliest brewer in the Palace's vast cellars didn't dare dilute the product for his own ends, for fear that one week the big man himself would be down there with them, watching the work and looking out for any wrongdoing.

Miraso took the sample, and placed it in the tray of an analyser in one corner of the room. The tray slid into the machine, and a series of numbers began to flow across the machine's screen, complex expressions of the sample's composition. Soon the software would translate the results into something more comprehensible.

The room was in near darkness to aid the resolution of the holoprojector set into the centre of the floor. Miraso stepped away from the analyser and watched as the projector flickered into life, information fed straight from the analyser to this three dimensional representation. A glowing green replica of the sample rotated in midair.

A low chuckle came from the darkness at the other end of the room. Miraso could see the faint glow of one red eye, the glint of metal in the shadows.

'If this is what I think it is,' said a rich, bass-heavy voice, 'then our employees on the door require a raise. Start with a free dose of hedeez for them both, I think they're going to need it.'

Miraso laughed politely. Her boss's low laughter echoed around the room.

The hologram focused on one of the seeds within the sample, and from that extrapolated a life cycle. The seed became a plant, growing into a tall tree, branches spreading out across the room. Miraso watched in fascination as blossoms grew on each branch, followed by lovely round fruit, which in turn contained the seeds. It was a beautiful demonstration of a life cycle, a wonder of natural development.

Heavy footsteps echoed across the room. Huge metallic fingers reached out to stroke the holographic leaves on the tree of light, as if touching the image of a long dead friend.

'As I thought,' the Silver Palace's owner said, a rare note of humility in his deep voice. 'The apple. The fruits of the tree are quite delicious.' He clicked his fingers, a hard noise of metal on metal, snapping Miraso out of the relaxed state the beautiful hologram had sent her into.

'Send the sample down to the labs and have them fastgrow a dozen trees in hydroponics.' Miraso heard a creak as her boss sat back in his chair. 'I expect apples to be the new delicacy by the end of the week.'

Miraso nodded obediently, and went to get the sample from the analyser. The hologram of the apple tree flickered as she walked through it.

'Oh, and Miraso,' her boss said with a familiar note of cunning. 'Fetch me whoever brought this sample to us. I suspect they will be interesting people.'

The beautiful singer had done a couple more numbers while the Doctor had been putting drinks on their account, and had then moved to a stool at the bar, where she proceeded to elegantly smoke a stubby cigar and drink deeply from a harsh-looking bottle of liquor. She looked down to Fitz, so he decided to lighten up her life. On a backwater planet like this, surely a cute girl like that would be impressed by Fitz's adventures.

'Hi,' said Fitz, sidling up to her with his best manly-yet-unthreatening walk. 'I'm Fitz Kreiner, traveller among the stars.'

'Really,' replied the singer, unimpressed. Fitz suspected she didn't believe it.

'Really,' echoed Fitz, using the age-old Kreiner trick of attempted sincerity. 'And I can prove it. Look at this.' He produced a crystal from his pocket, and held it out to the singer. The light refracted beautifully in its many facets.

'What is it?' the singer asked, awestruck. Now he was getting somewhere.

'A thought crystal, a present from the grateful people of a faraway planet.' Fitz dropped his voice to an awestruck whisper, leaning closer to the beautiful singer as he did so. 'Apparently, if you concentrate on the crystal, you can see into the minds of others.'

A frown of concentration passed over the singer's face. She looked deep into the crystal, raising Fitz's hands so that she could look straight through it and into his eyes. She was trying to read his mind.

'Pervert!' The back-handed slap she gave him nearly knocked Fitz off his feet. He watched her perfect bottom march indignantly away from him.

'Man,' said Fitz, examining the crystal with a new-found respect. 'Who would have thought you really worked?'

Anji laughed as Fitz was given the brushoff by the singer. It had been the first moment of brightness in an otherwise grey day, and it felt such a relief to have any kind of emotion other than fear and panic. The Doctor, in spite of himself perhaps, couldn't stop a wry smile as they watched Fitz's comical look of surprise as he sat admiring the crystal in his hands, idly rubbing his slowly reddening cheek.

'Poor Fitz,' Anji said to the Doctor. 'He should have learned by now never to let them know what he's thinking.' She sipped at her drink, which was cold and slightly fruity. She drank sparingly, suspicious of what stimulants might be in the tangy concoction. This was a club of sorts, after all.

'He wouldn't be Fitz if he ever learned things like that,' said the Doctor. 'It's part of his essential Fitz-ness.' He smiled with affection, but Anji could still see a lurking unease in his eyes, a discomfort with both where they were and, she suspected, the absence of the TARDIS.

'Good evening.'

Anji and the Doctor turned to find a young woman smiling at them. Anji couldn't help but use the woman's looks and style of dress as an initial indicator of character, and found herself impressed and not a little envious. She was tall, with long shapely legs and curves in all the right places. Her skin was pale but clear, and although she was as hairless as anyone else here her perfectly rounded scalp was beautiful in itself. Her lips were full on a wide mouth set into an appealingly broad and rounded face, although Anji was sure she could see a tint of suspicion in her deep brown eyes. While her clothes were the same red leather with silver trim as the Palace's staff, they were more casual and less militaristic, her red leather jacket opened to reveal a tight black vest underneath.

'Good evening,' replied the Doctor breathlessly. 'I'm the Doctor, and this is Anji.'

'And I'm Fitz,' yelped Fitz, crashing between the Doctor and Anji to shake the woman's hand rather too vigorously. Anji realised he must have run across the room to get to them.

'And this is indeed Fitz,' said the Doctor, gently moving Fitz out of the way. 'And you are…?'

'Miraso,' said the young woman, slightly perturbed by Fitz almost drooling over her. 'I'm Mr Silver's deputy, I'm involved in a lot of the ground level management of the Silver Palace and many of his other operations.'

'Mr Silver, I presume, being this place's owner?' asked the Doctor.

'Mr Silver is a businessman with many interests,' replied Miraso. 'This is just one of them.'

Anji thought that sounded like a rehearsed speech, and instantly began to wonder exactly what areas of 'business' this Mr Silver could be involved in.

'And how can we help you, Miss Miraso?' asked Fitz eagerly.

'Just "Miraso",' said Miraso a little tersely, her polite façade slipping slightly. 'And, as you are new members of the Silver Palace I thought I'd come down to greet you. Is everything to your satisfaction?'

The Doctor looked blankly at his drink, which he had barely touched, then back at Miraso.

'Wonderful,' he enthused. 'I hope my contribution is proving useful.'

'It's an interesting acquisition,' replied Miraso coolly. 'Mr Silver would love to discuss it with you, if you are agreeable to meeting him.'

'Well,' said the Doctor uncertainly. 'We were actually looking to speak to someone in the salvage business…'

Anji suppressed a smile at the Doctor's negotiating tactics. They seemed obvious to her, but worked a treat on Miraso.

'Mr Silver has salvage interests,' said Miraso a little too hastily, as if afraid of a refusal from the Doctor. 'Mr Silver has many business interests,' she added, repeating herself.

'Excellent,' beamed the Doctor. 'Then it would be a pleasure to meet with him. When would be convenient?'

Miraso shrugged, a little too casually for Anji's liking.

'How about now?' asked Miraso, and Anji's suspicions were raised even further. What sort of businessman was this Mr Silver, and why would he be free at a moment's notice to see the Doctor? Why was he so interested in an apple core? The Silver Palace was a gambling den, full of unsavoury looking characters – Anji had a vision of its owner being Joe Pesci, beating subordinates to death with a tyre iron.

'Excellent, I'll see Mr Silver at once,' said the Doctor pleasantly. He turned to Anji and Fitz. 'I think I'd prefer to handle this meeting myself. You two can stay down here and enjoy yourselves.' His meaning was clear – he didn't feel comfortable with the situation either.

'We'll be right here,' agreed Fitz, and Anji nodded.

Miraso beamed. 'This way then, Doctor.'

Miraso led the Doctor away towards a staircase at the back of the room, and Anji watched with unease.

'I don't trust her,' said Anji.

'Me neither,' agreed Fitz vacantly, watching Miraso's behind as it moved away. He let out a low sigh.

Anji cuffed him around the shoulder.

'We need to be on our guard,' she told him.

'I know,' said Fitz, looking down at her with a level gaze. 'Best if we split up. Keep an eye on the stairs, if the Doctor comes belting out we make a run for the door. Big crowd like this, not too many staff – we should get out of here fine.'

'You're smarter than you look,' said Anji.

Fitz grinned. 'I've been told that wouldn't be hard.' He backed away, heading for his side of the room, but didn't get very far. Anji watched as he bumped into a shorter figure in a long cloak. Fitz bounced back, raising his hands; intergalactic sign language for 'Sorry mate, please don't hit me'.

The shorter man wasn't interested. His hood fell back to reveal a humanoid face, pale with bits of circuitry crudely welded into his flesh. He pulled something resembling a length of springed cable out of his cloak, swinging it around so that it looped around Fitz's neck. With a click the cable sizzled with energy, and Fitz dropped to his knees in agony, clawing at his tethered throat like a wild dog on a leash.

Pandemonium broke out all around. Anji hadn't even noticed the grey-cloaked figures as a coherent group before, but she now realised they were all around, and all of them were taking hostages. Guns were levelled, blades held to throats. The attackers were a motley bunch, unimpressive aside from their grotesque modifications, the electronic devices wired into their flesh. There were protests, but the attackers soon silenced them with a few wild gunshots.

Anji exchanged glances with the Doctor, who had only reached halfway up the stairs when the attacks began. He gave Anji a nod that told her to stay calm, to wait and see. He began to edge his way down the stairs, Miraso behind him, trying not to make any sudden moves.

The room was reduced to a tense near-silence. Anji could hear someone whimpering behind her, but couldn't look away from Fitz, squirming in agony at the end of an electrified leash. The man at the other end of the leash was wild-eyed, triumphant.

'Where is the abomination,' he bellowed. His voice had a metallic edge, as if he were speaking through a vocoder. 'Where is Silver? Bring him to us now, or these feeble primates will all die.' He pulled on Fitz's leash, dragging Anji's friend to his feet. 'Starting with this one.'

Chapter Four
Fight Pub

Anji saw the Doctor edging around the room, looking for an opportunity to disarm one of the attackers. He didn't seem likely to make any sudden moves, as the situation was complex and difficult; too many hostages, and even with Miraso's help and Anji offering some kind of distraction, the Doctor could hardly disarm them all. Even worse, and Anji knew she was being selfish, geographically the last person the Doctor would get to would be Fitz, and looking at his strained face, which was slowly turning purple, Anji didn't want to think how his captor would respond to retaliation.

'Silver!' bellowed the man holding Fitz. 'Come out, Silver!'

A footstep rang out across the room, breaking the tense silence.

Heavy footsteps rang out, the booted feet of someone huge evenly making contact with metallic stairs, stepping into the hostage crisis with neither hesitation or urgency. Anji looked across, and felt her jaw begin to drop. The man walking down the stairs knew how to make an entrance. He was huge, for a start, neither fat nor outrageously tall but muscular, his rolling, brawny shoulders giving him a stooped aspect, even though he was probably standing perfectly upright. Any stoop would have been understandable – one of his arms was oversized, robotic, ending in a huge fist that hung down to knee level. Anji thought she could make out gun-barrel type attachments sprouting from the back of that great, four fingered hand. His other arm was that of a normal human but excessively muscular, and the hand wore a fingerless leather glove. Between the two arms was a barrel of a

45

chest barely covered by a green military vest, with a misshapen, alien-looking device attached to one side. The device boasted various cables and leads, the other ends of which plugged into both cybernetic attachments and human musculature. Compared to the rest of his body the man's legs seemed normal enough, almost short beneath such a huge torso; he wore dark combat trousers and military boots, with a weighty pistol strapped to one leg. As he emerged into the red-tinted light of the Silver Palace, the man's face became clearer, reflecting both sides of his nature; one side was human - real human, with eyebrows and close cropped hair - while the other side was a blank faceplate, a single lens glowing fiercely red in the place of an eye. A smudge of grease or oil ran down from that robotic eye socket, looking for all the world like a teardrop.

'I am Silver,' said the man, pausing on the stairs. It was a rather redundant statement.

The Doctor estimated there were just over a hundred people in the room.

The vast majority he presumed to be, in spite of the effect Endpoint had had on his mood so far, innocents. Potential victims, possibly incapable of defending themselves, certainly considering the state of intoxication they were in.

So, about seventy innocents to protect.

A subgroup of these innocents were the hostages, of which there were about a dozen, including Fitz. They were primary targets for their captors, in immediate danger. Silver was clearly the main target of the aggressors, but the Doctor didn't include him in the subgroup.

So, seventy innocents, twelve of whom were under immediate threat and needed protecting quickly.

Aside from the endangered innocents there was a smaller group, who the Doctor classified as potentially somewhat cannier, and could probably avoid harm without overt protection. The staff - apart from the one member who had been taken hostage - were probably capable enough in a disturbance to duck and cover. Miraso was definitely a bit of a fighter on the sly, and Anji had been travelling with the Doctor long enough to look after herself, at least for a few minutes if all hell broke loose. This group numbered about a dozen, and the Doctor didn't feel he needed to worry about them just yet.

Then there were the attackers, the hostage takers, the aggressors. The Doctor didn't know their motivation, whether they were right or wrong in their long term goals. They were recklessly endangering the lives of others. They needed to be stopped. There were twelve of them, all armed with a motley collection of weapons – electroleashes, stun pistols, microblades, force hammers – many of which had primary uses other than as weaponry. Their cybernetic enhancements, while primitive compared to Silver's arm, would undoubtedly give them enhanced strength, and probably greater speed. Their leader seemed a little unbalanced. Very, very dangerous.

Seventy potential victims, a dozen people who could look after themselves, another dozen who needed to be knocked out before they could harm anyone. All mixed together in a crowded, smoky environment, booze and litter messing up the floor. Difficult.

There was a final group the Doctor had to include. A group of two people, who between them were the only possible source of retaliation against the attackers, who no matter what would be able to defend themselves from attack and were the only hope of saving the innocents in the room.

Himself and Silver. Unfortunately, the Doctor had no idea whether Silver wanted to save anyone, or whether he would prove a threat himself.

So the Doctor remained still, poised, waiting for Silver to act as he strolled casually down the stairs.

The leash around Fitz's neck was a ring of fire, his nervous system generously spreading the pain through the rest of his body. He could barely move, but the unnatural strength of his attacker pulled Fitz to his feet, holding him steady. Blackness threatened to consume him, his vision receding to red tunnels. He barely registered the blurred face of Anji hovering before him, the look of concern. Unbearable pain tried to rob him of consciousness, and he wasn't sure whether the room had gone quiet or he had been deafened, or his mind was simply unable to process the sounds, unable to think of anything beyond how much it *hurt*.

Anji's attention was no longer on him, he saw through a red mist. She was looking past him, open-mouthed. And what was that sound, that thumping in his head? It sounded just like footsteps, echoing footsteps...

Fitz lost consciousness. He didn't even come around when his assailant dropped him to the floor, face down.

Anji lunged forward to catch Fitz, but she wasn't nearly fast enough. No one stopped her as she dropped to her knees on the filthy floor, scooping her arms under Fitz's shoulders and gingerly turning him over on to his back. She put her head to his chest. His breathing was ragged but constant. She thumbed his eyelids open, remembering both her first-aid knowledge and the sort of thing people did on TV under these circumstances. Anji couldn't see herself in Holby just yet, but Fitz seemed to be OK to her, pupils unfocused in unconsciousness, whites bloodshot but no evidence of anything worse. His nostrils were bloody from his encounter with the floor, but they'd all been there before. A few knocks came with the territory.

Shuffling backwards along the floor, Anji moved Fitz away from his attacker as carefully as she could. She took occasional furtive glances at the man, who was screaming gibberish at Silver, ranting about abominations and blasphemies and God alone knew what else. Anji wasn't interested. She needed to move Fitz out of the way, get them both back. Because when this Silver character reacted to these slurs on his character, Anji didn't want herself or her friend to be anywhere near either party.

She suspected it wasn't going to be a pleasant conversation.

* * *

A war in a neighbouring country can be ignored by millions. A dozen star systems could flare up and die, and the slow passage of light from the stellar inferno would take millennia to reach other inhabited worlds. But in the right context, a gesture can bring silence, can change the flow of events of everyone around.

A butterfly can flap its wings, an earthquake occurs elsewhere. But which is noticed?

A stand off. Members of the Brotherhood wield weapons, their leader rages, lives hang in the balance. A girl from millennia before nurses her friend, the only two members of their species in the room. Their descendants, used to violence as they are, still stand uneasy, waiting to act. A man with no past watches, waits to see what will happen, prepared to risk all to protect the lives of those whom he does not know.

Fingers caress triggers uneasily, muscles are tensed. A room full of people prepares for violence.

Then Silver raises his hand. His great steel fist opens out in a gesture for silence, and everyone in the room obeys.

'What do you want here?' asked Silver, his deep bass voice reverberating around the room. Anji felt an itching at the bottom of her spine. Even though the question wasn't aimed at her, Silver's voice was commanding enough to make her feel compelled to obey. It was a nauseating feeling, this urge to comply regardless of free will.

'We are the Brotherhood of the Silver Fist,' said Fitz's assailant, his synthetic voice lapsing into hysteria. 'We follow the true path of logic, the digital way, and we come to purge you from existence.'

'Really?' said Silver, unimpressed. 'Leave now. While you can.'

'Not with you alive,' came the reply, and the brother pulled a gun from within his robes, raising it towards Silver.

He pulled the trigger, and a ball of plasma streaked across the room, impacting with the staircase and reducing the handrails to twisted metal.

But Silver wasn't there. He had jumped, defying gravity and his own unwieldy appearance. He flew over the crowded room with surprising grace, flipping over in midair, perfectly balanced. His attacker desperately raised his gun, firing off another couple of shots as Silver hurtled towards him, but they went wide. Silver raised his fist, bringing it down towards his enemy's head as he came in to land. The result was a pile-driver blow, his fist coming straight down into his opponent's face and pushing his whole body back, Silver putting his entire weight behind his fist so that he landed in a crouch, hands hitting the floor. His attacker's head was trapped between one very heavy fist and one very hard floor.

Anji ducked and covered her head, only to feel something hot and wet spray across the back of it, hear a vile crunching as the impact rocked the room. She looked up again to see Silver in a crouch, the thick knuckles of his steel fist resting against the ground, blood and bone splattered across them. With great dignity he pulled himself into a standing position, surveying the crowd, as if challenging the dead man's allies to step forward.

'Who next?' growled Silver, and all hell broke loose.

Across the room, the hostage-takers moved their weapons away from threatening their hostages, ready to attack Silver. In that second the Doctor began to move. He shoulder-barged one of the attackers, sending the man flying across the room. The gun the man was carrying spun across the floor as its owner raised his hands to break his fall, and the Doctor kicked it out of reach.

One down.

Miraso ran in the opposite direction to the Doctor, running up behind the back of a confused Brotherhood member while drawing the stubby pistol strapped underneath her jacket. With one fluid motion she raised the pistol to the back of the man's head and pulled the trigger, the shot flying clear over the head of the hostage he'd been holding to his chest with a knife to her throat. Miraso pulled the corpse towards her as it fell, pushing the twitching knife arm away so the shaken hostage could slip out without harm, bloodied but otherwise OK.

* * *

The two humans lying on the floor, one cradling the head of the other – a baffling anomaly for sure – almost distracted Silver from the two cult members running up behind them. Almost. He raised his artificial hand and activated the gun built into the back. A heads-up display appeared over the image in his synthetic eye, outlining potential life signs. He locked on to the two attackers and released a couple of explosive charges, which flew over the heads of the two humans to hit the two men directly in the chest.

The female human was looking up at him in open-mouthed awe, and Silver nodded chivalrously, as if to suggest his actions were purely for the benefit of her defence.

Anji had nearly lost control of her bodily functions as Silver had raised his hand, the little barrels extending out of the back. For one split second, in spite of there being numerous targets more dangerous in the vicinity, she had thought he was going to kill her. It was an instinctive, primal reaction to having a weapon raised in one's presence, a gut reaction of fear and a desperate urge for self-preservation. It hadn't helped that Silver had fired a couple of shots over her head, and she'd swung around to see two members of the Brotherhood of the Silver Whatsit flying back, their chests opened up by Silver's exploding bullets, yet more blood spraying across the room.

She looked back to Silver, who nodded politely in her direction. Anji didn't know how to react, so strange was this almost dainty gesture performed by a giant war machine of a man. All she could do was nod in reply.

'Wurrrrhhh,' murmured Fitz, whose head was still lying in her lap.

'Wake up, Fitz!' barked Anji, slapping him hastily on the cheek. 'We need to move.'

'Wuz ate in,' mumbled Fitz blurrily, but he opened his eyes nonetheless. Anji felt the tension in his shoulders as he realised where he was, recognised the sound of gunfire and brawling. He began to scramble to his feet.

* * *

The Doctor ducked and weaved towards his second target, who still had a hostage and was holding a microblade. The man swung the blade around to threaten the Doctor, at which point his hostage elbowed him hard in the gut. The winded man staggered, and it was a simple enough process for the Doctor to distract him by waving one hand while snatching the weapon away with the other. The man snarled, revealing a plastic air filter instead of an airway inside his mouth, and lunged for the Doctor's throat.

Miraso's knees buckled under the weight of the corpse, but on hearing a clicking behind her she swung it around as a human shield, ducking down as she raised her gun. This new attacker had claws crudely implanted in the back of his hands, and as he swung them down they embedded themselves in the body of his late compatriot. Miraso, deciding on non-lethal force, chose not to use her gun and instead pushed up behind the corpse, so that her assailant couldn't get his claws free. He cried out as she pushed all three of them over, and he crashed down on to his back with the body on top of him. Miraso for her part rolled off, landing in a crouch and reholstering her gun. Before her attacker could push the corpse off him she ran up and kicked him hard in the face. His nose crunched nicely beneath the impact of her boot.

One attacker fired a stunblast at Silver, the energy bolt impacting on the naked flesh of his shoulder. A slight ripple of irritation spread across his skin, but otherwise there was no effect.

Silver turned to the man with the stunblaster, who had given up on the useless pistol and was running towards him with a forcehammer raised, letting out a less-than-logical war cry. Silver slapped him away with the back of his artificial fist, snatching at the handle of the forcehammer with his human hand. The forcehammer was heavy even for him, but he swung it around, muscles burning as he raised it in the air, proof that the enemy's weapons could be used against them.

'Citizens of Hope,' Silver bellowed, holding the hammer high as his opponent crumpled to the ground, knocked out cold. 'Defend yourselves and repel these attackers!'

Ignoring Silver's 'Henry V' routine, Fitz followed Anji as she scrambled across the floor, keeping low to avoid flying debris. She ducked through a doorway in the bar, flying glass landing in her hair as bottles exploded nearby. Fitz scurried behind, joining her by the drip-trays.

Looking past Anji, Fitz saw that there were two members of the barstaff already hiding there, covering their heads and holding their hands over their ears. Fitz couldn't blame them with this racket. His head still ached from being half strangled with an electric noose, now this. To make matters worse, he had passed out and didn't have any idea why any of this was happening.

Then again, he thought, what else was new?

Sharp nails dug into the skin of the Doctor's neck, clawing into his throat. Luckily for him his attacker's hands were completely human, unmodified. Unluckily for the Doctor the arms behind those hands had been enhanced, putting an unnatural strength behind the attempt to strangle the life from him. He would usually be able to deal with such an attack, close down his breathing to render the assault worthless. But since his illness...

The Doctor felt everything around him become distant, heard the hot rush of blood in his ears, saw the face of his attacker become less and less distinct, the expression of loathing less visible. Blackness crept in, reducing his vision to a tunnel. He desperately tried to pull those hands away from his neck, to twist the arms out of the way, but his grasping hands found only steel and plastic, no muscle or nerves to be pinched.

Then he was free, his attacker dragged off him by numerous hands. The Doctor scrambled to his feet, one hand instinctively going to his bruised throat. He felt unsteady on his feet, his single heartbeat racing to maintain the pace so recently kept by two. Around him, Silver was directing the crowds to repel the

Brotherhood, to cast them out of the Silver Palace. The Doctor's attacker was being carried on the shoulders of the rabble, flailing helplessly as the melee moved towards the exit. A couple of the other Brothers were on their feet, running away from angry crowds. The Doctor saw Silver picking up one of the fanatics, throwing him across the room with one swing of his huge robotic arm.

A cheer went out across the room, and Fitz gingerly stuck his head out from behind the bar. The weird part-robot guys in the cloaks seemed to have been repelled, with the aid of the big weird part-robot guy. Fitz presumed that this was a victory for what nominally counted as 'their side'.

Fitz staggered out from behind the bar. The Silver Palace was reduced to a battlefield; tables had been smashed to pieces, there was broken glass everywhere and there were occasional smoking patches where firearms had been discharged. There were a number of bodies lying around, but as they seemed to all belong to members of the group who had attacked – including the one who had held Fitz captive – Fitz found it hard to care too much, instead electing to divert his eyes and not think too hard about the humanoid remains around him.

'Good God,' said Anji in disgust. Fitz turned to see her surveying the wreckage, and noticed with concern the blood smeared across her forehead. He instinctively touched his own forehead and she frowned, echoing the gesture. She stared at the blood on her fingers with revulsion.

'It isn't mine,' she said simply, using a handkerchief to wipe the gore from her face.

'OK,' replied Fitz, unsure what to say. Anji seemed a little shell-shocked, but then he felt too shaken to judge.

'Are you two all right?' asked the Doctor, pushing through the crowd to get to Fitz and Anji, quickly looking them over as if checking for any obvious damage to a couple of valuable ornaments. To Fitz's alarm he could see a nasty black bruise growing on the Doctor's throat.

'We're fine,' he said insistently. He gestured to his own neck. 'Are you...?'

'Some slight bruising,' said the Doctor, a slight croak in his voice belying the sentiment. He tightened his cravat to conceal the damage. 'It will heal quickly enough.'

A chant was beginning to ripple through the crowd around them, one name repeated over and over.

'Silver! Silver! Silver!'

'I gather that's Silver,' said Fitz, nodding towards where the giant cyborg was climbing on to one of the few surviving tables.

'Yes,' said the Doctor, looking over at Silver with concern. 'It's him we have to deal with.'

Fitz didn't enquire as to which meaning the Doctor was ascribing to the phrase 'deal with'. Instead he turned to where Silver was clearly preparing to make a speech. In spite of the seemingly ludicrous robot arm bolted on to his body, which should have made him seem entirely lopsided, Fitz was surprised to find that Silver had a strange grace about him, a precision of movement perhaps aided by his computerised senses, as if he were more than a human with a couple of attachments. And that was another thing – Silver was clearly human, not an Endpointer. He had hair, thick and black, and one dark eyebrow that ran right up to the faceplate that covered the other half of his head. His skin was a rich, dark tone, and Fitz could swear there was a South American lilt to Silver's deep voice as he spoke.

'Thank you for your help in defending this, my home,' boomed Silver. 'Yet again it is shown that united against disorder we can bring reason to any situation. Unfortunately the results of this noble struggle mean that the Silver Palace will have to close for the next six hours for repairs. While those of you with restspace or outstanding intercreds may of course retire to the west corridor for this period, I am afraid I will have to ask the rest of you to leave for the moment.'

There were murmurs, albeit quiet ones, of discontent among the crowd.

'In gratitude for your help in defending this oasis of

civilisation,' added Silver. 'You will find that upon your next visit all of you here tonight will have a hundred extra credits on your account!'

The murmurs ceased and another chant of Silver's name went out.

'Thank you,' said Silver humbly, giving a slight bow. Gradually, the crowd began to disperse.

'He's certainly an impressive speaker,' said Fitz. 'These guys were lapping it up.'

'The fact that he can fire missiles from his wrists probably helped keep their attention,' commented Anji.

'In that case I'd be careful when you shake his hand,' added the Doctor.

Miraso was leading Silver towards them, leaning over to speak into his single ear. Fitz couldn't help be intimidated by the sheer size of the man, the raw power and presence he seemed to have. The only person Fitz had never known to have a comparable aura of authority was the Doctor – and Fitz was worried that the Doctor wasn't himself to that extent at the moment.

'Miraso has explained that you were responsible for bringing us an intriguing sample earlier today,' said Silver. Close up, Fitz found his voice even more overwhelming, like resting your head against a guitar amp just as someone strummed a power chord.

'Please,' added Silver. 'Let's talk in comfort.' He walked over to where a heavy wooden table had been knocked over in the fight, and picked it up with his artificial hand as if it were a paper plate, standing it upright and indicating for them to find chairs.

As they sat around the table, Silver ordered his staff to bring drinks, and had Miraso effect introductions between them. Silver seemed interested in them all equally, something Fitz didn't feel entirely comfortable with. There were times when the Doctor's tendency to be an attention-magnet was welcome.

'I gather you're travellers,' said Silver innocuously, pouring himself a glass of water from a large jug. His human eye looked straight across at the Doctor. 'Something tells me you're from further away than just some community of throwback inbreds.'

Fitz almost choked on his drink.

'We've come some distance,' said the Doctor levelly, evenly returning Silver's stare. He took the water jug and poured himself a glass. 'I'd be interested to know why you've come to such conclusions.'

'The unmistakable life signs of humanity,' said Silver. He tapped the rim of his glowing red robot eye. 'This allows me to see more than others. By the way, Doctor, I'd watch your heart rate if I were you. It seems rather over exercised.'

The Doctor didn't blink. 'Thank you for the advice,' he said flatly. 'I presume you intended to talk about something other than my health.'

Silver shrugged, a gesture that resembled a mountain range doing a Mexican wave.

'You are not from this planet, you are not from this time,' said Silver. 'I thought I was the last human this far into the future – and even I am a borderline case. To meet other time refugees like yourselves, others who are far from their place in history, is a rare luxury. I have to admit you three have intrigued me.'

'We're glad to be so entertaining,' said the Doctor. 'But there is business we need to discuss.'

Fitz had never seen the Doctor so cold. He hoped the Doctor wasn't going to blow these negotiations with his bad attitude.

'I'm always ready to discuss business,' said Silver, one eye narrowing. 'Please go on.'

'I have a box,' said the Doctor simply. 'It contains my personal possessions, and sank into the sea on the edges of Hope. I was told you might be able to retrieve it.'

Silver sat back, pressing his hands together in a thoughtful gesture akin to steepling his fingers. Of course, in this case the fingers of one hand barely covered the palm of the other. He paused.

'This will be very difficult,' said Silver. 'Very expensive and difficult, and you are strangers to this place with little to offer in terms of wealth. While I would like to offer my help without charge, Hope is a place of scarce resources and I am, I am afraid, a businessman at heart and need to protect my interests.' He paused again, leaning forward across the table. 'However, I am sure a mutually satisfactory arrangement can be made, so that your box may be returned to you.'

'And what do you want in return?' asked the Doctor suspiciously, leaning forward so that he and Silver were barely a foot apart.

'You work for me,' said Silver simply. 'The people of Endpoint, a few exceptions like dear Miraso aside, are savages. I need people of delicacy to work for me, and the three of you seem intelligent enough.'

'I'm not for hire,' said the Doctor indignantly.

Silver tapped his finger on the table so hard the noise echoed around the room. Everyone else had left, and the only other people there were staff, busy clearing the wreckage.

'You won't find anyone else who can retrieve something from those hostile waters, Doctor,' said Silver. 'I can tell you're a man of principles, the way you jumped to the defence of all and sundry back there proves it. And I can offer you a task that will fit with your principles, if you wish. Consider it a case of you helping me and me helping you, if it eases your conscience at all.'

'And what is this task?' asked the Doctor. 'I may act to defend others, but I'm not a fighter or a killer if that's what you're after.'

'I didn't think so,' said Silver. 'What I wish you to do is save lives. A number of murders have occurred. Now, death is no stranger to Hope, as you have probably gathered from tonight's fracas. This is a violent world, these are harsh times. But these killings are different, premeditated and surgical in their precision.'

'The head chopping,' blurted Fitz, only then aware that he had spoken out loud. He was worried about having embarrassed himself, but the Doctor and Silver were too busy staring out each other to look in his direction.

'Exactly,' said Silver. 'The decapitations, an unnatural and freakish set of occurrences beyond the everyday. They suggest an order, divine intervention. They represent something beyond my control, they are the actions of someone who demonstrably can act as they wish without my permission. This is not acceptable.' He leaned forward until the curve of his faceplate was almost touching the Doctor's nose. 'Hope is my city,' he seethed, almost grinding his teeth. 'I want these killings stopped. And I want you to find the perpetrator and stop them.' He fell back in his seat. 'Do this and you can have your box.'

The Doctor sat and thought about this offer, although Fitz knew there was no choice to make. Silver held all the cards, and they were at his table.

'It's a deal,' said the Doctor quietly, reluctantly.

'A deal it is,' replied Silver, holding his hand across the table.

They shook hands, the Doctor's pale hand dwarfed by the cybernetic hand that gripped it.

Part Two
Escalation

Chapter Five
Fear of Flying

If a bird breaks its wing, how does it survive? How does it hunt, how can it defend itself in a flat world without the power of flight, tethered by gravity in a way it never has been before?

It learns to run, thought the Doctor. To run, to jump, to negotiate the ground without the benefit of an aerial view, to hunt in the long grass without being able to swoop over it. No longer a creature of the air, it adapts, force-evolves itself to its new circumstances as a land-bound creature.

Either that, or it dies, crushed by a smaller world without the gift of flight.

The Doctor sat at the top of a tall tower, cravat tied over his nose and mouth, sore eyes peering out across the city of Hope as dawn began to rise. Having sealed the deal with Silver he had left Fitz and Anji to settle in at the Silver Palace and ventured out to survey the landscape he needed to familiarise himself with, to try and know it how this agile killer must know it. So he had climbed to the top of a mesh-covered pylon tower, gingerly avoiding the web of live cables that passed through it, and found a flat area on top of it where he could sit and wait for the dawn. And as he sat he thought about blind men finding their hearing enhanced, flightless birds learning how to run and beached fish finding they have lungs. Evolve or die. While Hope was a miserable, brutal place, he now appreciated that the people here had learned to survive in the face of seemingly endless adversity. It proved that adaptation and change could deal with the direst of circumstances.

The Doctor sat and he thought, and although his body was now more human than before, his thoughts were not human thoughts.

* * *

Although it was late at night for the residents of Hope, it was mid-morning for Fitz and Anji, so while the Doctor disappeared into the night to get the lie of Hope's land, his companions had stayed up watching – and, where possible, helping – the Silver Palace's staff with the post-brawl cleaning job. Broken items had been swept up, loaded into plastic bins and taken into the depths of the Palace where, if Hope was as resource intense as they were told, the pieces would be dredged through to find anything recyclable. Anji and Fitz – no doubt seeming bizarrely lively for such an antisocial hour, had eagerly helped sweep and mop the floor, occasionally getting into impromptu broom duels to the mild entertainment of those watching. Fitz had briefly played up his injuries, but had rapidly become so bored that cleaning seemed a good alternative to sitting around.

Finally, with floors polished and shrapnel cleared, the furniture had been put back in place. A couple of tables and a few chairs had to be completely replaced with new items, and this was done so efficiently that Fitz was left wondering exactly how often this kind of thing occurred. With the place back to normal most of the staff rapidly disappeared to their quarters, leaving only Miraso, Fitz and Anji sitting around the table Silver had set up an hour or so before. Fitz leaned back in his seat staring up at the ceiling. The lights were now dimmed, and he could see that above the lighting rigs the ceiling was a dome, with some kind of mural painted on it. It was hardly the Sistine Chapel; the brushstrokes were crude, and seemed to depict some kind of apocalypse, with planets exploding and ships fleeing.

'What's with the ceiling?' Fitz asked, never too afraid to speak his mind.

Miraso stared at him blankly, then looked up.

'Huh, that,' she said. 'Hope used to be pretty feudal a few generations back, and the Palace is built around what used to be some sort of meeting hall. The painting must come from that period, it's all the typical tribal history crap, where we came from and how we got here. You know, knowledge has been lost so often sometimes communities need to go back to the basics to pass things down.'

'Why don't you talk us through it?' asked Anji politely. Fitz glanced between the two women – Miraso seemed surprised by the suggestion, but not overtly suspicious.

'If you like,' said Miraso. 'I'm too wired to sleep anyway.'

She stood up, stepping backwards across the room to point at a part of the mural that illustrated a handful of planets orbiting a sun. The sun was a bright yellow with a little fleck of orange along one side, while the planets were all different colours.

'Right,' said Miraso. 'This is where we begin.'

Once, at the end of time, there was a solar system with several inhabited worlds. Races and peoples from across the galaxy lived there, although as time went on those species intermingled and essentially became one diverse people. While not a utopia, the standard of life in the system was good, and populations rose. As resources became tighter, space stations and other remote facilities were constructed in orbit around the various worlds, and one particular cold, watery rock, long named 'A245' but generally referred to as 'Endpoint' due to its reputation as the last place anyone would want to go, was designated as the place to offload all the waste of a highly populated system. Spent fuel rods, decommissioned military equipment, every possible kind of dangerous waste imaginable – it all ended up on the Endpoint, flooding the seas with poison and darkening the skies.

The fall of this system was due to no internal problem, no hubris or error on the part of those who lived there. They were simply stuck between two sides in one of the many wars that had raged since humanity's fall all those long, long millennia ago. Suffice to say a fleet of ships arrived in the system, knocking stations and moons out of orbit as these vast war-carriers sought shelter in their retreat from the enemy. An enemy who ploughed through the system, indiscriminately blasting planets to dust as they tore through their intended targets, leaving behind total devastation; all the decent planets had gone, cracked open by weaponry the inhabitants couldn't even comprehend. The space between those planets was left a minefield, huge chunks of debris colliding and inter-colliding, a Newtonian system that made the whole area impossible for space travel.

Not that the rest of the universe really cared. Hit badly by the war themselves, the empires and the factions had better things to do than send valuable ships into a star system reduced to a graveyard. It was too dangerous, there was no point, no hope that traces of civilisation had survived.

Little did they know that on the planet Endpoint, the last world orbiting that sun, the survivors of the cataclysm had gathered, fleeing in their habitation pods and their ships to the only place left to go. Debris rained down on Endpoint, the remnants of their now wrecked civilisations and fragments from the great ships that had doomed the system by seeking sanctuary there. And the people who had somehow survived the destruction of their homeworlds, who had survived the rigours of Endpoint's environments, began to use this wreckage to build. Over the centuries, something resembling civilisation re-emerged on the desolate surface of Endpoint. Communities thrived, people survived, tribes formed and alliances were made. While governments and townships rose and fell, life went on.

Miraso shrugged. 'And that's what its been like ever since. It isn't really an ending, I know, but that's what you get for asking for a true story.' She sat back down, rubbing the back of her neck. Fitz presumed it ached from staring up at the ceiling.

'Oh, I don't know,' said the Doctor, emerging from the shadows. 'I've always liked a deferred ending. It means you can make up your own mind over how the story ends.' Fitz noted a swagger in his step, a determination and purpose that had been absent earlier in the evening.

'How long have you been there?' asked Miraso suspiciously.

'Long enough,' said the Doctor. 'This place is fascinating. It's a wonder anything can live on Endpoint, never mind maintain a complex society here.'

'We pull through,' said Miraso.'I see you found your way back.'

'A traveller like myself learns how to get around new places,' said the Doctor.'You know, I'm quite surprised you still have the same guards at the door as earlier tonight. I'm surprised the Brotherhood didn't kill or seriously injure them in the attack.'

Miraso shrugged yet again. 'If they weren't resilient, they wouldn't make good door staff.'

The Doctor mimicked her shrug. 'I suppose that's true. Still, putting them back to work so soon after being attacked – that seems a little harsh.'

'This is a harsh world, Doctor,' said Miraso.

Fitz knew what the Doctor wanted to say; that the harshness of Endpoint was no reason to become harsh yourself, that a person should struggle against such an environment.

But the Doctor didn't say anything of the sort. Although less morose than before, he seemed tired; not just from experience past, but the sort of exhaustion brought on by what a person is facing.

'It's very late,' said the Doctor. 'Fitz and Anji need to sleep if they're to have any chance of adjusting to local time.'

Miraso nodded. 'Certainly. We'll put you in the spare staff quarters.' Miraso walked over to a door by the bar.'If you'd follow me.'

The Doctor dreams.

The great ship rocks upon the dark, stormy sea, but the First Mate holds the wheel steady and the ship maintains its course, cutting through the hostile waves. Whistles blow and sailors climb the rigging, struggling with ropes and adjusting the sails. Forked lightning licks the mast, sliding up and threatening to set the sails aflame, but the fire doesn't catch and none of the crew are hurt.

The Doctor looks out across the sea, but there is only the void, swirling clouds and foaming sea blurring into a mass of grey, occasionally illuminated by the flashes of primal energy that erupt from those massed clouds.

'Captain,' cries the First Mate. 'We're approaching the enemy.'

Before the Doctor realises he's been addressed, he straightens his brightly-buttoned jacket and marches to the prow. He looks out, and sights land ahead. A shining island, floating in the darkness. The enemy.

The Doctor, who barely knows himself by now, feels free of the restrictions of himself. He is a new man, unsure not only of what he is doing but of what it is his nature to do. He cuts free with a bold decision, pulling up his own anchor and setting himself adrift.

'Raise the cannons!' booms the Doctor, and gun barrels are raised, some from the prow of the ship, others from within the deck.

He raises his arm, feeling the wind and the rain lashing his bare hand. Nature is against him, but he can withstand the storm.

'Fire!' cries the Doctor, bringing down his arm. Cannon balls streak through the night, exploding on impact with the shining land. The shore ahead erupts into flames, massive destruction caused by the Doctor's order. Smoke drifts up into the clouds, is swept away in the storm. The ruins smoulder.

The Doctor stares at his own hand, the one which fell as he ordered the attack. How could he underestimate the strength he held, in a word and a gesture?

Powlin awoke at his desk, yet again. The yellow, sickly light of an Endpoint dawn seeped in through the small window in his office, tinting his vision a ghastly sepia. The whole place looked how he felt – aged, crumpled, worn out and about to split apart. He groaned at recollection of the previous night's events – another victim, and still nowhere near catching the creature that was perpetrating these bizarre, pointless crimes. Powlin couldn't even be sure of a human assailant, he now had a potentially bug-eyed killer who might even be able to survive in Endpoint's foul seas. Anything that survived swimming through that corrosive filth would probably be near unstoppable.

And what if he couldn't stop it? The Hope Militia was an independent body of law enforcement, funded through tax and sustained democratically. Powlin was ostensibly only answerable to the people of Hope as a mass, to a council of the city's leaders of an elected assembly, should one be called. In reality none of that was at all relevant to the day-to-day reality of this case. Powlin was required to answer to one man who, in spite of being officially a lone citizen, would be quite capable of removing Powlin from his post, from the city and from life itself. And no one would ever stop him.

Powlin imagined those eyes staring at him across the room. One eye expressing harsh disapproval, the other an unmoving red light, pointing at Powlin's head like a laser sight. When that red eye stared out of Silver's head Powlin imagined himself as a target, lined up in some heads-up display inside the cyborg's semi-computerised brain, a cross hair floating over his forehead. How much further could he displease Silver before he put that targeting to use, shooting Powlin through the head with a flick of his wrist cannon, one gesture firing an armour-piercing round straight through Powlin's skull? An appropriate end to his glittering career.

This was getting him nowhere. Powlin dragged himself out from the narrow space behind his desk, back and neck aching from sleeping sitting up. He sniffed his shirt – he smelt worse than last week's victim. Seizing a pile of fairly clean clothes from the corner of the room, he staggered up the rickety watchtower stairs, mumbling exhausted greetings to a colleague he passed awkwardly on the narrow stairwell. One floor up there was a shower room, based around a decontamination cubicle salvaged from a mining ship. Fifteen minutes later he emerged, scoured and wearing fresh clothing, a bundle of dirty clothes over his arm. With a slight spring in his step he descended the stairs three at a time, heading down into the depths of the tower. Past the office levels, past the holding and processing areas at ground levels 1–3, and down into the sub-surface level. Next to the mortuary and infirmary, in dim underground regions lit only by flickering gas light, were a number of small rooms where militiamen could perform any necessary domestic tasks. Powlin stuffed his dirty clothes into a cleaning machine, programmed it to blitz the filthy rags then proceeded to the small kitchen area. It was airless and dark, what air there was tainted by slightly stale food, but it was the nearest thing to a homely, domestic place the tower had.

Powlin found some stodgy but edible rations in the refrigerator, and prepared himself a fresh mug of caffy, then sat down at a chipped wooden table. It was an unsociably early hour, and the only other person in the room was an overweight militia woman unconscious across a couple of chairs, still half-strapped into her riot armour. Powlin ate quietly, trying not to wake her.

He was halfway through breakfast, eyes vacantly staring at the lurid green-painted walls, when the throwback witness from the night before burst into the room, ducking around the furniture to drop into a seat opposite Powlin. The Doctor, that was his name.

'Chief Powlin,' said the Doctor, grinning broadly. The man's eyes seemed bright green with enthusiasm, although Powlin could see the whites were slightly bloodshot. 'Beautiful morning we're having. You weren't in your office, and your neighbour pointed me down here.'

Powlin was about to ask how the Doctor had a free run of the watchtower in the first place, but was interrupted by the odd man leaning over the table to sniff at Powlin's caffy.

'Is that coffee?' asked the Doctor.

'Caffy,' corrected Powlin.

'But it's a hot, caffeineated drink?' the Doctor asked.

'Ye-s,' said Powlin, stretching the vowel. Where did this guy come from? 'There's a fresh pot over there if you want some.'

'Excellent!' exclaimed the Doctor, wild-eyed, slapping his palms on the table.

The unconscious woman across the room stirred in her sleep at the noise, mumbling to herself.

The Doctor scrambled across to the caffy pot, found a chipped mug and poured himself some. Powlin watched with interest. The Doctor seemed exhausted, strung out yet eager to keep pushing on, to stay awake and keep moving. Powlin guessed he wasn't sleeping too well. Bad dreams, perhaps?

'What are you doing here, Doctor?' asked Powlin as the man sat down, sipping his hot caffy tentatively. 'Remembered some further detail of what you saw?'

The Doctor shook his head, his hair – a part of his body Powlin couldn't imagine having – waving from side to side as he did so. 'No, no, no,' said the Doctor. 'I'm afraid my involvement in the case is rather more direct than that now.'

Powlin frowned. Was this madman about to confess?

'You see,' said the Doctor. 'Silver has hired me to find this killer for him.'

Powlin, who had been gulping his own caffy at the time, nearly spat it down his chin in shock.

'What?' he demanded. 'He has no juris… I mean he can't…' He trailed off, aghast. 'He could at least have killed me before replacing me.'

'Believe me,' said the Doctor. 'I'm as unhappy about this as you are, and I have no intention of interfering in the proper rule of law here. Besides, our own feelings, and those of Mr Silver, are a side issue. What matters is that people are dying, and we need to find this killer and stop him. Who captures the murderer is of no relevance to the potential victims.'

Powlin looked into the Doctor's eyes, and saw a certainty, a moral intensity he had never seen in anyone before.

'So,' said the Doctor, returning Powlin's stare. 'Can I count on your co-operation?'

Powlin nodded. 'Where do you want to start?'

Miraso only had a few hours sleep, but that was OK. She had made sure to take a nap the previous afternoon, to be fresh for the evening's activities. Those extra few hours had been a useful top up. As the working day began she was showered and dressed, eating a heavily sweetened cereal mash for breakfast –

one of the perks of her position. She was just finishing up when a call came through on her commlink – a summons from Silver.

Her boss's office was only a brisk walk away from her quarters, so three minutes later she was knocking on his door. A deep grunt from inside indicated that she should go in.

Early daylight was pouring into Silver's office, the holograms off and the blinds drawn. Silver's office windows were a sign of his personal prosperity, vast sheets of triple-bonded plexiglass, flawlessly clear and stretching out behind his desk. The outside was mirrored – Silver had a panoramic view of the city outside, but the city could never see in. It was very much a one-way relationship.

Silver was sitting at his desk, haloed by the light. A large plastibound book from his shelves was open in the palm of his vast metal hand, one finger of his human hand following the text across the page. The human side of Silver's face was fixed in concentration as he read. Miraso wondered whether he had noticed her, until he waved for her to sit down. She sank into the heavily upholstered chair, squinting slightly with the sun in her eyes. After a couple of minutes Silver closed the book, placing it gently in the centre of the desk.

'Apples and humans, both long extinct,' Silver said, drumming his fingers on the closed book. 'Both arrive here out of nowhere, in spite of our isolation from the rest of the universe. Our visitors have as good as admitted to being lost in time as well as space. And the only thing we know for sure about our visitors from far away is that they've lost a box. A box they are desperate to get back. What does this tell us?'

'My guess?' said Miraso. 'The box is somehow connected to their way home.'

'How?' prompted Silver.

Miraso shrugged. 'Judging by the size of the box described, it must be some kind of hyperspatial, possibly multi-dimensional link to wherever they come from. If they are from another time, then it might be a time-travel device.'

Silver smiled his best predatory smile. 'Exactly. And they have pointed us in the direction of this wonderful box of theirs. How generous. How stupid.'

'Do you want the box retrieved now?' asked Miraso.

Silver shook his head. 'No, I do not have enough information to make my move. Yet.' He swung his chair around, indicating the shelves of books against the wall, books just like the one he had been reading. 'Do you know what these volumes are?' he asked.

'Books that I'll die if I touch,' Miraso replied. It was a statement, it wasn't something that distressed her. She had no intention of breaking Silver's rules.

'These are the chronicles of the knowledge installed in my brain by those who upgraded me, who made me what I am,' said Silver, almost wistful. 'I have lived longer than was ever expected of me, and as time has gone on I have required more of my personal memory banks for my own memories.' He tapped the side of his faceplate with a metal finger, the clash ringing out. 'Before I have deleted each file installed here, I have made physical records of the salient points, so that I may have access to some of that knowledge if I needed it.'

'And can I ask what these files concerned?' asked Miraso.

'If I wasn't going to tell you, I wouldn't have brought it up in the first place,' said Silver. 'These were records of the fragmentary sightings and encounters humanity had had, up to this point, with advanced alien technologies – I was sent in search of those technologies, so that I could bring them back to my home time, where they were needed most. There are oblique references to travellers coming out of boxes.'

'What kind of references?' asked Miraso, intrigued now.

Silver looked her straight in the eye. 'References to chaos, to destruction. To gods in human form and to the arrival of time refugees as a precursor to armageddon. We must be very, very careful with our next move, Miraso. We do not wish these people to become our enemies.'

The Doctor had thrown himself into his investigation of the case, and to his surprise Powlin found himself being carried along, reviewing evidence with fresh eyes.

'So many victims over such a short time period,' said the Doctor. 'All decapitated cleanly, the bodies left where they fell with no attempts to conceal the crime.' The Doctor moved around the images and pages of notes on Powlin's desk, looking for a particular item. 'Ah, here we are. Prior to last night there were no eyewitnesses, but damaged roof tiles near one of the killings suggest tremendous agility and resilience, as the killer seems to have jumped several storeys from the crime scene, landed on another building and kept running.' He put the paper down. 'Interesting.'

'Interesting?' echoed Powlin angrily. '"Interesting" suggests your interest being drawn along, that the information gives you some fascinating places to go to. But it's taken me nowhere. I have no why, no who, no nothing.'

'But you do have a "who",' insisted the Doctor. 'Maybe not when it comes to the killer, but certainly when it comes to the victims.'

Powlin shook his head. 'No connection between the victims. They were as far apart as can be in a small town like Hope. The only thing they have in common is that they all wandered into our killer's path. They were all alone, far away from witnesses, and then they were dead.'

'Don't you see,' said the Doctor, standing up in the cramped office and pacing agitatedly. 'This very lack of connection between the victims, the seemingly random nature of the attacks takes us straight to motive. There is no psychotic pattern, no personal vendetta, none of the other possibilities inherent in the usual serial killer profiles.'

Powlin was exasperated. 'How does that help us?'

The Doctor smiled, leaning across the desk. 'It tells us one thing about the reasoning behind these crimes. They are not prejudiced or psychotic – they are functional. Someone is murdering these people for a coldly thought out, rational reason.'

* * *

Another morning and, thanks to the vagaries of time travel, a morning less than a day after the previous one. Anji was woken from her brief rest by unpleasantly harsh sunlight coming through an uneven, tinted window. The window was high up in the wall, but as the wall of the small room wasn't that tall in the first place, the light still shone right into Anji's face.

Anji rolled over in the small, cramped bed and bumped into the wall. No space, not like her bed in the TARDIS, or the one in her old flat. Space was clearly at a premium in Hope, especially when it came to staff quarters. The walls were rough and metallic, and the room was smaller than some of the cells Anji had been thrown into in her time with the Doctor. All the same, there was a vaguely homely feel to the place, as the previous occupant had painted the room in warm colours, obviously trying to make it cosy rather than confined. The result was a child's dream of a room, an oddly shaped and confined space straight out of a storybook. Unfortunately for Anji, she was rather bigger than a goblin or a moomin and kept bumping herself trying to move around.

With her back turned to the window, Anji felt the light from that alien sun on her neck. It was an odd feeling, unlike the sensation of feeling the sun anywhere back on Earth; not like the blazing sun of the tropics, the baking sun of Spain, or the ozone-enhanced sun of a summer in London. Anji found herself smiling at the memory of that day in Green Park, a couple of years ago now. Having more thoughts of Dave made her smile, then frown, then squeeze her head into her pillow, uncertain of *what* she should be thinking.

Anji pulled herself up on to one elbow, sighing deeply. She felt slightly queasy, in that uncertain state where she didn't know whether to sleep some more or get up. Which would be better, which would be worse? She elected to get out of bed and face this new day. And preferably find somewhere out of the sun.

Through these mean streets, thought Fitz, walks a man who is not mean. A man who is not cruel, but may possibly be quite cowardly, if things really did get too mean. OK, so maybe Fitz wasn't Raymond Chandler's idea of a rock-hard detective, determined to get to the truth in a morally uncertain world. But did Philip Marlowe ever have to deal with acid seas, toxic fogs and being half strangled by some loony half-robot death cult? No, he didn't. If he did, maybe Marlowe would have acted a lot more like Fitz. Then again, maybe he wouldn't.

The previous night Miraso had led them down narrow corridors and up winding stairs to the staff quarters, where the Doctor had wished them a brief good night and disappeared into one of the empty rooms. Fitz had never known the Doctor to be much of a sleeper, but these days who could tell? Perhaps he just needed quality brooding time, and Fitz was happy for him to take it by himself. Anji had also gone straight to bed, leaving Fitz alone in his own small room, staring at the blotchy, low ceiling. A Town Called Hope, he thought. There was a song in that, but without his guitar he couldn't really work on a tune. Besides, he might have difficulties rhyming anything with 'cyborg'.

Fitz fell asleep, half-formed lyrics drifting through his head, and was woken early in the morning by the pacing of the Palace's staff as they started the day. He wandered out into the corridor, greeting a couple of the red-uniformed staff he had met the night before. A quick poke around in the Doctor's room revealed he was gone, though the bed had been slept in – the sheets were twisted out of place, so either no one had cleaned the place lately or the Doctor was having uncomfortable nights. Fitz couldn't blame him, he'd slept with his feet propped midway up the wall in an attempt to stretch himself out. Leaving the residential part of the Palace behind, he'd quickly found the dining area, which was like any other works cafeteria in the universe, and blagged himself some stodgy broth for breakfast. Eavesdropping on the staff revealed little, just the day-to-day trivia of any workplace. So, breakfast consumed, Fitz hit the streets to do some real detective work.

And so he found himself, skin tingling in the harsh sun, trying to think what Philip Marlowe or any of those other hard boiled 'tecs would do next. Follow the lead, find a snitch and gain some info. Follow those leads, trace the clues relentlessly until the case was cracked. And, most of all, follow his well-honed instincts. And everyone had instincts. Fitz mentally reviewed the evidence, and found that one thing in particular didn't sit right with him, even by the twisted standards of this place called Hope. He rubbed his bruised throat, and wondered whether it was his own bitterness drawing him to false conclusions.

Nah. This whole Brotherhood of the Silver Fist thing didn't sit well. As a man with few beliefs, Fitz considered most religious types pretty cranky, but these guys took the biscuit. They despised Silver as an abomination, yet had modifications that made them just like him. Fine distinctions were par for the course when it came to religious schisms, but this defied all internal or external logic. And these guys were supposed to be all about logic, weren't they?

Fitz needed to learn more, he needed information, a voice on the streets who would know what's what. And he had already met someone straight from the gutter. That's where he would start.

While the Doctor and Fitz went out in search of Hope's secrets, Anji decided to stay indoors. Nearly drowning in an acid sea hadn't endeared her to the idea of leading the outdoors life in such a place, and the Silver Palace had an aura of safety about it. Perhaps it was the very presence of Silver himself – he was a frightening figure, but the fear he inspired seemed to envelop and protect his staff, warding off the chaos outside. On the other hand, that sense of safety may have come from the Palace being more of a fortress than anything else, its outer walls seemingly impregnable, its air processed to protect against poisons and pollutants.

More likely it was both. The building echoed with his presence, was an extension of his own metallic yet human persona, the echo of his militaristic manner reverberating through each stick of utilitarian furniture, the polished metal fittings reflecting his faceplate. Anji wouldn't have been surprised if she had been told that they were symbiotically linked, that somewhere in the depths of the Palace Silver was plugged into the very structure of the place, his breathing regulating the air conditioning, hidden cameras acting as his eyes.

For some reason, she didn't have any problem with meeting that gaze. She wondered why. Perhaps it was shock, an emotional residue from Silver despatching her assailant the previous night. Stockholm Syndrome, or something like that.

Whatever the reason, Anji found herself feeling strangely at home in the clattering corridors and mismatched rooms of the Silver Palace. Her status seemed to currently be 'staff member without portfolio', and with no task ascribed to her she was free to wander the corridors, being politely ignored by everyone she met. Her first stop was to retrace her steps of the previous night, to return to the Palace's public main hall and re-examine the ceiling mural that Miraso had shown them. Anji tried to imagine the apocalypse that the Endpointers had fled, tried to work out a hypothetical social construct or economic model to explain their life here on this polluted rock, but she couldn't get any further than a society based on constant struggle, the relentless fight for survival that living on Endpoint entailed. Social and economic norms must have broken down and established themselves on a basis of immediate, painful expediency. Feudalism one week, communes the next, depending on how the wind blew. All in the name of survival, the constant pursuit of a hard-wired, primal urge to live.

As the day grew longer the hall began to fill up with the citizens of Hope rich enough to start their revels at lunchtime. Anji found herself becoming slightly self-conscious, aware of furtive glances in her direction. Fair enough, she thought. Humanity was an extinct species, and she could imagine the fuss if a velociraptor had wandered into her local back on Earth and sat in the corner with a pint of mild. If there was one thing Anji had learned during her travels with the Doctor, it was that dead things walking around tended to be the start of trouble.

Deciding to postpone trouble until at least mid-afternoon, Anji resumed her exploration of the Palace, away from the public gaze. Much of what she found was mundane; an office where the administrative work that kept the Palace running took place, kitchens where food and drink were prepared in a riot of steam and motion, dank corridors lined with barrels, storerooms full of boxes. Eventually, though, Anji found something of interest, an area of the Palace where rough metal gave way to clinical white walls, bright strip lights banishing the darkness from every corner.

Laboratories. Having travelled with the Doctor for quite a while, Anji knew the drill by now. She found a rack of protective clothing and pulled on a light blue environment suit. The suit was baggy, designed to go over full clothing, and sealed across the chest, a simple breath mask built into the hood. Anji rubbed the visor clean with her gloved hands, and proceeded through a glass panelled door into the labs proper.

The lab she entered seemed to be deserted, although Anji suspected the equipment operated itself most of the time. Certainly, the complex rig set up across one wall seemed to be quite happy unattended, bleeping and bubbling by itself. Anji took a closer look, and found some kind of breeding project. A spiny plant was growing in a vat of bubbling liquid, breeding like cells in a petri dish. She didn't recognise the sprouting green plant, but it looked fairly innocuous. On a bank of screens what looked like 3D models of DNA strands were rotating. Genetic modification of crops had been a tiresome news topic when Anji had left Earth, and she suspected that was what was going on in the lab, albeit in a highly advanced form. To the right of the breeding tank was a glass-fronted refrigeration unit, in which sat a fat black flask. Checking in either direction to see that no one was about to burst in, Anji gingerly took the flask out of the fridge and placed it on the workbench. It looked like a thermos flask to Anji, which made the contents either a vital sample frozen in liquid nitrogen – or someone's coffee.

Anji twisted the lid open, and felt a vaguely cold sensation around her thickly gloved hands – liquid nitro it was. She pulled out the lid, and the entire sample slid out, fixed into the inner casing with clamps, frozen solid.

Anji blinked. It was the Doctor's apple core, frozen with liquid nitrogen. She quickly resealed the flask and placed it back in the refrigeration unit, then stared at the growing plant in the tank. She could vaguely make out the branch patterns of an apple tree. These people clearly thought growing apple trees was vitally important. Anji realised that with Earth and humanity gone, there probably were no apple trees any more. The Doctor had blithely restored to life what was potentially a long-dead species, without even thinking about it.

Were there cosmic laws against this kind of thing? Was that the right thing to do? Anji looked at the baby tree, suspended in nourishing gel. It seemed harmless enough, almost benevolent, to bring apples to a world that didn't have them. What could be the harm in that?

But she also remembered the stories about apples she had been told when she was young. There was Adam and Eve, Snow White, and she had vague recollections of a Greek myth involving golden apples. The prevailing symbolism wasn't good.

There was a breath-filtered cough behind her. Anji swung around to see a lithe figure leaning against the doorframe, dressed in an identical suit to hers. She recognised Miraso's sparkling eyes behind the visor.

'Checking on the progress of your friend's sample?' asked Miraso, nodding towards the miniature apple tree. 'Our scientists tell us the growth is progressing well, without mutations. We'll be ready to plant by the end of tonight.'

Miraso stepped across the room, and Anji couldn't help noticing how tall Miraso was compared to her.

'So you can safely leave this one to grow on its own, can't you?' said Miraso, firmly but without undue threat. 'Besides, I'm sure we can find you a more profitable way of spending your time.'

Anji didn't like the sound of that.

* * *

Pazon, Fitz thought, was exactly the kind of untrustworthy, shady friend he needed right now. The market place was quieter in the afternoon, and so Fitz sidled up to the man's stall and ordered a mildly unpleasant-sounding soup. Pazon ladled out a thick broth into a metal jug, and accepted one of the tokens Fitz had picked up at the Silver Palace in return. They were officially gambling chips, but according to one of the Palace's staff members they acted as valid currency almost anywhere on Endpoint. The slashed 'S' logo Silver used made the chips look like cartoon dollars.

Fitz sipped his soup; it tasted all right, with a faintly vegetable taste. He decided to try to draw Pazon into his confidence, engage him as a source of information.

'Having a good day?' Fitz asked.

'Bloody awful,' whined the rat-faced man, scrubbing his pots with a dirty-looking cloth. 'Why do you ask?'

Fitz shrugged. 'No reason. Just making polite conversation.'

Pazon swivelled around, fixing Fitz with his beady little eyes. 'You really must be from out of town.'

'Yes,' said Fitz. 'Conversation is a strange custom unique to my people.'

Pazon made a throat-clearing sound in reply.

'Don't you have anything to say?' asked Fitz.

Pazon shrugged. 'Not unless you're paying for the conversation.'

Fitz gave up on the subtle approach, and slapped another chip on the bar. 'Let's talk.'

To Anji's surprise, Miraso had taken a great interest in her work. Once Miraso had gained an appreciation of what Anji used to do for a living, she had dragged Anji over to the accounting offices, where Anji had spent the rest of the day discussing various local markets, getting a grip on the vital resources and the trading that took place on Endpoint. It had been mentally exhausting, trying to stretch her head around a whole new economic system, and by the end of the day all she wanted to do was stare into space.

Which was fortunate, as neither of her companions really needed her company. So she sat at a table in the Palace's main hall, and watched them at work.

In one corner, Fitz was singing in what, to Anji's uneducated ear, seemed to be Chinese. The people around Fitz seemed to be enjoying it, drunkenly trying to sing along to something they had never heard in their life before. At another table the Doctor was deep in discussion with Powlin, the sour faced militiaman, poring over various papers and printouts. Anji had joined them briefly, but the images of gruesome crime scenes they had been flicking through had put her off.

Her thoughts drifted back to that afternoon, to her conversations with Silver's accountants. Something didn't sit right. There hadn't been anything beyond her understanding – if anything the rational, resource-based nature of supply and demand on Endpoint was easier to comprehend than a complex consumer society like twenty-first-century Earth, with its disposable incomes and disposable resources. No, it was something slightly more fundamental about the questions they had asked. The perspective from which they addressed economic questions.

It was as if they weren't following market forces at all, that they weren't interested in predicting economic patterns. The questions they had asked Anji had been in an attempt to determine what economic trends they could *create*.

A family sits down to eat, and he watches through red lenses, following their heat signatures. This family, living in small, barely insulated accommodation on the edge of Hope, can only afford one proper meal a day. The parents work in the gas mining plants, the children scavenge in the streets and gutters. They wear full clothing indoors, to protect against the cold seeping into their ramshackle home.

These facts are of no relevance to him as he clings to the wall of their homespace, looking in through the crude window. He sees only four soft targets, the chance to fulfil rising quotas. Hand over hand, he climbs above the window, making no noise. A steel bar is bolted on to the wall, a context-less clue to whatever this homespace had been in a previous existence. A life pod? Part of a space station habitation unit? It is stripped of equipment and meaning now, rebuilt as a home by the wretches inside it. To him it means nothing – he holds on to the bar with both hands, pushes himself back with his feet.

He swings forward, impacting with the window feet first, crashing straight through in a shower of glass fragments. His four targets – two adults, two children – have little time to react, torn between fight and flight.

He does not allow them time to decide.

Chapter Six
No More Time Outs

Miraso insisted on hard work from her staff, but wasn't a stickler for timekeeping when it came to non-rota staff. Providing the work got done, who cared? So she was used to having the administrative sections of the Palace to herself in the early morning, the accountants and auditors and administrators usually rolling in some time later.

So she was surprised to come in that morning to find Anji already there, piles of ledgers and other paperwork teetering around her. The human had somehow managed to get the terminal on the desk working, and had laid out a few simple spreadsheets.

'Got everything you need?' asked Miraso. It was intended to be sarcasm.

'Not quite,' said Anji. 'I really need a more thorough tour of Silver's resources to make any clear judgements on how his investments can be expanded.' She paused. 'That's if you still want the job done.'

Miraso nodded. 'Once we're up and running this morning, I'll get one of the guys to show you around.'

'Excellent,' said Anji. 'That'll be really helpful.'

Powlin found the Doctor's refusal to carry a weapon unusual, with several possible implications. The most impressive was that the Doctor didn't need a gun, that his offensive capabilities were physical and mental. A gun could be taken away, or could jam. There was no substitute for being able to defend and attack when no obvious weapon presented itself. Powlin, for his part, clutched his gun with his back to the wall, looking across at the

Doctor, who was adopting a similar, albeit unarmed, posture on the other side of the door.

They were about to burst into a crude living unit bolted on to one of the towers on Hope's eastern perimeter. Neighbours had reported a brief but loud disturbance the previous night, and the two adults living there had failed to turn up for work that morning. These two facts, alongside the isolated location of the living unit, suggested a possible link to their case, and the Doctor had insisted they follow it up. Powlin was rather more worried there was something more obvious going down – a drug deal, a home invasion or suchlike. So he kept his gun to hand, just in case, and tried to block out the witterings of the street kids hanging around nearby, rag-shrouded scavengers who were drawn to possible misfortune like flies to carrion.

Powlin swung around to face the door, and fired a light impact explosive charge directly at the lock. Fragments of rusty metal flew out in all directions as a section of the door was blasted to pieces, and Powlin gave the door a solid kick, keeping his gun raised.

He needn't have been so cautious – the Doctor's instincts had been right. Four bodies lay prone on the floor, furniture was smashed to sticks, broken glass was scattered around them. Blood had pooled and dried, and even in the half-light of the dim room Powlin could see that the bodies lacked their heads, and one of the adults had fallen with the severed neck pointing to the door, the top of the spine poking through red flesh. Powlin lowered his gun slackly to his side as he walked carefully into the crime scene. This was carnage.

'Out!' shouted the Doctor, slamming the door into the faces of the street children, who had been pushing past each other to get a look at the gruesome display. Powlin gave the Doctor a questioning look.

'This isn't a sight for children,' said the Doctor, moving past Powlin for a closer examination of the bodies.

'Doctor,' said Powlin, holstering his weapon. 'Those "children" have probably seen more death and violence in their short lives than you ever have.'

'Oh, I doubt that,' replied the Doctor, his serious tone leaving no room for disagreement. 'Whatever schedule our killer is working to, it's just picked up a notch,' he added, and it took a moment for Powlin to register the change of subject.

'You're telling me,' said Powlin redundantly. 'Multiple victims is unheard of, especially only a day after the previous attack. Think this might be a copycat killing?'

The Doctor shook his head. 'No, these incisions are the work of the same killer. But there are anomalies.' He gingerly slipped a hand into a space between two of the bodies, and picked up a slim plastic capsule.

Powlin looked at it blankly. 'What is it?'

'A disposable casing from a medical shot, discarded when an injection is made,' said the Doctor. 'Now, from what I've seen on Endpoint, I doubt anything is "disposable", am I right?'

Powlin took the casing and examined it. 'Only time I've been inoculated, the syringe went straight into the steriliser and was used again.'

'I thought so,' said the Doctor, nodding enthusiastically in spite of his gory surroundings. He began to search around the clothing of the adult female corpse, and eventually lifted up an arm for Powlin to examine. 'Look, there.'

Powlin followed the Doctor's finger, and could see a small, clear bead peeking through the grey sleeve. The Doctor pressed the material around it down, and Powlin could see that the bead was at the end of a slim dart sticking into the woman's skin.

'Tranquilliser shot,' said the Doctor, standing up and letting the corpse drop back to the floor. He bounded over to one of the dead children, and started doing a similar examination. It looked like he was playing with a headless ragdoll, flipping it around. 'There, another one. Our killer's getting sloppy, leaving physical evidence. He wanted this crop of heads quickly and efficiently, so he came in through the window, firing tranquilliser shots from a medium range dart gun, a device not uncommon in outbreak situations but incompatible with any medical technology I've seen in Hope. He removed the heads, and left without clearing up after himself.'

'Sounds like he doesn't care any more,' said Powlin.

'Possibly,' said the Doctor. 'Or that whatever he's doing with these heads, our killer thinks the end of the project will make any retribution for his crimes seem irrelevant.'

The previous day, Pazon had finally – after some not inconsiderable remuneration – given Fitz what he knew on the Brotherhood of the Silver Fist. It seemed that most of the populace of Hope knew who the Brotherhood were, as their previous attacks on Silver, and the miserable failure of such attacks, had been the subject of a number of news items on the local mediastreams. Pazon had pointed out a flat, television-type screen on a nearby stall, which was showing images of Silver despatching one of the Brotherhood the previous night. The Brotherhood were generally regarded as exactly what Fitz had suspected – dangerous fanatics who were capable of anything.

Pazon had given Fitz a location to go to, a deserted area beneath two bridges where Pazon had heard that members of the Brotherhood met. Fitz had spent the rest of the afternoon staking the place out, watching from a darkened alcove but with no result. While the odd person had walked through, often moving hurriedly as if afraid of what might lurk in the shadows (Fitz felt vaguely affronted by this), no one stopped or held any assignations there, secret or otherwise. By dark he was bored and cold, and returned to the Palace.

But the next day he was back, painfully aware that this was his only lead. So he returned to his alcove, waiting to see if anyone came by. For the first couple of hours, Fitz gained nothing except aching lungs from Hope's polluted air. But around midday he was in luck. A hooded figure shuffled into the centre of the open area, looking furtively around but completely failing to register that Fitz was present. Fitz watched the figure closely, and was sure he glimpsed a flash of metal beneath that hood. A few minutes later a second, similarly attired figure, arrived. The two exchanged a muttered conversation, which Fitz could not catch, and a box was exchanged. The second figure dashed off down a pathway, leaving the first holding his newly acquired box.

Fitz realised he had to act now, before his only lead wandered off again. He remembered his last encounter with the Brotherhood, imagined the choke hold he had been put in, and hoped this meeting would go better. There was no one here to rescue him if it all went wrong.

He stepped out of the shadows, footsteps echoing on the metallic walkway. The hooded figure turned to him as he emerged.

'I wish to help you destroy the abomination,' said Fitz.

Anji had been given the full tour – or as full as they were willing to show her – of Silver's operations. She had seen the laboratories where genetic specimens were grown, where new discoveries became new crops, new products, new genetic upgrades for existing species. She had been taken into the storage areas of the Palace, where there were weapons and vehicle parts, computers and mineral reserves. She had seen the atrium at the Palace's centre, where the light was enhanced to allow plants and flowers to grow in an elegant and well-tended garden. She had seen the kitchens and the vaults of valuables and the generators and the transmitters and the offices and the wine cellars. And when her guides brought her back to Miraso's office, she was exhausted. She had politely declined the monorail trip to the edge of Hope where Silver owned a dockyard, where ships went out to trade on his behalf with the other communities on Endpoint. Anji had seen quite enough, and was willing to take their word for it, and read about other Silver-owned properties. A flick through the portfolios showed Silver had business interests in most of the communities, connections and investments everywhere.

Miraso was elsewhere when Anji returned to the office, and so Anji was free to examine the map of Endpoint and compare it to Silver's list of properties. One in pretty much every major community, and by far the largest of those communities was

Hope, where Silver's headquarters was located.

Anji sank into Miraso's chair, lost for words. Silver effectively owned a controlling share in the entire planet. He owned communications, power suppliers, food producers. He donated the lion's share of funding to the supposedly independent citizens' militia organisations in each community, so the forces of law and order effectively belonged to Silver as well. His headquarters, the Silver Palace she was currently residing in, lay at the heart of the largest city on Endpoint. It was his capital, his seat of government even though he didn't officially govern anything. No wonder she couldn't find room for expansion in his investments – Silver pretty much owned everything anyway, if he expanded any further he'd only have himself to trade with. There was nothing really to stop him taking complete and immediate control of Endpoint.

So why didn't he? Anji couldn't quite work it out. Silver hardly seemed the insecure type, or the sort who would avidly believe in the rule of democracy. Perhaps it wasn't political power he was after, perhaps the answer to Silver's desires lay in his scientific investments, the raising of dead species and the improvement of existing ones through genetic engineering. Was it Silver's wish to conquer life and death? Unless Silver had that power already, of course. This was far into Anji's future, she had no idea what technology might be commonplace, or at least available to someone of Silver's resources. If he could take a genetic sample from an apple core and grow apple trees, what else could he raise with appropriate DNA samples? Anji had seen *Jurassic Park*, and although the cinema had been full of kids and the occasional cackling lunatic she had appreciated the basics of the plot. Although that had been a film, pure science fiction, it had been based on real science, and she herself had seen the first cloned sheep in the newspapers. And she had certainly seen weirder things on her travels since then.

Which left Anji with two questions – how far did Silver's power extend, and how far did he want to expand that power?

* * *

The Doctor's visits to the lavish offices of the powerful usually began with him being dragged in by his hair. A polite request was a radical, but not unwelcome, change. Miraso had caught him on his way into the Silver Palace after a day of sweeping the crime scene for evidence and attending autopsies. Silver's request was reasonable enough, and the Doctor let Miraso lead him through a winding series of corridors to a door high up in the building. Before she could knock the Doctor pushed the door open and walked through it, waving cheekily at Miraso as she stood there, hand raised to tap on the door politely. He let the door shut in her face, walked straight to a free chair and slumped into it without being invited to sit. Some basic standards of insolence needed to be maintained, even in the face of the most seemingly polite authority figures.

Silver raised his single eyebrow at the Doctor's presumption, but let the impertinence slide.

'Doctor,' he said, his voice reverberating around the room without actually being loud. 'I'm glad you could join me.'

'A pleasure,' replied the Doctor, shuffling himself into a comfortable position in his seat.

Silver raised his eyebrow again. He sat behind a large, highly polished desk, illuminated in the fading early evening light by a spherical lamp. Silver's faceplate gleamed in the warm glow. The Doctor allowed his eyes to wander, taking in the rows of books on the walls, the fine furnishings. For a cyborg, Silver's tastes were exceptionally human.

'I have been monitoring communications channels throughout the day,' said Silver, picking up a slablike remote control in his robot hand. 'Take a look.' He pointed the remote at a viewscreen on the wall and pushed a chunky button. The screen presented a fuzzy image of a woman, talking in panicked tones about how there were bodies piling up in the streets, how nowhere was safe. Silver pushed the button again and the screen split in two, a man appearing on the other half of the screen describing killers on the loose. Silver pressed the button twice, and the screen split into quarters, then eighths, images of people in each part of the screen, voices overlapping in various levels of hysteria.

'Panic is setting in, Doctor,' said Silver. 'These latest killings, the murder of this family – people are beginning to believe that this killer is beyond capture, that no one can stop him. Their faith in the status quo has been shaken.' He pressed another button, and the babbling faces disappeared, to be replaced by footage of Silver himself, firing over Anji's head and sending a member of the Brotherhood of the Silver Fist flying. 'This is what people should have on their minds,' said Silver. 'Images of dissent and terrorism being swiftly defeated. Uplifting images that make them feel that their world makes sense.' He turned the screen off and placed the remote control back on his desk. 'I want you and the militia to give them back that sense of perspective, Doctor.' Silver's artificial eye flared red as the Doctor met his gaze.

The Doctor threw an evidence bag on to Silver's desk. Silver picked up the bag, examining the contents.

'Recognise these?' asked the Doctor.

'From a previous life, yes,' said Silver. 'They're disposable meditabs.' He threw the bag back to the Doctor, who caught it out of the air. 'Did you bring these with you?'

'No,' said the Doctor. 'I found them at the scene of the crime this morning.'

Silver frowned. 'Nothing is disposable on Endpoint.'

The Doctor nodded. 'As I thought. Which makes these rather an unusual find. Could someone have landed here without you knowing?'

Silver leant back in his chair, steepling his fingers under his chin. One hand was comically larger than the other.

'It would technically be possible to break through the barrier clouding this system,' said Silver quietly. 'If you had a hyperspace tunnel. But to land here without me knowing? No. With weather like ours, atmospheric disruption is constantly monitored – no ship could land without being noticed.'

The Doctor nodded. 'Regardless of where your killer comes from, I doubt they're an average citizen of Hope.'

Silver paused, thoughtful. 'Clearly not. And as an outsider

yourself, Doctor, you are perfectly placed to catch him for me. So how do you intend to go about this?'

The Doctor sat forward in his chair. 'I know where he hunts, I know the times he kills,' he said. 'I intend to be there, and hunt him down before he kills again.'

That evening, Fitz joined the Doctor and Anji at what was rapidly becoming their regular table in the Silver Palace's main hall. Anji had a brightly coloured cocktail, but after his embarrassing musical performance of the previous night, Fitz decided to stick to something a little tamer. Besides, the music was provided this evening, harsh electronic sounds with a pumping bassline echoing across the hall. Fitz found it a little loud for his liking, but when he saw Anji nodding her head appreciatively he wondered whether his own reservations were due to getting old – it just didn't sound like music to him.

'What are Batman and Robin up to?' he asked Anji, nodding towards the Doctor and Powlin. He thought it was a reasonable analogy, considering the Doctor's increasingly solemn mood, and the way the militiaman followed him around like a puppy.

'We're planning to try and stop these brutal murders, thereby saving many lives and perhaps get a chance to leave this place,' said the Doctor, not looking up from the maps he and Powlin had been poring over. 'Why, what have you been doing?' he added, as if Fitz had spent the last couple of days playing British Bulldog down the park.

'I've been following my own leads,' said Fitz indignantly. The Doctor could be a cheeky sod, sometimes – if he knew that Fitz had arranged to attend a Brotherhood meeting in a couple of days time, then he'd be more impressed. But Fitz decided to take a leaf out of the Doctor's own book and not reveal anything until he had dazzling results to show for his efforts. Fitz could be the mystery man too.

'Good good,' said the Doctor, still not paying any attention. 'Just try not to get yourself killed, will you?'

'OK,' said Fitz, trying to give Anji an askance look, but she was involved in the music, or deep in thought. He couldn't quite tell.

Fitz decided to return to the bar. Perhaps he needed a stronger drink after all.

Night fell, and the Doctor and Powlin patrolled the perimeter of Hope.

The Doctor ran across the rooftops, heart pumping and lungs bursting as he jumped the gaps between buildings. He crawled across pipes and swung from beams, watching any passers-by down below, searching for the shape of a possible killer. Meanwhile, Powlin and his men patrolled at street level, torches searching out anywhere the killer might be hiding.

In the early hours a shrill cry rang out on the western side of the city, near to where the Doctor was crouched on a transmitter mast, looking out across the footways below him, observing the area for signs of anything suspicious. At the sound of the cry he slid down the mast, ran across a pipe and dropped down on to a walkway. He paused to catch his breath, listening out for any further noises. He heard a couple of shouts, the sound of a shot being fired and a brief yell. The noise was from his left, but fell silent as he ran towards it, heading for an area in the shadow of several tenement blocks.

The Doctor arrived to find no sign of life, skidding to a halt on a metal platform, a crossroads suspended between the blocks. One woman and two militiamen lay dead, their weapons smoking as they lay on the ground. Of the killer, and the heads of his victims, there was no sign.

Chapter Seven
Secret Origins

Miraso seemed happy to let Anji have the run of the Silver Palace's information resources, and so Anji spent the morning attempting to research Silver himself. She had some measure of his current power from examining his finances and the technology he had access to, but she knew little about the man himself. So she took a portable information unit and wandered around the Palace, in search of some quiet place to work. Anji soon found the perfect place – the atrium-stroke-greenhouse in which plant samples were grown. To her delight she found that the first few full-size apple trees were growing, planted in an area surrounded by a rough bronze grass. Still, it was soft enough for Anji to sit under the nearest tree, and the harsh Hope sunlight was filtered enough to be pleasantly warm.

She sat under the tree, in this strange indoor garden, and flicked on the information console. Looking for answers, she found little. There was no coherent story to it all. Instead Anji got lost in her own questions. Where had Silver come from? Was Silver his name, or a nickname due to his metallic nature? Where was he born? Who were his parents, or did he come out of a tube? What had his childhood been like?

The heat thrashes the barrio during the afternoon, the sunlight pouring in through Humberto's window. Maria don Silvestre's only son is too weak to go to school, to play with the other children, even to stand up, walk over to the window and close the blinds to stop the harsh light causing reflections on his monitor screen, interfering with his work. If nothing else he 'can move his hand over the keyboard, manipulate the code on screen. The poisonous waters of this small, dirtball town attacked him in his mother's womb, took away his chance to live in the sun, to live any kind of normal life. His mother works eighteen hours a day, and although she does her best for her only son she is never there enough.

The old computer she found him is his best friend, closer to him than any living thing, any person at all. It does not stare at his sickly complexion, or feel nervous in the presence of a child permanently attached to a respirator. Instead, it responds to his commands, his persuasive coding and occasional, delicate repairs. His mother had been nervous about leaving her son with a soldering iron by his bed, and with good reason – Humberto would love to hurt himself, to feel anything real. But to him the iron is a medical tool, designed to heal his beloved machine. To use it to cause harm, even to his worthless self, would be sacrilege.

Besides, soon he will be beyond harm or healing. Humberto has read the paranoid ramblings on the communication channels, of what the World Council does to those who interfere with their military technology. Black skimmers swoop at dawn, missiles tearing through the huts where technoanarchists prepare their viruses on wrist-tops. The anarchists reach for their guns, but plasma beams tear through the huts, ripping them to pieces. World Government One, Anarchists Nil. That's what happens to dirt-poor criminals who mess with the rich and the powerful. They get wiped out.

Well, better to go out in style, to be noticed by those above in their environmentally sterile habitation blocks, breathing their clean air instead of the filth outside. Better to be seen by God for one second before he rubs you out than never be noticed at all.

Humberto may well be delusional, locked away for so long with only a computer for company. For what he wants is to be worthy of destruction, to offend the powers that be. He is fifteen years old, with only months left to live, and wants to commit the last great crime of the thirtieth century before he dies.

* * *

Nothing. Anji couldn't find a damn thing on Silver's origins. Everyone knew who he was, but he seemed to have walked out of nowhere. His features were human, a product of a bygone age as far as the Endpointers were concerned. Looking through his public appearances on the communications channels of Endpoint, Anji noted Silver's militaristic manner, his combat trousers, polished boots and rigid bearing. Endpoint wasn't organised enough to have a proper police force, let alone armed forces. Where the hell did Silver pick up the army way?

Humberto looks in the mirror before he leaves the barracks, admires his reflection. Each button of his uniform shines in the half-light of a winter's night, reflecting the multicoloured sparkle of the occasional firework. It's millennium eve, the end of 2999 and the dawn of the year 3000. Humberto has just passed his twenty-first birthday, he's a handsome young officer, the Tactical AI Division's brightest star. Caught hacking into the Central TacNet five years before, he had been whisked out of his barrio home to an elite training centre, where a sickly young man had been given artificial lungs more efficient than any organic lungs, the best drugs the military could afford – which were the best in known space – and the chance to play with the most powerful hardware and software in mankind's possession. In the whirl of events the reason for his transgression and his desire for death were swept away, and through a physical fitness regime, all the physical traits of the old Humberto disappeared too. His mother was proud not to recognise him, delighted in this new son of hers.

And so Humberto was a good soldier, appointed to barracks just outside of Melbourne, his days as a hacker long forgotten. Leaving his quarters he strides purposefully down the path to the base's gates, intending to enjoy the once-in-a-thousand-years party. It's a beautiful Australian night, and his friends are waiting.

He has no idea that a resentful teenager in a Sun City basement is hacking into the TacNet mainframe, just as

Humberto did before. But this teenager will be more successful, his unwitting application to the military will cause a technological meltdown that will kill thousands across Australia's wealthy east coast. Humberto will be one of the survivors. Just.

A scan of the communication channels in Hope revealed many archived threads of conversation concerning Silver's legendary fighting ability. The computer interface Anji was using was straightforward enough, and she flicked through endless grainy images of Silver punching people's faces in with his metal fist, firing the gun on the back of that hand. There had been an assassination attempt a couple of years back, and a bullet had bounced clean off his faceplate, not leaving a scratch.

No one seemed to know how Silver got to be the way he was, who had fitted those implants. Would someone do that to themselves voluntarily, no matter how powerful it made them? Or was Silver just a glorified guinea pig, on the run from the lab?

Maria don Silvestre thought herself too old at the best of times. Her son had provided for her well, and when he suffered an accident in Melbourne the army looked after Maria. But she knew that the hard years before those had aged her, that in her fifties she had the health of a woman twenty years older. As she pulled herself through the airlock, bobbing weightlessly against the walls, she felt ancient and fragile. So, weightlessness was good for arthritis, was it? Not if your brittle bones were shattered boarding the station.

The army had treated Maria well, as the only next-of-kin of a promising young officer. Now she had come to the Zero G Hospital facility orbiting the Earth, to see how they were caring for Humberto himself.

Two men in blue overalls were waiting for her.

'Senora don Silvestre,' said one, pushing himself over to help her. 'Welcome to Zero G. I'm Dr Venni, and this is Dr Haigney. Shall we see Humberto now?'

Maria spent an hour with Humberto, talking to him but receiving no reply. He lay, suspended in a web of dripfeeds and cables, unmoving. The view from the vast window was spectacular, the sharp blue curve of the Earth gleaming below them, but Maria paid it no attention. She talked to her son and watched for any sign of life, for a twitch of his remaining hand as she squeezed it, a flicker of recognition in his eye. But the undamaged side of his face was as blank as the side wrapped in bandages. As the two doctors had warned, the brain damage was severe.

Maria re-emerged from Humberto's room, leaving a nurse to reapply bandages. She found Venni and Haigney floating in the corridor outside, waiting for her.

'I am grateful to you for bringing me here to see my son,' said Maria. 'But I doubt that is the only reason.'

'You are correct,' said Dr Venni. He was a dark-skinned man with a high forehead that creased with concern as he spoke. 'As our reports to you have explained, conventional treatment can do nothing for Humberto. However, there are more radical methods we can attempt. But these involve complicated issues.'

'Issues?' Maria echoed.

Venni paused, making sure he said the right thing. 'We could attempt to revive Humberto by introducing new technologies to his body, by allowing a sort of liquid computer we have been working on to merge with his brain, hopefully repairing the damage. There is a strong chance this may lead to recovery, but Humberto would no longer be fully human. He would partially be that technology, and we could not allow that technology to do as it wished. Also, if something went wrong then that technology – which is potentially very dangerous – would have to be shut down, regardless of the consequences for your son.'

'You would have to kill him,' said Maria. It was a statement, no more.

'This technology is alien,' said Dr Haigney, speaking for the first time. 'It may help your son – we think it may be the only substance with even a chance of healing him. But if something

goes wrong, then it will have to be destroyed. And if the operation is a success, Humberto will not be free to do as he wishes, he will be required to do as we say. If we perform this operation, it will be a high security military procedure. Your son will no longer be a man, he will be a military experiment.'

'Because of the waiving of rights involved,' added Dr Venni, 'we will do nothing without your permission.'

Maria thought of her son, lonely in his childhood sickbed, the joy he had taken in his work for the military, and how he was in a worse situation now than when he was confined as a child. Anything had to be better than this.

'You have my permission,' said Maria. 'When do you start?'

Anji couldn't help wondering what it was like to be more than human, to have cybernetic extensions and additions. She raised her hand, imagining a steel fist in its place, able to crush boulders. But would it be able to feel, would she get any feedback from the hand? If she did, would it feel the same as a normal hand, or would those feelings be the electronic pulses that passed information around any computer system?

Her researches showed that Silver was alleged to have some kind of liquid intelligence flowing through his brain, a liquid data storage system that vastly enhanced his mental capacities. This raised further questions – if data was constantly exchanged between the mechanics and the man, then to what extent was he human and to what extent computer? Could he see in binary, could he break down a smell or a taste into calculations, electronic synesthesia converting every sensation into computer code? And, presuming Silver hadn't been born with a baby robot fist and half a baby robot face, what was it like to wake up one morning more than just a man?

He is aware, but not quite awake. Something is stopping him from attaining total consciousness. Yes, there. Security software circling his thought processes, locking off his access to certain areas.

Software? He can see code? What is this?

He remembers the explosion, combat bots running loose in a civilian area. The memory is more than memories used to be, a picture-perfect rerun of the scene retrieved from his memory with digital precision. He rifles through the archives of his memories, seeing how far he can go. Many have been lost, somehow, but those that exist are accessible in ways that no human mind could manage.

He vaguely recollected an afternoon as a new recruit, a smile in a crowd. As he thinks of that day now his enhanced memory plucks out that moment, and he can see not just the smile, but her red hair, the silky whiteness of her dress. He can focus in on follicles in her hair and the pores in her skin.

What is he, a creature of pure data, downloaded from poor Humberto's shattered skull into a hard drive somewhere? Is he a file on someone's wrist-top, a transmission bobbing around the Earth?

No, there is physical awareness, muscles and bone and skin. And something else, a dead weight. The security programs push him away from these areas but he dodges them, his aptitude for programming enhanced now that he is part computer himself, the edges of his person blurring into information space. The security programs were there to keep him unconscious, partially, but there are others – command codes to keep him in check, instructions to follow orders with compacted files of names and faces to be ever obeyed. There are kill-switches built into him, he realises.

Enough of that. He does not know what has happened to him, but he knows he wants freedom, at least the freedom to wake when he chooses, if nothing else. Besides, these security programs are crude things, primitive attempts to program the advanced technology of his mind. Whatever that may be. So he gets rid of them, composing countermeasures in his head like brief arias, which flit around the crude command programs, dismantling them with the poetry of blades, a concerto for ones and zeroes. The doors fly open, and with a sudden awareness of breath he can wake up.

The world around him sweeps in at the same time as an awareness of self, while his countermeasures continue their work, feeding back into the datanet monitoring him to find out more about his situation. As he opens his eyes – one human and weak, the other a precise visual feed with numerous options for enhancement, scanning and tracking – he is simultaneously overlaying his own medical records on to a heads-up display. Humberto don Silvestre, experimental operation, alien technology. He turns to examine his new arm at the same time as he reads about it, and instantly overlays that information on to the arm's controls, feeling the capacity to crush steel, to extend the barrel of a gun from your own body. He feels the power of the wetware liquid storage system flowing through his own brain – a substance the scientists could barely comprehend, but of which he himself has mastery.

He releases himself from a web of cables, floating precisely in the zero gravity, the physical calculations for every move pre-empting any human clumsiness. The medical monitoring equipment is rigged to inform the doctors when he shows signs of life, but it was easy enough to hack through the datanet and turn those fail-safes off. He looks out of the window, into the stars, only his link to the datanet still attached, a cable plugged into the side of his skull. Otherwise, he is free, all command protocols disarmed, no restraints to hold him back.

He watches the stars, remembering his human life with complete digital recall, contrasting who he was then to who he is now. He knows he is not the same man. He brings up Humberto don Silvestre's medical records once more, this time allowing the military computers to detect his invasion of their systems, to note his presence. Before disconnecting he makes one alteration, deleting most of his former name, editing his surname until only one word remains. He reaches to the back of his head with his new metal hand, gently disconnecting the cable. It is done, he has been reborn, renamed.

He is Silver.

* * *

Searching for Silver's origins, Anji realised, was a waste of time. He had never elected to tell anyone about them, so the archives, communication channels et cetera were full of nothing but rumour and innuendo. No one was even certain how long Silver had been on Endpoint, when or how he had arrived. He must have just appeared one day, certainly there seemed to be records from a time before he existed. He clearly wasn't a child of Endpoint, they didn't have the technology. So he must somehow have arrived there. But how?

The attack came in 3006. The invasion began with a full scale landing in Detroit, which gave the invaders a beachhead in North America. Washington fell shortly after, and most of the major missile bases went down soon after that. Within hours what was once the United States of America was overrun, and the rest of the world did not even know who these attackers were.

Only hours after the first strike Maria was rushed into an underground bunker beneath the base at which she and her son had lived for the last couple of years. She was the mother of Silver, one of the military's finest and most respected, and even in a time of crisis she was treated with the utmost reverence. A corporal showed her to a quiet waiting room, a beige-painted place with leather seats and a drinks machine. She sat with a plastic cup of bitter coffee, letting it go cold between her hands. The sound of sirens echoed in the distance, occasionally footsteps clattered past at hectic speeds. It was the end of the world, she was sure of it. Two facts came to her with startling clarity: firstly, that as Silver's mother and a resident of this base she was one of the safest people on Earth; and secondly, that this would not make the slightest bit of difference and she would be dead within hours.

The door burst open and her son walked in, striding towards her. It was all she could do not to flinch. She loved Silver, and she was terribly proud of him. But all that strength, all that intelligence... she could not help but be slightly in awe of him, even though he was her own son.

'Mother,' said Silver, dropping to one knee before her. He placed his hands on her shoulders, squeezing gently and with mathematically precise affection. The human side of his face was a mask of distress. 'I am being sent away,' he said simply.

'Away?' Maria echoed.

'Yes,' said Silver. 'The war is lost on Earth already, and the High Command are sending us out in search of ways of liberating our world. They have an experimental time device, mother. We are being sent out into history, into the future, across all of time and space, to obtain reinforcements or technologies to save humankind. Grey has already been sent into the past, and I am being sent into the future to bring tomorrow's technology back with me. I will return, Mother, I promise.'

And then, in spite of Silver's ability to manipulate human emotions as if they were simple raw data, Maria knew without a doubt that he was lying. Whether he knew himself, she did not know, but either way the promises he was making were lies. He would not return from this trip, as he had no reason to. Humanity had not been his race when he had been locked in his sickbed as a child, and although his few years as a young officer had brought him close to the human race, the operations that saved his life and made him Silver had cast him out once more. He was a man apart as he had been a child apart, and as something other than a human being he would have no reason to return to this doomed Earth. He would go out and find his own place in the universe. She hoped he might perhaps breed a race of people like himself while he was out there. She didn't like to think of him being all alone, forever. Behind that faceplate she still saw a little boy cut off from his peers, isolated from those around him, happier with the company of machines.

She touched his metal cheek. To her surprise she realised it wasn't cold, but had a warmth beneath it, like an overworked engine.

'Good luck,' she told him. 'I hope you find what you need.'

Silver looked up at her then, and a pretence seemed to drop. His expression was curious, as if he had detected the double meaning in her words.

A sergeant burst through the door.

'Sir, they need you now,' said the breathless young man.

'I must go now,' said Silver, taking her frail hands in his metal fist.

'I know,' said Maria, squeezing his hand impotently.

She watched as he turned and walked out of the room, certain that she would never see him again.

Anji had spent the whole morning researching Silver, and had got precisely nowhere. She sat beneath the apple tree, chewing on a pen and wondering about the various possibilities. The more she thought, the more lost she became, unable to come to any conclusions, questions simply leading to further questions. The information unit lay open on her lap, paused on a still shot of Silver, snatched from the public information channels. Anji closed her eyes, the lids red in the midday sun.

A shadow loomed across her. She opened her eyes, blinking at the bulky figure standing over her, a dark form gleaming at the edges.

Silver looked down at her, his eyebrow raised quizzically. Anji looked down, and realised he had seen the image of him on the screen. She snapped the info-unit shut, her cheeks reddened. She hadn't felt like this since school, when Miss Kemp had caught her with a picture of Bros taped to the inside lid of her desk.

'I've been doing some research,' said Anji quickly. It was the truth, but she kicked herself – his next question was inevitable, he was going to demand to know why she was investigating him.

'So, Miss Kapoor,' said Silver, demolishing her expectations. She hadn't even expected him to remember her name. 'What would you like to know?'

Chapter Eight
Turning on a Dime

'She should be here,' said Fitz, protesting.

'Well, I can't find her,' said Miraso, wandering into the main hall. An area had been cleared with a white board at the front, on which the Doctor had attached a number of images and maps. Miraso took a seat next to Fitz. Anji's place was empty.

'Anji doesn't know we're having this meeting,' said the Doctor. 'She can hardly be expected to turn up now.'

'Still,' grumbled Fitz. 'I think she should be here. We could use her right now.' Because if you were talking rubbish, Doctor, she'd know and I wouldn't. Fitz kept that last thought to himself.

'Can we start?' asked Powlin, attempting gruff impatience. But Fitz could see the childish eagerness, thinly disguised behind that harsh exterior. Like a dog waiting for its master to throw a stick.

'Very well,' said the Doctor, snapping on a projector. The screen behind him lit up with a series of medical diagrams. The Doctor sipped from a mug of caffy, and Fitz noticed how tired he looked.

'Let's begin,' said the Doctor, putting down his cup. He fumbled it slightly, and brown liquid sloshed over the table.

The Doctor didn't seem to notice his own clumsiness.

Quid pro quo, Agent Kapoor, thought Anji as she sat beneath the tree looking up at Silver, who was haloed by the midday sun. If she were to ask him a question, what would he require in return? She decided it was safer to begin with a statement, a compliment.

'It's wonderful what you've done here,' she said, indicating the indoor orchard. 'All this from one little apple core.'

Silver looked around himself, then up, as if basking in the

sunlight for the first time. 'I suppose it is remarkable what can be done,' he said, and Anji was surprised his voice wasn't louder. Instead it resonated, each word drilling through her. 'The technology at my disposal here, even in this planet's recent dark ages, is so far in advance of what we had in my day.'

'And what was your day?' asked Anji. She bit her lip, feeling a twinge of embarrassment, as if she had wasted one of a genie's three wishes on a clean toothbrush. She just hoped the first answer came for free.

Silver lowered himself on to the ground, sitting next to Anji beneath the tree, the human side of his face in her line of sight. She could see the traces of slight cuts on his skin, which made him seem slightly more normal. Powerful as Silver was, he wasn't invulnerable. Gods didn't have scars.

'I am from the year 3006,' he said eventually, turning to Anji with an enquiring expression, as if he expected her to have some response.

'I'm afraid that's rather after my time,' she replied. 'I left Earth in 2001, and the year 3006 isn't one I've dropped into on the way here.'

Although Anji couldn't be sure, she would have sworn Silver looked briefly relieved. But if he had such feelings, or feelings at all, he covered them up fast.

'Time travel,' said Silver, as if savouring the words. 'I have only experienced it once, when I travelled from my native time to this one. The freedom must be incredible.'

'As free as swimming in an ocean,' replied Anji. 'During a storm.'

Silver laughed a deep, metallic chuckle. In spite of herself, Anji found she was laughing with him.

'It occurred to me,' said the Doctor, 'that our killer must have a purpose in the acquisition of the heads he takes from his victims. Now, presuming that we are not dealing with a ritualistic killer – and all the patterns would indicate we are not – then there must be something within those heads that is of use to the perpetrator.'

Fitz stuck his hand up. The Doctor raised an eyebrow.

'Memories?' asked Fitz. 'The victims might all have seen something, and the killer might need those memories.'

'Good idea, very good,' said the Doctor, and Fitz's chest swelled with pride. 'Good, but it wouldn't make any sense. So disparate are the victims that I doubt they could have any useful shared recollections our killer would need to gather. Besides, our killer seems to have a gift for observing the areas he inhabits. I'm sure such a stealthy individual would be able to gain access to anything our victims had seen if he needed to.'

Fitz shrugged a 'whatever' and sank back into his chair.

'I was certain the answer was more basic,' said the Doctor. 'Something biological. Now, Endpoint's medical records are sketchy at best, but I spent the night going through as much of the available research as I could get my hands on. And I found one characteristic unique to Endpointers, a physiological oddity that might explain our killer's head obsession.'

The Doctor stepped back and inserted a new slide into the projector. A crude cross-section diagram appeared of what looked to Fitz like a human head. An area towards the bottom of the brain had been coloured in a rich golden yellow.

'This,' said the Doctor. 'Is the vivactic gland, which research indicates floods the body of an Endpointer with a unique hormone-chemical cocktail, referred to by most medical experts as *Kallisti.*'

Miraso shrugged. 'So what?' she said. Powlin seemed equally confused as to the relevance of this. For his part, Fitz had no idea what any of them were going on about.

'You may well consider the vivactic gland to be as common as a heart or lungs,' said the Doctor. 'But I assure you it is not common at all. No other species I have encountered has such a gland, which seems to have evolved as a direct and strong response to the harshness of the Endpoint environment. Kallisti makes Endpointers stronger, faster, more resistant to poisons. It increases your healing capacities. To be quite honest, I suspect that it isn't an evolutionary product at all, but the result of smart geneware responding to extreme conditions. Perhaps that geneware was implanted by your ancestors. Perhaps it was the result of humanity cross-breeding with a heavily genetically re-engineered species. Nevertheless, the result is the same. Any other species with military ambitions would kill, probably kill in the millions, to produce their own vivactic glands. Now, past research shows the gland withers rapidly when removed from the brain, that Kallisti breaks down in contact with air and becomes useless, impossible to analyse. A researcher would need fresh samples of the vivactic gland, preferably still inside the heads of the donors.'

The Doctor pulled a chair over and sat down, waiting for a response to his theory.

'So,' asked Powlin eventually, 'who would want to perform this research? All Endpointers already have these traits, and we're isolated out here. Who else is there, and where have they come from if they're here?'

The Doctor paused. 'I have no idea,' he said finally, slumping slightly.

Miraso gave out an audible groan of disappointment.

'What is it like?' asked Anji, lying back in the grass. The accelerated growth of the apple trees was continuing, and blossom fell down from the branches. 'To have as much power as you have, to be able to make any decision and see it happen, to wield absolute power on this planet. What is it like?'

'It fills me with despair,' said Silver, without hesitation.

Anji frowned. 'Despair? How can being able to do anything lead to despair?'

Silver paused before responding. 'Because I have done everything that can be done on Endpoint,' he said. 'I have reached a pinnacle of success, and there is no danger of me falling. I cannot expand my power because there is nowhere else to go, no more power to have. All that is left is keeping the machine well maintained, making sure the system continues to work. Threats like these murders your Doctor is investigating provide brief distraction, but they are irritating problems rather than serious challenges. I have explored every facet of this world, conquered every territory, bought every resource. There is nothing new to discover.'

'But surely there are always new discoveries,' replied Anji. 'Scientific discoveries, if nothing else. Like these trees.' She tried to stop herself, aware of what was emerging from the back of her mind, unbidden. The thoughts that she had been suppressing for the last couple of days. She realised the path she was leading herself down with her next question. 'I mean, there's always new places to go with science, technology, medicine. You can't do everything, can you? You can reintroduce a dead species like the apple tree, with enough material.' She tried not to say it, but she did. 'But you can't actually raise the dead, can you?'

Silver turned to her, looming over her once more. Perhaps her question had challenged him in some way. Anji was painfully aware her fragile neck would snap like a twig between those steel fingers.

'This planet's resources are limited,' said Silver. 'But the technology here can do whatever those resources allow. There are no new discoveries to be made. And yes, given the correct genetic material I can "raise the dead", as you would say. It is a resource intensive process, and there is no one indispensable enough to revive, but it would be possible to create a copy of any living being within our laboratories.'

Anji was grateful she wasn't given a chance to speak, that he kept talking and didn't allow her to ask, to take things too far.

'Imagine you had done everything you ever could, Anji,' said Silver. 'Then what?'

Anji tried to think about that, but Silver answered for her.

'Nothing,' he said. 'You do nothing, forever.'

'This gets us nowhere,' groaned Miraso. 'We still have no plan of attack against the killers, no coherent defence against them. We know nothing about them.'

'No,' said the Doctor, jumping to his feet. His eyes gleamed and his body seemed energised as he stepped towards Miraso, pointing a slim finger. 'But we do know about *you*.'

'What?' replied Miraso. 'How does knowing me help?'

'You, Powlin, all of you,' said the Doctor, waving his arms expansively. 'I've been observing all of you, and that's how I know how to break this case.' He suddenly pulled Fitz out of his chair, so that the two of them were opposite Miraso and Powlin, who were sitting up in their chairs, leaning forward. Fitz didn't like their expressions.

'Look, Fitz,' said the Doctor, pointing at Miraso and Powlin. 'They're different from you, but they're alike, the same species. What do you notice about them?'

'They seem really pissed off?' replied Fitz, uncomfortable with the Doctor dragging him around by the collar.

'Exactly,' said the Doctor, spinning Fitz around to face him. 'They're aggressive, defensive, always prepared for an attack, always suspicious, always puffing themselves up, making themselves look big.' He threw Fitz back into his chair.

'That's partially the Kallisti talking, of course,' said the Doctor, addressing all of them once more. 'And partially a response to the hard lives you lead here. But it's a definite trait, nonetheless. Just look at the names of your towns – Hope, Survival, Triumph. All that posturing in the face of adversity.' He dropped down to his knees in front of Miraso. 'Remember what you just said: "no plan of attack", "no coherent defence". A combative culture permeating your every word. So it's understandable that certain things would never occur to you. It would never occur to any of you to act weak, to lay yourselves open to attack.'

Fitz chuckled, which seemed to rile Miraso slightly. He covered his mouth. He could see where this was going, but the other two couldn't. Yet. The Doctor had to take them there by hand.

'Why would we want to lay ourselves open to attack?' asked Miraso.

The Doctor placed his hands on her shoulders.

'Because,' he said quietly, 'the best way to trap a predator is to look like prey.'

* * *

Silver slowly got to his feet, and offered his steel hand to help Anji up. With a slight gesture she was dragged upright – it was like being given a helping hand by a fork-lift.

Silver was looking her straight in the eye. Clouds passed overhead, and for a second both his eyes seemed to glow red in the brief gloom. Then the sun passed over and the illusion was gone.

'You want something from me,' said Silver. 'You ask questions about my power, about what I can do. You coyly ask about the technology, the sciences available to me. This does not seem like simple curiosity. What do you want, Anji?'

She didn't answer, instead staring at her feet. The moment she had thought about, toyed with in those half-dreaming moments before sleep and after waking, the decision she had realised could come the moment she had looked around the Silver Palace's laboratory.

'Simply ask, Anji,' said Silver, his rich, deep voice almost seductive in its intensity. 'If it is possible, I'm sure we can come to some arrangement. And most things are possible for me.'

'I had a friend,' said Anji, matter-of-factly, as if telling an anecdote that was leading nowhere. 'Dave. He died, and I'd like him back. I have a hair of his, I keep it close to me.' She looked up at Silver, making eye contact, opening up to him. She had started now, there was no point in holding back. 'If you had the hair, could you bring him back?'

'I wouldn't be able to restore his memories, or even guarantee he would have the same personality,' said Silver. 'This new "Dave"… he would be a different person, genetically the same but with a different upbringing, different influences. He would not be the man you knew.'

Anji shook her head. 'This isn't for me. I don't want my boyfriend back. All I want is for him to be able to start again, to live another life. What happened to him was pointless, random, stupid.' She felt weak tears crawling down her cheeks, her skin itching in their path. 'He deserves another life. Not the life he had, but another life.'

Silver nodded. 'Then this I can do. But it will be a complex, resource-intensive operation, expensive even for me. I must ask for a high price.'

'What do you want?' Anji asked. The first full grown apple fell out of the tree, rolling across grass and blossom to land at her feet. She realised she hadn't much to give. Would he ask for her soul? No, that was stupid...

'This box,' said Silver. 'The one I am retrieving for the Doctor. I presume that it is his time machine, correct?'

Anji shook her head. 'It's not mine to give,' she insisted. 'I can't take it for you, and I wouldn't know how.'

Silver stepped closer to her, laying his human hand on her shoulder.

'That's not what I'm asking for,' he said. 'I'm sure the Doctor's craft has numerous security measures to prevent the likes of me from walking off with it. No, all I want you to do is wander around inside with a scanning device, gathering data for me. The Doctor need never know, and after you and your friends have left I will be able to use that knowledge to further my own studies. I want to leave this planet, that's all, and this information could help me.'

He squeezed Anji's shoulder, leaning closer to her, his voice dropping almost to a whisper.

'We could help each other.'

'This is bloody stupid,' said Powlin, muttering into the mic taped inside his breather. He was based on one of Hope's higher buildings, where a signal could get through to any place in the city. If he gave the order, an assault team would get it without fail, following his word to the target area. Wherever that turned out to be. 'This is just asking for trouble.'

'That's the bloody point,' hissed Fitz on the other end of the line. He and the Doctor were staggering around various grotty alleyways and dark corners of the city, making themselves targets. The Doctor seemed insistent that with the killer's timescale seemingly accelerated, a couple of vulnerable potential victims would be too tempting to miss out on. Powlin could see the logic, but there was still something about setting yourself up as a target that sat badly with his nature.

'You're just bitter you didn't think of this yourself, Powlin,' said a deep voice down the line. Silver was on the roof of the Silver Palace, heading his own private group of armed men. If anything kicked off nearby, Silver would supposedly respond to Powlin's request. In reality Silver was overseeing the entire operation. Powlin could almost feel Silver's cold, filtered breath on the back of his neck.

The rooftop was ice cold, and Powlin paced impatiently. A handful of his men were aiming sniper rifles around, just in case. The Doctor had planned the operation so that each team was at the centre of as many possible routes to as many possible flashpoints as was, well, possible. Virtually the entire perimeter of Hope was within five minutes of a fast response team. The only problem was that the Doctor refused to allow anyone except himself and Fitz to act as targets – he wouldn't allow any other moving targets on the perimeter. Miraso had tried to argue that this just meant the killer would pick off *real* drunks instead, and that it would be more effective to have several groups of targets. But the Doctor was adamant. Powlin was beginning to think the Doctor was looking forward to getting his hands on their killer.

Sometimes, Fitz wished the Doctor had less faith in him. When he had volunteered to accompany the Doctor in his ramble through the outskirts of Hope, showing displays of physical incompetence and vulnerability to tempt the murderer to come down and make a bid for their heads, Fitz had presumed the Doctor would refuse. He'd expected the Doctor to say it was too dangerous, that he shouldn't put himself at risk. Instead the Doctor had instantly agreed.

'You're the only other person capable of doing this,' he had told Fitz. 'You're the only person who I know can look after themselves in these circumstances.'

While the Doctor's faith in Fitz's ability to defend himself in the face of a knife-wielding maniac serial killer was touching, it wasn't a faith Fitz shared. If they bumped into this guy, Fitz was a dead man. He just knew it. The best he could hope for was a no-show, that the operation was a complete disaster.

'Wraaargh!' bellowed the Doctor, dressed in rags, as he collapsed into a pile of rubbish. Fitz rolled his eyes at this ham acting.

'Come here you,' Fitz rambled, staggering over and offering the Doctor a hand. He hoped that, whatever was lurking in the dark, it saw through the Doctor's bad acting and left them well alone.

Miraso had never seen Silver so interested in a project like this before. Previous criminal activities and disruptions of the natural order had been dealt with swiftly, with only brief intervention by the big man. Now he was up on the roof with her and the men, giving direct orders to Powlin and the others. It wasn't natural; it was a disruption of order in itself, this abandoning of Silver's detachment. Soon people would begin to think he was just a man – and from then on, chaos.

It was the strangers, thought Miraso. Silver had begun to take too much of an interest in them, and was letting everything else slip. So he was up on the roof, with the Anji girl nearby, monitoring the Doctor's plan. At least Silver seemed to have the sense to completely ignore Fitz, presumably because he saw him as neither asset nor threat.

'I thought you were completely isolated out here?'

It took Miraso a second to realise Anji was talking to her. 'What?' she demanded.

'All this weaponry,' said Anji, indicating the huge amounts of heavy weaponry on the roof, some pointing down over the battlements, others pointing to the skies, some prepared to launch missiles at other cities. 'This planet is isolated, so why so much weaponry?'

'It's for the eventuality of an attack from people outside the Palace, but on Endpoint,' said Silver. He had somehow found a dark greatcoat from somewhere, one which had a large enough sleeve to fit his fist through.

'Still, you could take out a small army with one of these cannons,' said Anji.

'You misunderstand,' said Silver. 'These weapons are for an attack from the people of Endpoint, a full-scale rebellion. Not just a small rebellious force, but everyone. There's enough weaponry here to take down the entire population, if necessary.'

There was a brief but difficult pause.

'You really do think of everything, don't you?' said Anji.

Miraso couldn't tell whether Anji thought this was a good thing or not.

The imaginatively named Long Pier was one of Hope's most desolate and precarious outcrops, and so the Doctor had decided it was a vital stop-off point in their tour of Hope's lower points. The Pier was a slender web of interweaving walkways stretching out across the sea, with several levels linked like a snakes and ladders board. A few flaming gas torches were strung out along the Pier, and there were a couple of visible fires, but mostly it was oppressively dark.

'Doctor,' whispered Fitz as they approached. 'I don't think we're going to have trouble finding a murderer in there, I just don't know whether it'll be the right one. I'd hate to be decapitated by the wrong person.'

'You feel vulnerable,' whispered the Doctor in reply. 'That's understandable. It's a vulnerable place out here. The people who live here must live with that fear constantly. And tonight they're an obvious target. We have to protect them.'

With a slightly more purposeful stagger, the Doctor walked on to the Pier, somehow managing to reel around while watching his step.

Fitz cursed and followed behind, letting the pretence slip a bit. Powlin was right – this was madness. As they walked further on to the Pier, Fitz realised they were in a multi-storey shanty town. Tiny homes built of crates, things moving in the dark, people beneath every possible bit of shelter. As they approached one of the fires they had seen from a distance, Fitz saw figures moving around the flame, staying close. Fitz could understand the appeal – it was freezing out here, where winds tore across the surface of the sea, a slim structure like the Pier barely blocking their path. Fitz kept walking towards the flame, drawn to it, until the Doctor laid a hand on his arm.

'I don't think we want to challenge them to their source of warmth,' said the Doctor quietly, and as he said that Fitz could make out the raucous voices ahead, the tones of barely suppressed violence. No, Fitz didn't want to challenge them after all. He stuffed his freezing hands under his arms instead.

'Down there,' said the Doctor, pointing to a stairwell. Fitz could barely make it out in the dark, and could only just see thin slivers of light reflecting from the railings. He let the Doctor lead the way as they descended the stairs, until the sky above seemed to be completely blotted out. They seemed to be in a void of beams and girders, not unlike the ones they had climbed up after losing the TARDIS.

Fitz's hand felt freezing cold, and he instinctively pulled it away from the railing. He yelped in shock as strips of skin were pulled away, stuck to the rail. The Doctor was over Fitz in a second, examining his raw hand with a pen torch, all thoughts of his mock-drunkenness forgotten.

'You'll live,' said the Doctor, turning to examine the railing. 'This must be conducting an incredible amount of cold.' He 0suddenly snapped upright, flicking the torch off. Fitz was left alone in the silent darkness.

'There's been a temperature drop in the sea,' said the Doctor. 'It's frozen again.'

Fitz's eyes were adjusting to the darkness. Dim light was seeping in, and he could just make out his silvery breath in the air.

'This is the place,' said the Doctor.

'Oh goody,' said Fitz, nursing his sore hand.

A scream rang out, and the Doctor was gone, the vapour of his breath hanging in the air behind him. Fitz swore and gave chase, trying not to bump his head, fall to his death or in any other way kill himself in the rush. The Pier was a labyrinth of dark corridors, and Fitz could see shapes moving, disturbed by the screams, preparing themselves for attack.

Ahead, the Doctor slid down a nearby pole like a fireman. Swearing again, Fitz jumped for the pole and clung on, letting himself slide down until his left foot impacted on unstable, shaky boards. Fitz let go of the pole and reeled backwards on the unstable surface, partially dazed by the twenty-foot vertical slide, and partially distracted by smoke. In Fitz's ear Powlin's voice was babbling on, demanding to know what was going on. But Fitz was too tired, too out of breath, to speak coherently.

There was a fire burning, and Fitz had the impression of ragged figures in the firelight, adults and children. Someone was slumped nearby, and Fitz saw splashes of red. He didn't need to look closer. He hadn't time to look closer – he had a more pressing concern.

The Doctor was wrestling with a tall, white-clad figure, one with wide, black eyes. Fitz recognised their target from Powlin's description, and from the flash of the man jumping over him on the ice. They'd found him, and Fitz shouted that this was the case, hoping that the throat mic was still working. He needed to get the signal out just in case, to bring Powlin's men to their location as soon as possible.

Fitz ran over to the tarpaulin pulled across the beams of the Pier wall, a makeshift protection from the elements raised by the people there. He scrabbled for a gap and pulled it open, dragging out the flare gun he had been given earlier and jamming it through the gap. His breath ragged, one eye on the fight between the Doctor and the killer, he pulled the trigger.

The last thing he saw was the Doctor falling back, his head lolling dangerously close to the raging fire. The killer was straddled over him, one hand clamped around the Doctor's neck, the throat mic torn away and hanging off his collar. The killer's knife was raised, firelight casting his shadow on to the ceiling.

Then the flare gun's recoil knocked Fitz off his feet and he collapsed to the ground, facing away from the fight. As he scraped his raw fingers on the rough floor, pulling himself to his feet, he heard a sickening crunch of bone and a yelp of anguish. He turned to see the knife skidding across the floor towards him, the ghostlike figure of the murderer backing away from the Doctor. Now it was Fitz's friend who loomed in the firelight, and for one second he didn't know who to be frightened of and frightened for.

Then, in one second of clarity that brought him to a halt, Fitz realised that the killer was wearing some kind of costume. The black eyes were lenses, the muzzle a breath filter. And from within the zip of his white coat, he was producing...

'Doctor!' Fitz shouted, running forward, trying to get to the Doctor before the man could fire his gun, trying to do anything to distract him.

The distraction tactic worked. The shock of Fitz's cry caused the killer's aim to shake, and his shot went wild.

Instead of shooting the Doctor, he shot Fitz.

The Doctor heard Fitz crash to the ground and ran to him, turning his back on his assailant. He dropped to his knees, looking for help. The inhabitants of the Pier had all fled, and Powlin's men were doubtless still a few minutes away from finding them. The only person present was the corpse of the one victim the Doctor hadn't been in time to save. He was determined that Fitz wasn't going to double his failure. He flashed a look over his shoulder. The gun had been dropped to the floor and the killer had disappeared.

The Doctor checked Fitz's pulse, his breath. Both fine. He searched for a gunshot wound, but there was none. Then, with immense relief, he noticed the dart stuck into Fitz's neck. A tranquilliser tab.

The Doctor was torn for a second. Fitz needed looking after, but help was on its way. The Doctor would have called for help from Powlin, but his throat mic appeared to have been lost in the fight. Meanwhile a serial murderer was escaping. Fitz would have to look after himself. The Doctor ran into the darkness where he had seen his enemy flee, listening out for any clue.

To his right he heard the sound of a loose beam snapping. He ran towards the sound, pulling aside a crude wall made of flimsy board. He stuck his head out into the open air, and in the dim light saw his prey, the former predator in the all-over environment suit, scurrying down the outer wall of the Pier. As the Doctor had suspected, the water below was frozen. A coincidence? Perhaps not, but the Doctor didn't have time to worry about that. He dragged himself over the ledge and dropped, reaching out to grab a bar ten feet below. His arm protested, nearly coming out of its socket, but his grip didn't loosen. He hung there and kicked out, a blow meeting with his enemy's head. He watched this man, this creature, this monster, jerk back and fall, landing with a crunch on the ice some way below. The Doctor pulled himself up until he had a proper footing, then began to climb down towards the ice. A glance down a few seconds later showed that the white clad figure was pulling himself up, and so in spite of the risks to his bones – not to mention of crashing straight through the ice and being burnt alive by acid – the Doctor let himself drop the last ten feet or so. He felt his ankle nearly crack, and there was a painful jolt in his right knee, but he pulled himself up and ran after the killer, pursuing him across the ice.

The Doctor's target was staggering, one arm limp at his side, but still moving. The Doctor himself was winded, and every part of his body ached, screamed for him to stop, to just let the fugitive escape, to catch him another day. A few months ago the Doctor would barely have noticed the exertion, but now he just felt tired, and his vision blurred as he ran through the mist. But he didn't stop, he kept running after the man ahead, because how could he overcome the evils in the universe if he couldn't overcome his own frailties?

Ahead something loomed out of the fog, and the Doctor found himself climbing up the side of a black metallic shape sticking through the ice. He didn't let himself think about it, following his target up the surface of the thing, which felt like iron beneath his fingers, slippery and cold. He found a railing at the top, and pulled himself over it, dropping on to a flatter surface. The killer was just ahead, dragging open a door of some kind built into the metal floor. Bright, electric light poured out of the hatchway, illuminating that muzzle of a face. The Doctor threw himself at the man, and both of them dropped down into a confined space. The door slammed behind them, and the Doctor wrestled with the killer as the lights around them flashed red. The Doctor could feel a change in pressure, a tingling on his skin. They were in an airlock, with decontamination scans sweeping over them. The whole room lurched violently, and the Doctor realised they were in a submarine of some kind, beginning to descend below the ice, into the sea. The air in the airlock was being filtered, and the new air was oxygen rich, cleaner than any in Hope. The fresh air made the Doctor giddy, and he received a kick in the shins for allowing himself to be distracted. With his last effort the Doctor raised his fist and put all his strength into one blow, bringing his knuckles down into the killer's masked face. His wrist seemed nearly to snap with the power of the blow but the recipient crumpled to the floor of the airlock and finally stopped moving. The Doctor had his man, at last.

But where was he? The airlock lights turned green, and the Doctor pushed open the inner door, emerging into the cramped environment of the submarine. There was no one around, the crew presumably being elsewhere.

The Doctor pulled the man in white out of the airlock, laying him on the floor. He gripped the muzzle of the man's mask, his aching fingers working the release mechanism beneath the chin. The gasmask came off in one motion, revealing a very human face beneath. A bruised and scarred face, one with a slightly bovine expression, but human nonetheless. Not an Endpointer, or a mutant, or some kind of killing machine. Just a human being.

The Doctor found a bench built into the wall, presumably there for crewmembers to sit while they removed their environment suits. The Doctor blearily noticed three empty suits hanging from the wall opposite as he sat, feeling the aches run through him as the tension in his muscles dissipated. He looked at the man he had pursued all this way, across the city and below the ice, the man who now lay unconscious on the floor. The killer who had struck fear into one of the most fearless places the Doctor had ever known.

Just a man, after all.

Part Three
Beyond the Sea

Chapter Nine
Downward Spirals

The submarine's descent is rapid, moving away from the city of Hope, where metal struts reach up from the sea bed. The sub is heading towards areas where the sea is deeper, a descent into dark valleys where the pressure would crush any life, places where no light has ever shone. It moves on an automated programme – a small vehicle designed for a crew of ten, it now relies on the most basic of artificial intelligence protocols: follow the signal, avoid the obstacles. The sub weaves its way around the reefs of diamond-like coral, one of the few species to survive in Endpoint's corrosive, poisonous waters. Below, on the sea bed, lie wrecks of spaceships and habitation areas, rafts and leviathans, all equally useless now, all lost to this brutal sea.

The submarine continues, through impenetrable darkness, following the signal, the signal that lights the way home.

Torches swept the Pier as militiamen and Silver's personal guard worked together in their manhunt, exploring the flimsy structure for signs of the Doctor, Fitz or the enemy they had been pursuing. Anji stood on the dockside, hovering near to Silver, aware that his looming presence would keep away anything lurking in the dark. It was her first trip outside the Silver Palace since the Doctor had made his deal with Silver, and it just reminded Anji why she hadn't wanted to see the rest of Hope again. Even the cramped living spaces of the Silver Palace were better than sprawling squalor like this.

The Doctor's encounter with the killer they were seeking, which everyone had partially heard over the Doctor and Fitz's mics before they cut out, had put everyone into a state of frantic disturbance. Powlin was shaking down the tramplike figures of the Pier's inhabitants, bawling at them and threatening to kick their dustbin-fires into their lean-to homes, destroying everything they had. Miraso was pacing up and down, directing the search over her mic. Anji had been so frantic that, even if there was nothing practical she could do to help the Doctor and Fitz, she had to be out here, ready for whatever happened.

Only Silver was unmoved, standing silently, waiting to make his next move. The only motion from him was the flapping of his greatcoat in the cold sea breeze.

'Got one,' said Miraso urgently, one finger to her earpiece. 'Four floors down, towards the west side of the Pier.'

Silver nodded. 'Let's go.' He strode ahead, leading the way to a nearby ladder, Anji and Miraso close behind. As they got further into the Pier Anji was surprised to see Silver start to jump around, like a child playing hopscotch. He was surprisingly agile on his feet. As a board creaked beneath her foot she realised Silver was carefully moving across the areas that could hold his weight, jumping over any unstable panels.

The cold, the fear, a night exposed to the foul air of Hope – it was all too much for Anji, and as they descended into darkness she began to feel detached and disorientated, unsure of where she was. Torchlight flashed around her, but not enough to make any sense of where she was. She simply followed the red glow coming from Silver, and tried to keep her footing.

They left the staircase and entered an open area, heading for an orange glow ahead. A fire, burning in a pit of inflammable material, the rim of the area scorched and hardened. Anji saw a ragged, headless figure, blood pooling around the neck, and a brief burst of panic stuck in her throat. She broke into a run, but a few hasty steps later she realised the body didn't belong to either of her friends – it was the wrong shape, too bulky and flabby, to be either the Doctor or Fitz.

One of Powlin's men approached, seemingly uncertain of protocol but absolutely certain that Silver was to be deferred to nonetheless.

'The head for this one is over there,' said the nervous militiaman, and Anji rigidly avoided following his pointing finger. There were some things she didn't need to see.

'We don't think the killer got any heads this time,' said the militiaman. 'It's difficult to call, our only witness is out cold.' He stepped out of their way, and with a gasp of relief Anji saw Fitz lying on the ground, unconscious and slightly damaged but with his head still attached to his shoulders. The lines on his face seemed stark in the flickering firelight, a cut on his cheek glistening with dark, wet blood. Anji was eager to run over there and examine him, but a hand on her shoulder stopped her. Silver walked over to Fitz, dropping into a crouch. He swept his eyes back and forth over Fitz, and Anji realised Silver's robotic eye was performing some kind of scan.

'No broken bones or serious internal damage,' said Silver. 'We need him awake. Miraso.'

Silver stepped back, and Miraso stepped forward, straddling Fitz and leaning over into his face.

'Wake up,' she shouted, slapping Fitz's face. 'Wake up, now.' She slapped him again, and Fitz's head jerked to one side. Anji winced. This was too much, Miraso was hurting him.

'Leave him alone,' protested Anji, moving to pull Miraso away from Fitz. She felt herself jerk back, a rock solid grip around her arm.

'We need to find the Doctor,' said Silver, red eye flaring in the dark. 'Only Fitz can tell us what has happened to him. We need him awake.'

'She's hurting him,' protested Anji, but she couldn't slip out of Silver's hold.

'Wake up,' Miraso was still barking, slapping Fitz's face from side to side.

Suddenly Fitz's back arched, his eyes opening wide. His hands clawed at the ground, as if he was dragging himself out of some inner pit.

'A-teen!' he screamed incomprehensibly, panicking, not truly aware of where he was. 'She said, she said she wa–'

Miraso, still sitting on Fitz's chest, grabbed him by the scruff of the neck.

'Where's the Doctor?' she demanded. Fitz's eyes began to roll, so she slapped him again. 'Where did the Doctor go? Where is the man you were chasing?'

'There was a fight,' said Fitz blearily. 'The Doctor fought the white man, but the white man shot me. I was shot.' Fitz looked confused, and he tried to move his hands to check himself for bullet wounds. 'That's all I remember.'

Fitz slumped back to the ground, and this time Miraso left him there.

'I think he's been tranquillised,' said Miraso, brushing her hands on her trousers. 'We're unlikely to get any more out of him.'

Silver nodded to a nearby militiaman. 'Have him stretchered to the Silver Palace at once. And don't damage him.'

'Fitz said he was shot,' said Miraso. 'But he seems to have been tranquillised. If he was shot with some kind of tranquilliser, they could have done the same to the Doctor.' Anji could see a theory developing in Miraso's mind as she spoke. 'The Doctor thought this killer might be gathering Kallisti from Endpointers, because it's unique. Well, the Doctor's a unique specimen himself, an offworlder.'

Anji realised what Miraso was implying. If this killer had the Doctor, then he had access to an alien tissue sample. The Doctor could be subject to all kinds of experiments. Anji didn't want to think of the kind of analysis they might put him through.

'You're right,' she said out loud. Silver turned to her with a questioning gaze. 'We need to get the Doctor back.'

The Doctor hadn't realised he was asleep until he awoke. The exertion of all that chasing and fighting, combined with the warm, pressurised atmosphere of the submarine, had caused him to drift off. The clanging of a bulkhead door woke him up, and he jumped to his feet, smacking his head on an overhanging pipe. He swore in a language he didn't even understand himself, and tried to cram himself into the alcove above the bench.

'Castillo?' a male voice was calling. 'Castillo, you imbecile, we're nearly there. Get the samples ready for Stephens.'

The Doctor stayed perfectly still in his alcove, hoping that the voice would go away. He didn't know whether he could face another fight, his whole body seemed to be aching. He tried to tense his muscles, but they felt weak.

A door creaked open.

'Castillo, I said –' the voice went suddenly quiet, the speaker clearly having seen the unconscious killer on the floor. Before the Doctor could move the door slammed. There was the sound of a wheel being turned.

The Doctor didn't consider this a good sign. He let his head rock back, felt the warm metal of the pipes behind him on the top of his head. He let his mind and body relax. He suspected that whenever he next saw someone, he would need all the energies he could muster.

The guards on the door at the Silver Palace parted for their master, the doors sliding open as he approached. Anji tried to keep pace with Silver, who had been silent since they left the Pier. She feared her dependency on Silver and his power, especially now she had lost the Doctor. But at the back of her mind she was aware that the Doctor was a Jiminy Cricket, who would coax her away from bringing Dave back. Without the Doctor there, she would be able to make a clearer decision. And the fact that his absence helped her situation made her feel guilty, even though she knew the Doctor could look after himself.

Anji expected Silver to stride straight through the main hall, ignoring the Silver Palace's nightly clientele with their drinking, gambling, and other organic pastimes. Instead he stood in the centre of the room, and from where he stood, an aura of silence spread as the people grew quiet, aware of his lingering presence, unwilling to disturb him, equally unwilling to show fear at his presence by backing away, in case that only served to anger him.

Soon, the whole room was silent, as if everyone there had been frozen in time. Every eye turned to Silver, waiting for him to move.

Anji watched him close his eyes, a lid falling over the human eye, the other going temporarily dark. Silver reached up his human hand and rubbed his temple, deep in thought.

'Miraso,' Silver said quietly. 'Get these people out of my Palace. Clear the entire room.' He began to raise his voice, opening his eyes to address the rest of the Palace staff. 'I want all non-essential equipment powered down. Someone tell the power stations to divert all energy to here. Cut off everything except life support. And put out announcements on all the communication channels – they will be going off line in twenty minutes.' All around him glasses were being left on tables half full, games of cards and dice were being abandoned as people backed away, heading slowly but steadily to the exits.

Miraso nodded. 'It'll be done. Within the hour all communications and power will be entirely at your disposal.'

'Good,' said Silver, shrugging off his greatcoat. There was a nervous tension in his muscles, Anji could see them squirming under his skin. 'We're going to activate SatNet.'

Anji had no idea what that meant, but from Miraso's expression she gathered it had to be big.

As he heard the submarine docking, the Doctor backed himself into a corner, preparing for the inevitable. Within minutes the outer airlock door opened, and a dozen white, environment-suit clad gunmen dropped through the gap, running straight for the Doctor with their tranquilliser guns, firing darts in his direction.

The Doctor thought he did quite well, all in all. He managed to take down the first five of his assailants, dodging the darts as they shot past him, bouncing off the walls. But the sixth managed a lucky shot, and the dart jammed in the Doctor's thigh. He reached inside himself, preparing to metabolise the drug and dispose of it harmlessly within his system.

He only realised he couldn't do that anymore when he fell over, dead to the world.

* * *

The room had cleared, and Silver's staff were busy running around, powering down all non-essential equipment as he had insisted. Silver himself sat at a table, steel fingers drumming impatiently against wood.

'My grandparents told me about the last time SatNet was activated,' Miraso said quietly. 'The power drain left Hope without any resources for a month. One of the reactors on the north side went into meltdown. Hundreds of people died.'

'I know,' replied Silver. His tone made it clear that he was not open to arguments.

'What's SatNet?' asked Anji.

'It's a series of orbital satellites,' replied Miraso. 'It takes a huge amount of power to operate them, even briefly. I can't see any reason why anyone would want to use it. The risks are colossal.'

'Anji,' said Silver firmly, holding out his oversized hand. 'Please take my hand.'

Reluctantly, Anji reached out and held on to Silver's hand. It felt cold, slightly scratchy.

'You felt a slight tickle, didn't you?' asked Silver, taking his hand away.

Anji nodded.

'That scratching sensation disguised a minute injection into your hand,' explained Silver. 'You now have a nanobot in your bloodstream transmitting your position. I put a similar device into the Doctor when he shook on our deal a couple of days back.'

'And SatNet is the only system that can pinpoint the signal,' finished Miraso. 'It's a lot of effort to find one man.'

Silver turned to Miraso. 'That one man and his current location is the key to a mystery that is undermining our entire way of life. I wish to banish uncertainty from Hope and from Endpoint as a whole. The Endpointers will have the certainty that I can protect them from anything. And I will do whatever it takes to re-establish that certainty.'

'No matter what the cost?' asked Anji.

'Precisely,' said Silver. 'Some things are worth any price asked, aren't they?'

* * *

A voice echoed in the darkness.

'How is the patient?'

I'm not the patient, he thought. I'm the Doctor. But he couldn't speak, couldn't move. He couldn't even see.

He slid back into an anaesthetised haze.

Some time later, he found he could see. He opened his eyes, then closed them again. It was bright out there, huge lights hanging from the ceiling. He rolled over on to his front, bringing himself up on his hands and knees, using his own body to create a shaded area to look at. This was harder than it should have been – he rolled to his right and bumped back, having hit some kind of barrier. He shuffled to the left and tried again, this time successfully. The concrete beneath his palms felt pitted and damp. He could hear dripping water, the clicking of machines. He opened his eyes, looked down. The backs of his hands seemed blurred. Contrary to the saying, he didn't know them at all. It was as if something was moving under his skin.

'The sense of disorientation you are feeling is understandable,' said a cold, clipped voice. 'Your presence represents a threat to our environment here. As such, you have been subjected to a full nanoscan. Your entire body is being picked over, cell by cell, for any material potentially harmful to us. Don't worry, providing you survive, it will be over soon.'

Oh, good, thought the Doctor, collapsing to the floor. If this was a temporary state, he was willing to sleep it off.

More time passed, and the Doctor was woken by the same sophisticated voice that had informed him of his condition.

'As you can see from these scans,' the voice was saying, 'our patient here is not human, and neither is he one of the surface mutations. He has many totally alien qualities, although most of these would seem to be dormant, the patient's basic life signs operating at human normal. One might speculate that this condition is perhaps due to a recent operation – there are signs of surgery around the chest area, although I would hesitate to guess what kind of surgery has been performed.'

'Just a little exploratory self-surgery,' the Doctor said, rolling up into a sitting position. He found himself in a glass bubble on a rough concrete floor. He blinked, taking in the sights – a lab of some sort, in a concrete structure strewn with pipes. A handful of ageing humans opposite him. 'As you said, my insides are terribly interesting, so I thought I'd cut a hole, pop my head through and have a look. Unfortunately for me, it was terribly dark in there and I forgot to take a torch.'

The humans were staring at him, seemingly surprised by his presence even though it was him they had been discussing. The Doctor noted their deathly pallor and weak posture. They had been living in darkness for some time. Their clothes, however, were impeccably neat, and the Doctor found himself adjusting his cravat in retaliation.

'You know, I'm surprised you left me in my own clothes,' he said. 'Isn't it standard to strip the subject naked, dehumanise him? Isn't that the way you treat people when you lock them in cages, experiment on them?' His voice began to rise, anger slipping in. 'Don't you do everything you can to deny their humanity, to excuse what you do to them?'

'Why?' said one of the humans, stepping forward. He was the man who had just been speaking, and he had more confidence than his fellows. He wore a white lab suit, and his dark hair was slicked back and thinning. His nose was long and sharp, his eyes a watery blue. He must have been in his mid fifties.

'Why would we need to do that?' said the dark-haired man. 'When you so clearly aren't human anyway.' He stepped forward to examine the Doctor with interest. 'Besides, we weren't going to touch you. God knows what you might have carried in from the surface.'

'We're below ground,' said the Doctor, then remembered how he had got to where he was. The submarine. The sound of dripping water as he lay there. 'No, not below ground, at the bottom of the sea. This is some kind of deep sea bunker.'

'Quite correct,' said the dark-haired man. 'This is a deep-sea, self-contained environment free from the pollutants of the rest of this wretched planet. I'm Stephens, by the way, and I'm in charge of the project you so rudely interrupted.'

'Project?' said the Doctor. 'Is that what you call it, slaughtering innocent people for some pointless scientific endeavour?'

'Those aren't people!' hissed Stephens, spitting as he leaned over the case in which the Doctor was enclosed. 'They are mutants, an aberration of the human race. *We* are the people here, and only my project can give us any hope of leaving this bunker. So don't attempt to take a high-handed attitude with me, whoever you are.'

'The Doctor,' said the Doctor calmly, relaxed now he had successfully riled Stephens, passing his anxiety on. 'You do know you people have got all the clichés wrong, don't you? It's supposed to be the humans who live on the surface and the mutants who live underground, not the other way around.' He smiled what he hoped was an infuriating smile.

'Ah, but one thing remains the same,' said Stephens with a cruel smile. 'The humans still hold the knives.' He nodded to a nearby operating table. 'And it's the animals who get dissected.'

The Doctor's smile faded.

Anji found Fitz in his room among the staff quarters, lying on his bed and trying not to move.

'How are you?' she asked.

'Nauseous every time I move,' Fitz replied. 'So in general I'm trying not to move much. What's it like out there?'

'Boredom Central,' replied Anji. With all resources diverted to Silver's project, the Silver Palace was almost entirely dead. No customers, no life, just subordinates scurrying to perform various dry technical tasks.

'At least you've been in the centre of things,' moaned Fitz. 'I'm on the outskirts of Boredom – nothing ever happens here. How's the Doctor?'

'You mean you don't know?' said Anji.

'Know what?' asked Fitz, pulling himself up on to one elbow, in spite of his previous determination not to move.

'The Doctor is missing,' she replied. 'You're the last person to have seen him. Silver is trying to trace where he's got to. We think he might be in the hands of the killer, whoever that is.'

'What time is it?' asked Fitz, rolling off the bed and on to his feet. He waved from side to side slightly, and Anji had to help him to stay standing.

'Almost sundown. Why do you ask?'

'Because I've got one lead left that might help us,' said Fitz. 'And if I don't get going I'll miss my assignation.'

Anji watched, concerned, as Fitz staggered out of the door. Something told her there was no point trying to stop him.

They gathered in Stygian darkness in one of the city's foulest meeting places, dark within the struts of Hope. Their piety and faith burned even as they were shrouded in shadow, waiting for the new member of their number, the one who wished to transcend. Eventually he came, an innocent wandering into their presence. He made a gesture of supplication and indicated his inferiority.

'Hey,' said Fitz. 'Sorry I'm late.'

The three Brothers accepted the man's apology for his human weakness. They bowed to him, acknowledging acceptance. Soon they would make him more than human. As the three brothers led the way through low corridors to their sacred place, the man experienced uncertainty in the face of the challenge ahead of him.

'Are you sure you know where the hell we're going?' asked Fitz.

The Brothers nodded again. This crisis of faith was understandable. The step into the light was a distance of many miles, an effort of will. Even the strong faltered. It was only more evidence of the human weaknesses that needed to be erased, a cry for help and salvation. In faltering, the faithful demonstrated how much they needed purity.

In the sacred place they gathered. It was their sanctuary, a haven for the Brothers. The three led the potential new follower through the hooded ranks, and as they passed those hoods were thrown back, revealing proud modifications and enhancements. The new follower showed his admiration.

'Nice box on your face,' said Fitz. 'Does it get Radio Luxembourg?'

'Behold,' said one of the three. 'Behold the shrine of our queen.' They bowed down, presenting the magnificence before them.

'That's nice,' said Fitz, looking at the box on the stage. 'It's really... shiny.'

The faithful gathered around their new potential member, and presented their knowledge to him. He listened patiently as they outlined the tenets of their faith, their principles and belief. He listened to tales of their victories and achievements, sacrifices and sufferings, all with the greatest of respect. He listened as the Brothers told him their secrets, of their journeys through the city's undertunnels, of the twisted creatures that lived down there, howling their demented pain.

Then, when he had listened enough, they asked him if there were any theological issues he would like them to resolve, any questions of faith he had before he committed himself to the cause.

And so the newcomer asked his questions. He asked why Silver was their enemy, when he seemed to represent everything they strived for? And while some among the Brothers refused to hear this heresy, others found they could not answer his question, and were disturbed. While he was at it the newcomer also asked why the Brotherhood claimed to be committed to the abandonment of all human emotion yet always seemed so bloody angry? Yet again, some of the Brothers were angered while others listened to the newcomer's words with interest.

So, with his audience at least partially warming up, the newcomer asked more questions, picking apart the belief of the Brothers bit by bit, pointing out the contradictions, whether they be implicit, explicit or obvious to any idiot, as he put it. And by the time he had finished speaking half the gathered brethren were baying for his blood, while the other half were baying to give up on this whole religion lark and go home instead.

A question had become an argument, an argument a schism,

and soon that schism turned into a punch up. Limbs, cybernetic and otherwise, flew in anger. Faces were bruised, heads were knocked together, and a lynch mob tried to sacrifice Fitz on the altar. The only thing that stopped a raised microblade from being plunged into his chest was the appearance of the Brotherhood's Queen, her digital visage floating above the altar, staring out across the melee.

'My followers, you must not fight!' declared the holographic face regally. 'What has brought you to this sorry state?'

'The newcomer, our Queen,' said one Brother, prostrating himself while pointing to Fitz. 'He questions our sacred tenets.'

'Newcomer?' said the face of the Queen, metallic voice echoing around the chamber. The face turned to Fitz. There was something terribly familiar about that tone of voice, the curve of the Queen's silver face…

The Queen blinked when she saw Fitz, and he could swear he saw that godlike face appear slightly thrown by the whole situation.

'Cast out the infidel from this sacred place!' declared the Queen, returning her attention to her followers. 'He is not worthy of a clean death from you.'

For once, Fitz was glad to be looked down upon.

I'm getting very sick of standing around on this roof in the cold, thought Anji. It was like being in a play, rotating between two or three settings, with flat backgrounds lifting up into the rafters and props being wheeled on and off as required.

The latest bit of set decoration was currently being prepared by Silver's lackeys – a wide satellite dish seemingly constructed from tinfoil and spit. Apparently SatNet could only be activated by a focused energy-data stream transmitted at a certain time of day to the primary satellite. The primary satellite would then pass the data and energy around the chain, step by step, creating a global network covering the whole of Endpoint. A fairly straightforward business on any other advanced world – with Endpoint's environmental and resource problems it was a

Herculean task. Technicians were checking the satellite dish, while Miraso had emerged from the depths of the Palace in communication with the power plants via her headset.

Silver monitored progress through a flat console he held in the palm of his metal hand. Cables trailed from the console to the dish, and Silver's human fingers raced across the keyboard, tapping in co-ordinates. The collar of his greatcoat flapped in the wind, partially concealing his face.

'Nearly there,' he said, his voice carrying in spite of the wind. The satellite dish adjusted itself, whirring loudly, as Silver tapped the keys. 'We will have contact in five minutes. Miraso, are power levels ready?'

'I'll check,' replied Miraso, turning away to mutter instructions into her headset. Finally she turned to Silver and nodded. 'On your signal.'

Silver turned to Anji.

'I suggest you step away from any live power lines,' Silver said. 'They are likely to be severely overloaded, and there may be a breach.'

Anji didn't like the sound of that, so she made sure to step away from anything that resembled a cable or power line. Difficult to do with so many snaking across the roof to plug into the base of the dish.

'Nearly there,' said Silver again, tapping away. 'Activate primary power feeds.'

Miraso passed on the command. A steady hum began to build up. Anji began to feel slightly woozy. There was a dry taste of ozone on her tongue. Electricity in the air.

'Feed in the secondary and tertiary power sources,' said Silver. The energy levels began to increase, the sound coming from the dish rising. Anji could swear it was beginning to glow. She felt her skin crawl, tickling like tiny electric shocks. She rubbed her arms, felt static on the fabric.

'Seconds to go,' shouted Silver over the roar. 'Feed in all other power.'

Anji felt faint. The pressure was building around her, a heat

138

haze distorting the air.

'Now!' shouted Silver, punching a key. The dish made a noise like a plane breaking the sound barrier as a stream of blue erupted from its centre, piercing the sky. It shook, and the power lines around it writhed like snakes. The roof was lit like the eye of a lightning storm, energy crackling in the air.

'We have contact,' stated Silver. 'Data transmitting.' He paced the roof, each footstep reverberating. Anji reached to steady herself, then remembered she was standing away from all the walls, and nearly keeled over. Her nerves seemed to be tingling deliriously with the power around her.

'Nearly there, nearly there,' boomed Silver, a stream of green neon data from his monitor screen reflecting in his faceplate. The dish seemed to be shaking loose from its moorings, the cables thrashing even more fiercely.

'Nearly…' said Silver. Anji felt ill, as if she would black out at any moment. The dish seemed to be close to collapse, teetering over her.

'Got him,' shouted Silver. 'Miraso, all power off.'

The dish ground to a halt with a shower of sparks and a burst of blue plasma as the power was cut. Somewhere in the distance there was an explosion, and across the city Anji could swear she saw a ball of fire erupt. She barely got a glimpse – as the power was cut a jolt ran through the air and she was knocked off her feet, her face scraping against the synthrete floor, her elbow smarting as it bumped the hard surface. She choked – the air was filled with smoke, enough to break through her protective barriers.

Anji felt a strong hand under her arm, pulling her to her feet. Silver held her up, and for a second they seemed like the only people in the world, two islands in a never-ending sea of grey smoke. Two figures in long coats, one huge, one small. They looked at each other for a second.

'Was it worth it?' she asked.

'We seem to have lost power,' said Silver. 'I suspect what we just heard was one of the power stations overloading. Many lives may have been lost, and our resources will be seriously depleted.'

He looked at Anji, and his red eye narrowed to a scarlet pinprick.

'But it worked,' he added. 'I have found the Doctor.'

Chapter Ten
Human Factors

'Well, you look like shit,' said Anji, her face underlit by the candle in the centre of the table.

'Thanks,' replied Fitz, staggering across the main hall to sit opposite his friend. He had escaped the Brotherhood's lair only to find the entirety of Hope had lost power, with gas explosions puncturing the darkness. He had run through the dark streets, trying not to lose his footing and plummet to his death while avoiding the fights and looting that had broken out wherever the citizens had realised there was a crisis going on. The power failure had clearly been seen as a sign of weakness in the status quo, and like the roughly bred survivors they were, the people of Hope were trying to take full advantage of that weakness. Fitz didn't want to get caught in the middle when old scores were settled and inequalities readjusted. So he ran, and dodged, and tripped and bruised himself along the way, but eventually he had managed to find the Silver Palace again, wave at Silver's guards and stagger into its darkened hall. The hall was lit with scattered candles, and Anji was the only person left up and about, sitting alone.

Anji pushed a bottle and a glass across the table. Fitz left the glass and took a heavy swig from the neck. The liquor stung his throat, and burned away at a little cut in his mouth where he'd bitten the inside of his cheek. But the sudden, shocking pain seemed an improvement to the dull throb he felt throughout the rest of his body.

'So, how was your day?' asked Anji. She seemed slightly drunk, albeit neither overly happy nor morose. Perhaps she felt numb too.

'Well, today I was taken into the confidence of a cult of dangerous religious fanatics,' said Fitz. 'When they took me into the depths of their lair, I caused a schism in the ranks and was only saved from becoming a human sacrifice by the intervention of their living god. What about you?'

'Oh,' said Anji. 'I just watched Silver divert the city's entire power supply and blast it into space, thereby causing a complete city-wide power loss and the possible collapse of society into complete anarchy.'

They sat in silence for a while. Fitz felt his exhausted body begin to sink forward in his chair. If he didn't go to bed, he'd probably just collapse on the spot.

'Time to make a move,' he said, dragging himself to his feet.

'Hmmm, yeah,' said Anji, swilling liquid in the bottom of the glass, watching the candlelight refract. She seemed lost in thought. Fitz hadn't the energy to retrieve her, so he stumbled off to his room in the staff quarters. It was on the way there, halfway up a winding stairwell, that he encountered Miraso coming the other way, a gaslighter not unlike a zippo burning in one hand. He backed down the stairs to let her past, holding on to the railing, slightly apologetic. The flame's light flickered across her face, lending it an unreal quality, and Fitz found a strange sense of recognition washing over him.

'Thank you,' said Miraso, pushing past him as they reached the bottom of the stairwell.

'A pleasure,' said Fitz, giving her a low bow. His back ached miserably as he did so, but a comment like this required full theatrics. 'My queen.'

How many heads, thought the Doctor as he watched the scientists at work. How many heads had been hacked from the shoulders of innocent Endpointers to allow these experiments to take place? He sat, trapped within his secure area, looking out across the laboratory. Just another guinea pig to these people. How many others?

He had been right about the significance of the vivactic gland.

142

Watching the scientists perform their tests, he could see the sample glands they had at their disposal. They were tiny things, and each represented another dead Endpointer.

'Why so many?' he asked.

'Pardon?' replied a nearby scientist. He was younger than some of the others, but he still seemed enfeebled, weaker than he should be. His blue eyes were watery and strained behind his spectacles, his dark blond hair patchy and receding, even though he was only in his early twenties.

'Why collect so many vivactic glands?' asked the Doctor, raising his voice. 'Surely you must have had more than enough sample material after the first dozen glands?'

'Ah,' said the scientist. He didn't seem to regard the Doctor as hostile. He had probably never met anyone from outside his working group before. 'Well, Doctor, the problem with Kallisti – the substance excreted by the gland – is that it breaks down into different chemicals as soon as it leaves the gland. That's part of its unique properties, the ability to provide such a rich cocktail of hormones to the body. But it also acts as a kind of genetic copy protection. Kallisti is proving very hard to analyse and synthesise because it breaks down so quickly. It seems to have been engineered that way.'

'Interesting,' said the Doctor, sitting back in his cage. 'Thank you...?'

'Richard,' said the scientist.

The Doctor forced a smile. 'Thank you, Richard.'

The Doctor let the young man get back to his work, taking note of his slow response times and slightly dim attitude. With the equipment at their disposal, the humans should have managed to find their way around the Kallisti problem by now. He watched their fumbling hands, working on samples within sealed containers, gloves built into the boxes. Their physical and mental aptitude weren't up to the job. Judging by the similarities between the humans he had seen, they were also more than a little inbred. He remembered the almost simian brow of the human who had been killing the Endpointers on the surface.

Hardly great breeding stock.

Interesting, thought the Doctor. It seemed that the species wasn't quite what it used to be. Just as he seemed to be getting closer to them, they were sliding down the evolutionary ladder.

He knew he could give them the Kallisti if they wanted it, synthesise it himself and stop the humans' harvest of Endpointers. The question was, to what purpose would the humans put that knowledge if he gave it to them? Which would be the worst crime, allowing the killings to continue or allowing whatever they planned next?

'If it's any comfort to you,' said Fitz. 'Of all the gods I've met, you're one of the prettiest.' Miraso's face being that of the Brotherhood's queen had thrown him for a couple of minutes, but Fitz Kreiner wasn't the kind of man to be shaken by something like this for too long.

'So now you know,' replied Miraso, as friendly as ever. 'So what? I'm a god for a couple of hours a week. What's it to you?'

'I guess I just need to know why,' said Fitz. 'Why lead a group who want to hack your boss's head off and wave it around on a pole? Is this some kind of power play on your part?'

'Don't be stupid,' replied Miraso. 'The Brotherhood were Silver's idea, Silver's creation. I'm just responsible for the day to day running of the project, including the occasional masquerade like this evening. Like so many things I do, it's a task Silver hasn't got time to waste on, but which needs doing all the same.'

'But why?' asked Fitz, slumping on the stairs, his boots dragging on a lower step. 'What's the point of it all?'

'Opposition needs to be seen to be expressed,' said Miraso, sitting on a step a few down from Fitz. 'People need to feel that there is an alternative to Silver, and by giving it to them we avoid the inconvenience of a real opposition forming. It's a win-win situation. The public get to see that there is opposition out there, but at the same time see how much of a better bet Silver is. And those who do genuinely oppose Silver are dragged into the Brotherhood's sphere of influence, where we can direct their action in harmless directions.'

'Apart from that suicide run the night we got here,' said Fitz. 'That seemed less than harmless to the people who took part. Are you happy with sending people to their deaths?'

Miraso shrugged. Looking up at Fitz from the lower step, she seemed almost innocent.

'They want to be martyrs, they get to be martyrs,' she said. 'As I said, everyone wins. And things run as they should do.'

'Yeah,' said Fitz, pulling himself to his feet. 'A real sweet deal all round. Good night.'

Fitz was almost out of her sight when Miraso called to him, a note of warning in her voice.

'The Brotherhood are dead men walking, Fitz,' Miraso said. 'Don't do what they do, don't go where they go, or you'll end up the same.'

Fitz didn't reply. He walked away, heading for his room, too emotionally and physically tired to think about anything any more. As soon as he lay down on that uncomfortable bed he was fast asleep.

Silver had found the Doctor. Anji wasn't sure quite what this signified in terms of Silver's offer, how it affected her feelings about the situation. Surely the potential return of the Doctor should have reminded Anji of her loyalty to him? It prevented her from fooling herself into thinking that the Doctor wouldn't return, that giving Silver the secrets of the TARDIS wouldn't make any difference.

But of course the Doctor would return, deep down she had never really doubted that. He was a survivor.

Anji sat at the table in the darkened hall, candlelight flickering. She stared into the shadows, thinking of the Doctor, how closely he guarded the secrets of the TARDIS. She owed it to him not to betray that trust; after all, he had saved her life numerous times. Normally, nothing could swing the balance against that loyalty.

But then there was Silver, who had also done much for Anji. He had delivered the Doctor's whereabouts, he could still be instrumental in retrieving the Doctor himself. Silver was nothing if not transparent – he made promises, he acted on them. There was no reason for him to lie, nothing to stop him from achieving whatever he wished. Silver was simply too powerful to waste time on lies and broken promises. Words were followed by actions, what he wished for came to pass. And he had used that power to find the Doctor, at great expense to himself.

All that effort to retrieve Anji's friend. She owed Silver some degree of loyalty and respect for that, surely?

Then there was the other man in her life, the one she had known long before the alien and the cyborg. Thinking of Dave, putting him next to the Doctor and Silver, made it all seem like some soap opera romantic dilemma. Who would poor Anji Kapoor choose; the modest boy from down the road, the eccentric academic or the tall dark stranger with the bewitching red eye? Of course, it was nothing like that at all. The Doctor and Silver were both people who had, to differing extents, won her trust in the face of extreme circumstances. The Doctor was a friend, someone she liked and respected. Silver was someone she looked up to, and she had to admit she was slightly in awe of. Neither relationship was particularly personal.

Whereas what she had with Dave had been the keystone relationship of her adult life. OK, maybe not the love of her life – she had been far too young, and way too cynical to think it would last forever, and had been on the verge of leaving him at the time of his death – but it had certainly been a defining relationship in her emotional life. Her loyalty and love for Dave wasn't forged from being thrown into trenches together. They hadn't become close due to escaping from some alien prison together, or facing some similar adversity. Passion had not been ignited while dodging bullets. They had been together because they wanted to be together, because they had trust, and affection, and lust and hope and warmth. Anji could have done anything; she was young, smart, talented. What she had chosen to do was be with Dave, and he had chosen to be with her. And ultimately that was more important than the Dunkirk spirit of travelling through the most dangerous times and places in the universe, a bond stronger than that between people saving each other's lives in the face of war and disaster. It had been love, freely entered into, without secrets and barriers.

Torn between her friend and her lost lover, Anji sat through the night, unable to walk away from her thoughts, unable to go and sleep.

Dawn came, and Miraso had not slept. Her mind felt worn, exhausted, while her body was running on caffy and sulph-shakes, eyes wide open with a stimulant rush, unconsciousness artificially suspended. The world around Miraso was starting to take on an unreal, dreamlike state. Welcome to the land of the half awake, thought Miraso.

She entered Silver's office to find him surrounded by red-clad underlings, who were scurrying about carrying bits of equipment and sealant guns. Silver was being sealed, bit by bit, into a makeshift survival suit to allow him to survive in the toxic oceans of Endpoint. His feet were up on a stool, clad in more flexible boots which could act as flippers. Someone was checking the boosters attached to the back of the heel, little bursts of flame threatening to singe the carpets. Layers of protective, rubbery shielding were being attached across Silver's vulnerable areas, wherever the skin showed. The gaps between shielding and whatever implant protruded from the skin were then covered in sealant glue fired from a gunlike device, gas hissing as the sticky substance was liberally applied. A length of tube stretched from Silver's chestplate, at the end of which an oddly moulded breather mask was being tested, specifically designed to click into Silver's faceplate, covering up the human side of his head.

'You don't need to do this,' said Miraso. 'We could send an expedition down there, rebuild one of the hab capsules and use it as a diving bell. I'm sure we have enough equipment to build a robot probe or two, something suitable for deep-sea investigation.'

'And how long would these plans take?' asked Silver. 'Days, weeks, all with unreliable results and a likelihood of death for all concerned. I am the only person capable of undertaking this mission with a high chance of survival, and who can resolve the situation immediately.'

'But you're too important for something like this,' complained Miraso, realising how plaintive she sounded. Like a child trying to persuade her father not to dance in public. 'It's beneath you.'

'I believe he who rules should not just be able to rule, to give orders,' said Silver, brushing his subordinates aside. 'He should be able to do everything his subjects can, and more. He should stand when others kneel, run when others are too weak to even stand. He should assert his right to rule through stretching the boundaries of the possible.'

Silver stood over Miraso, arms crossed over his chest. With his extra protective equipment on, he was even bigger than before. The rising sun shone off every metallic detail.

'I will do this impossible task in full public view,' said Silver, red eye flaring. 'And in doing so prove that no one is superior to Silver.'

'I believe you have been interrogating my staff,' said Stephens, waking the Doctor from his meditative state. 'I hope you have found humanity to your interest.'

'Oh, this is hardly my first brush with humans,' said the Doctor flippantly, pushing his dirty hair out of his eyes. They had kept him in this box for what seemed like days, the same air being recycled again and again, the overhead lights never dimming. He wasn't at his best, but he put up a brave front. 'I have quite a long history with the human race. I have visited many points in your species' history. I lived among humans for years before I even realised I wasn't one of them.' The Doctor realised he was perhaps saying too much in his dazed state, but was aware that he needed to draw Stephens out somehow, find his vulnerable point.

'Fascinating,' said Stephens, tilting his head as he watched the

Doctor. 'A time traveller. No wonder you are so much more impressive than those bovine mutants who roam the surface of this rock.' He couldn't conceal his interest. 'So, Doctor, what do you know of humanity?'

'That they are an immensely creative and adaptable species,' replied the Doctor. 'In the time I spent among them, cultures and ideologies rose and fell, whole new areas of science and knowledge were discovered. They fought wars, created nations, and made their first ventures into space. And, in my travels since I left that distant century, I have discovered that adaptable, creative spirit to have continued into space, into the future. Even this far towards the universe's end, it still exists.'

Stephens smiled. 'So, you may disapprove of our methods, but you acknowledge that our humanity has its advantages?'

'Oh, I didn't mean you,' replied the Doctor. 'What creativity, what adaptability, do you have? None whatsoever. You have cloistered yourselves away from the wider universe, protected your bloodline and in the process created an enfeebled species forced to crawl under rocks until the end of time. No, the true inheritors of the human spirit are those "mutants" you despise, the Endpointers. They have shown all the survival instincts and resourcefulness of their human ancestors. They are the true holders of the human legacy, not your inbred, murderous kind.'

'Doctor,' said Stephens, backing away from the Doctor's enclosure. 'You do not know how much I am looking forward to cutting you open.'

Fitz staggered into the main hall that morning to find Anji, Miraso and a number of the other Palace staff watching a large screen erected above the bar. Fitz couldn't help noticing that the Palace didn't seem to have heating and lighting, but had a television running. He asked Miraso if she was certain she had her priorities straight.

'Surely getting the power back is the most important thing?' he asked.

Miraso shook her head. 'We made certain to get communication channels open first for damn good reasons,' she said, standing with her back to a pillar, eyes glued to the screen. 'The people need to see this. They're Endpointers, they can survive a little hardship. What they need right now is to be reminded who the boss is around here.'

The screen buzzed, and resolved into an image of a bulky figure, standing in front of a railing. The murky sea was visible behind him. Fitz realised it was Silver, albeit with all his human parts covered. A diving mask covered the human side of his face, a green visor covering that eye. Weapons and tools were attached to his metallic, rubbery clothing, while oxygen pipes were strapped to his body.

The image stayed steady, albeit remaining a bit fuzzy. Miraso slapped her fist into a palm and hissed 'yes', clearly pleased with the result.

'Citizens of Hope, people of Endpoint,' said Silver, his booming voice unobstructed by his mask. 'I have exciting and disturbing news for you all. I have discovered evidence of an unknown force living beneath the sea, within the territory of Endpoint. We believe that this force may be connected to a series of violent incursions into Hope in recent months. This cannot be allowed to continue, and as the waters here are too hazardous, too poisonous, for any normal person to survive, I have decided that I, Silver, will have to perform this operation myself. I intend to find this threat to our lives, and if necessary destroy it. This is, I believe, the least I can do.'

Silver nodded to the camera, then turned and leapt over the barricade. Whoever was holding the camera ran to point it over the edge, only to get fog-obscured glimpses of ripples on the water's surface.

Miraso stood up, waving for the screen to be turned off.

'He's on his way,' she said.

Silver's descent beneath the sea was not so much a swim as a careful process of controlled sinking. The Doctor's location was far beneath the waves, but on the horizontal plane only a short distance from Hope. As he sank, Silver flapped his feet gently, moving slightly forward as he descended. He had lost visibility as soon as he was a few feet beneath the surface, and had switched to sonar, with an overlay of the global positioning data from SatNet. The Doctor's last known position, or at least the last known position of the tracker Silver had placed in his bloodstream, flared below Silver in the distance, down on the sea bed.

For a long time he sank, not encountering anything. The protective clothing was resisting the corroding effects of the sea, although sensors indicated gradual tarnishing of his faceplate. For anyone else, floating through impenetrable darkness would have induced an aching feeling of loneliness. But for Silver, in so many ways unique, it was not an unusual sensation. His computer-enhanced brain had time to process a billion thoughts during this sensory deprivation, but none of them disturbed him enough to interrupt the steady movement of his swimming.

As he approached the sea bed, Silver noted an increased pressure around him, threatening to crush his chest. Fortunately his chest plate was built to withstand much greater pressures, and an increase in power flow compensated for any drag caused by the pressure. The sonar with which he viewed this sea bed world was far too sensitive, fragments of swirling matter and sand blocking his view. Something large loomed ahead, somewhere near the Doctor's location. Silver activated the jets on his heels, moving smoothly towards his target. The shape ahead solidified into some kind of structure, a vast bunker built into a rock slope, jutting out like a tooth, solidly rooted in the rock.

Silver raised his human hand to his mask, his arm difficult to manoeuvre under all the layers of protective material. His finger pressed a rubber bump on the side of his diving mask, a covered switch which allowed him to cycle through possible wavelengths. Standard visual and infrared were worse than useless. Eventually his heads-up display was ablaze as he cycled to a view of power sources in the immediate vicinity. Silver's enhanced mind overlaid what he was seeing with other information, and interpreted the row of cigar-shaped structures floating next to the bunker as submarines of some kind, their power sources glowing warmly.

Silver swam towards them. Some form of undersea structure, a series of submarines. Where the two joined there would be airlocks and boarding tubes, an ideal area to break in. As he swam Silver began to check the functions on his robotic fist. This would require some of the more robust weaponry…

When they came for him, they came in force. The Doctor watched as thugs gathered around his contained area, Stephens at their centre. The Chief Scientist stepped forward to address the Doctor.

'Now, Doctor, you've told us about how low we've sunk,' said Stephens. 'Well, here we have humanity's fighters, descended from long family lines of bruisers and battlers, guards and soldiers. Imagine how low they can sink, what violence they will inflict on you. So play nice, Doctor. You're out of your league now.'

The Doctor didn't reply, but settled into a crouch, a tiger preparing to leap.

'Very well,' said Stephens, turning to address his men. 'Take him, and don't use the tranqs – I want him to feel this.'

Stephens activated a remote control, and the clear barriers around the Doctor began to retract into the ceiling. Dizzying, purified air slid in beneath the walls, but the Doctor didn't allow himself to be distracted. Stephens's thugs were moving in, batons at the ready, clothed in simple clinical overalls. The Doctor was sure he recognised the killer he had chased across Hope among them, although frankly their appearances were much too similar for him to differentiate. What had Stephens said about family lines? These men looked like they had been inbred to increase their fighting capacity. A pure strain of the worst of humankind.

When the cage above him was a few metres above the ground, the Doctor sprang, grabbing the inner rim of the cage as it retracted into the ceiling. The thugs looked up, confused, as he continued to rise. There was nowhere to go – the cage would retract fully, a couple of feet more, then stop. But nonetheless the Doctor clung on by his fingertips. It lifted him up until his feet were dangling a couple of metres above his captors heads. The cage ground to a halt, and he hung there, looking down.

Stephens shook his head, bored. From his perspective the Doctor could see the old scientist's bald patch.

'Get him down from there,' said Stephens wearily. 'Now!' he snapped, and the thugs moved into action. They started jumping, trying to grab the Doctor's shoes, trying to hook his trouser leg or hit him with their batons. But the Doctor swung himself out of their grasp, playfully avoiding them. They moved in tighter, jumping higher. The Doctor tensed, pulling his knees up to his chest.

Then he let go, wrapping his arms around his knees. The Doctor dropped like a stone, landing on top of his captors, sending them reeling. One was knocked unconscious, the rest went flying. One landed face down, the Doctor's entire weight pressing on his back. The Doctor rolled off on to the floor, landing in a catlike posture and springing to his feet, striding towards Stephens, who was between him and the door. The other scientists were backing away, while the thugs behind him were swearing as they regrouped.

'Get out of my way,' the Doctor told Stephens firmly. He moved to push Stephens out of the way, but to his surprise the old man ducked under his arm, aiming a low punch that hit the Doctor in the ribcage, sending him spiralling off course. The Doctor slammed into the wall, flipping around to face Stephens with a confused expression.

'We are fighting for our survival here, Doctor,' said Stephens, slipping into an offensive stance, one palm raised. 'Even a man like myself has to have combat skills implanted. The body may be weak, but the will to fight back will always be there.'

The thugs were back on their feet and advancing, while the other scientists had gained confidence from Stephens's words, and had stepped forward to back him up. The Doctor glanced around desperately; there was nothing to use against them, no useful equipment, not even a fire extinguisher or an alarm to set off.

The Doctor tensed, preparing to defend himself. His assailants advanced towards him. The Doctor counted fifteen of them.

Before they could attack an alarm went off, a wailing siren that caused wincing from the humans. The lights went out, emergency red lighting clicking on.

'Perimeter breach!' said the younger scientist, the one called Richard.

'Find out what it is,' barked Stephens in reply, and Richard ran over to a monitor screen, tapping on a keyboard to cycle through the viewpoints of numerous cameras.

'I know what it is,' said the Doctor levelly. The gathered humans stared at him as one.

'Your future,' the Doctor said. 'And it's here to meet you.'

Chapter Eleven
Storm Front

They had been taught from birth that they were superior, that they were the guardians of the universe's greatest culture. They had been cryogenically preserved, to rest until a time when they could retake their dominant position. Those who had been revived to man the bunker had never faced the outside world, had only known of it what they had been told. Of one thing they were certain: their humanity put them above the detritus who lived on the surface, that their inherent superiority would allow them to fight off any savage attack from above. Nothing could defeat them.

This certainty was crushed by the unstoppable threat of one man, a former human who now constituted a sub species all on his own.

The rupture had occurred at airlock seven, an unknown intruder breaching the boarding tube connecting the airlock to one of the small subfleet docked at the bunker. The intruder had then wrenched open the airlock's external door, entering the airlock and locking himself in. At this point all guards were summoned to the area and the bunker went on red alert. A motley collection of armed men had gathered in the dank corridor, not daring to approach the entrance to the airlock, standing there fearfully with weapons raised. None of them had ever left the bunker since their revival, most had been born on the last of the human colonies, then shipped out on ice. They were not prepared for an incursion from outside their hermetically sealed world.

The airlock door burst open with a fiery explosion, and a room full of toxic, acidic water burst forth with a cloud of stinging vapour. The sea water sloshed down the corridor in both directions, and the humans fled, most far too slow to avoid the waters flowing over them, stripping their skin, burning through their clothes, leaving them scarred and dying on the floor, twitching in mute agony, their throats too scorched to cry out.

The lucky ones were only splashed, their injuries merely disfiguring rather than crippling. One half-blind soldier, one hand virtually incinerated, tried to crawl away as the intruder stepped out of the airlock. He was too slow, and turned in horror to see the intruder emerging from the steam. Humanoid but broad shouldered, its surface slick and metallic, it bristled with nozzles and boxes. One eye glowed red, the other was a pale green square, its face a gas-masked muzzle. Vapour rose off its form, a barnacled, armoured monster from the deep.

The half-blind soldier collapsed, overwhelmed by pain and fear. The beast stepped over him, following an invisible trail.

The sound of gunfire echoed down the corridors as another group of guards tried to intercept the intruder.

'Surrender now,' said the Doctor. 'I'm sure I can make an arrangement for you.' He stood with his back to the wall, his attackers hanging back, unsure what move to make. Stephens was leaning over a monitor screen, observing the action near the airlock. The Doctor had occasional glimpses of the battle on the screen, enough to know that it was Silver attacking the base. Single-handed, by the looks of it.

'Richard,' hissed Stephens. The young scientist was instantly at his side. 'I want you to take a team down to the cryochambers. I want a hundred strong men revived, with full update memory implants covering current situation plus weapons training. Give them a massive revival booster, triple the normal dose.'

'That could kill them within days,' complained Richard. 'That kind of dose is bound to cause major organ failure.'

Stephens spun around, grabbing Richard's jacket and pulling him to his face.

'I don't care,' shouted Stephens. 'I want them alive, energetic and ready to kill. Take them to the armoury then get them to kill this cybernetic mutant bastard before he razes this bunker to the ground.'

'Or,' replied the Doctor, 'you could find out what he wants.'

'I know what "it" wants, Doctor,' replied Stephens. 'What else could it want but to destroy us? Humanity's enemies have found us at last.'

'I think isolation has driven you mad, Stephens,' snapped the Doctor. 'You're not as important as you think. Just another dead species. If anyone out there remembers humanity, they believe the species is extinct. No one is going to be interested enough to try to hunt you down.'

'Shut up,' Stephens told the Doctor. He turned to Richard. 'Are you still here?'

'On my way,' replied Richard, running to the door.

Stephens turned his attention back to the monitor. 'Now, where are –'

His sentence was cut off when the door exploded, sending Richard flying into the corner of the room. A bulky figure emerged through the smoke.

'I think now might be a good time to reconsider your tactics, Stephens,' the Doctor suggested.

No one came to the orchard all day, so Anji was left undisturbed. Power supplies were still intermittent, and Miraso was still marshalling all available staff to deal with that problem. No one had any reason to visit Silver's indoor orchard, where the first apple trees in millennia were growing. This was fine by Anji. It left her with her thoughts, although whether this was a blessing or a curse was something she was entirely undecided about. Fitz was the only person who knew where she was, and he was under strict instructions to leave her alone unless there was news about the Doctor or Silver.

Since when did those two have equal ranking in her mind? Her thoughts had entwined them together, the twin heads of the decision that stole her sleep and left her an incoherent wreck.

Anji lay in the shadow of an apple tree, coarse grass beneath her. Her tired mind was a muddle of past and present, new experiences leading back to long neglected memories. As her head tilted to one side, the feeling of grass against her cheek reminded Anji of that summer's day with Dave in the park, watching the tourists. Nothing really had happened that day; they had lazed around in the park, eaten ice cream, seen an unremarkable film. But the normality of it all, the fact that it had been a day made special by each other's company rather than any remarkable occurrence, flagged it as a special day in her memory.

The irony was not lost on her, that while she was denied the normal life she wished for, Dave's death meant that he could not be with her visiting the future, going to alien worlds, doing all the things he'd read about in all those science-fiction stories. She would never even get to tell him about it. No chance for him to be jealous, or impressed, or have any other reaction. If she ever returned home he would not be there to welcome her. There were so many things she could tell him about that he would love to know, so much knowledge she had picked up that Dave would have listened to raptly, but she would never get to tell him.

The sheer, brutal unfairness of it all suddenly hit her. Lying on her back, Anji choked slightly on her tears. But she didn't have the will to sit up.

Silver raised his robotic fist, gun barrels on the back whirring as they pointed at Richard's head. A red dot targeted the centre of the human scientist's forehead.

'How many humans in this base?' Silver asked.

'Ninety seven active,' replied the young scientist, wide-eyed with fear. 'Dormant... I'm not sure.'

'I think you'll find the active figure is down to fifty five,' said Silver, lowering his hand. His head twitched, and with one fluid motion he drew his gun with his human hand, spun around and fired three shots into the wall next to the Doctor's shoulder. A low groan issued from the corridor outside, followed by a hollow thud.

'Make that fifty four,' said Silver, holstering his weapon. 'Trying to sneak up. Stupid. Any more wish to try?'

The gathered humans stayed perfectly still, perfectly silent. Richard was among them, too scared to try to complete his errand for Stephens.

'I didn't think so,' said Silver. He reached to his face, and tore the diving mask away from the human side of his face. Rubbery strips of sealant clung to the edge of his faceplate. 'Doctor, it is good to see you. I have come a long way.'

'Yes,' said the Doctor. 'And killed far too many people. Was that really necessary?'

Silver shrugged. 'I found you. But have you found me my killer?'

The Doctor stepped back, making an expansive gesture. 'This entire project was responsible for those killings.' The Doctor leaned past a couple of scientists, who backed away quickly, and picked up a glass test tube, which he threw to Silver. The cyborg gingerly caught the tube between giant fingers, and held it up to the light. Silver's red eye widened, clearly scanning the tube's contents.

'The vivactic gland,' said Silver. 'Interesting. It seems your theory was right, Doctor. Congratulations. You have fulfilled your side of our agreement. I will retrieve your box as soon as possible. Now.' He turned to the gathered humans. 'Who is in charge of this project?'

There was a difficult silence.

'Mr Stephens,' said the Doctor coldly. 'I think you should take credit for your excellent work, don't you?'

The old scientist grimaced and stepped forward. He retained his defiance as Silver stepped slowly towards him.

'Silver,' warned the Doctor. 'I don't want any more deaths. There have been enough of them on Endpoint of late.'

Silver slowly turned his head to the Doctor, impassive, and turned back to Stephens. He towered over the old man.

'Mr Stephens,' boomed Silver. 'I wish to see the facilities in my new bunker.'

* * *

Richard found himself dizzied by the thought processes of the two beings from the planet's surface. The young scientist had been given the task of showing them around the bunker, as requested by Silver, Stephens being too old for the task. And so Richard had taken them around the main locations, constantly amazed by how little he needed to tell them. He had always been taught that no one could outthink a human being, but Silver and the Doctor only needed to glance at the highest technology they had to understand its operation and application.

While touring the cryochambers Silver had made an estimate of the number of humans frozen there – he placed the figure at around two thousand – while the Doctor suggested alterations to the cooling system. In the control centre the Doctor had fixed a monitor problem that had been plaguing maintenance for months. Silver had closely examined many items in the armoury, while the Doctor had seemed keen to keep moving.

So Richard had not been surprised when, as they were cutting through a storage area used by the guards for recreation, the Doctor had suddenly stopped, knocking over a makeshift card table to expose the rounded, brass object beneath it. Richard realised with a jolt that the card players had probably died in Silver's attack.

'Do you know what this is?' the Doctor asked, examining the brass object.

Richard checked his inventory. 'Unidentifiable item, purpose unknown,' he read.

'It looks like a cloud seeding pod to me,' said Silver. 'The kind used in heavy-duty environmental re-engineering. A few of these could fundamentally alter a planet's atmosphere.'

'That would make sense,' said Richard. His inventory said that even Stephens had been unable to identify the pod. 'We are supposed to be equipped to create a new Earth in the future, to recreate a planet as our new home.'

The Doctor marched towards him. 'And did it never occur to you that these resources might be better used to solve the environmental problems on this planet? That alleviating the suffering of others might be a more humane option than hoarding your resources for some supposed future glory? No, of course it didn't. Forget I said anything.' The Doctor waved a dismissive hand in Richard's direction and wandered away.

Silver pointed a finger at the pod. 'Find me the rest of these,' he said. 'And soon.'

'Let me guess,' said the Doctor, spinning back around to face them, sulk dissipated, enthusiasm restored. 'We're going to do a spot of decorating?'

The day had been one of confined tension, while the inhabitants of the Silver Palace had waited for news from Silver. Miraso was still having difficulty arranging a return to normal power supplies, and so heating and light had been intermittent. The failure of the air conditioning had begun to lend a stale taste to the trapped air within the Palace. Fitz considered this an apt metaphor for their situation; like the air there was nowhere for them to go, all they could do was swirl around within the same space, bouncing off one another at random.

Anji's behaviour hadn't helped matters. She seemed fixated and distant, lost in her own thoughts, although she was making some effort to disguise this. A shallower man would have taken those forced smiles at face value and not let himself worry about it, thought Fitz, wishing he were a shallower man. In the end he had let her wander off to the orchard on her own. Fitz wasn't a man to get in the way of anyone's quality brooding time.

During the afternoon Fitz found himself snapping at the Silver Palace's staff, and decided he needed to get away from everyone else. He had returned to his little room in the staff quarters, lying on the bed with his hands folded beneath his neck, staring at the bumpy ceiling. The room was featureless and, with the power out, somewhat dark. No sounds could be heard in this isolated part of the Palace. Sensory deprivation led to a thoughtless state, and that meditative, trancelike condition in turn led inevitably to sleep.

Fitz woke with a jolt, the sound of thunder echoing through

his brain. He was just beginning to wonder whether the thunder had been part of a dream when the room was briefly illuminated by light from outside. Fitz scrambled on to his feet, as another deafening peal of thunder rang out a few seconds later. He looked out of the small, misshapen window. Out in the fog he could see blobs of light rippling up in the sky. A darkness seemed to be expanding above, while simultaneously occasional flashes struck out from within.

Storm clouds, growing in time-lapse, their development unnaturally accelerated. Inevitably, the clouds burst, and rain began to hammer down, echoing off the metal rooftops of Hope.

A man needs to defend his property, thought Pazon, sitting on the floor of his stall and cradling a stout stick resting in the crook of his arm. He had bolted the stall up when the power had gone out the day before, pulling down the shutters and locking himself in the small shack. Apart from brief sorties out he had remained there, weapon in hand, ready for the looters who inevitably worked their way around Hope in times of crisis to reach his patch.

Thankfully, he had yet to be seriously disturbed, and the square had remained largely deserted, the occasional lone citizen running past, not stopping to find out who might be in the shadows. There had been a scuffle a few hours ago, and Pazon had sneaked a glimpse through a gap in the shutters. A crowd of swaddled figures had been kicking and punching another man, muffled curses and screams echoing in the silence. Eventually, the mob had dragged their victim away, leaving Pazon in silent darkness once more. He didn't even want to light a candle, for fear of attracting attention. All he could do was sit there, waiting for the power to come back and life to resume its normal course.

He was almost dozing off in the darkness when the clattering began. It sounded like little feet scurrying about, and in his half-asleep state Pazon briefly thought that children were marauding his stall. He clenched his stick, ready to go outside and fight them off. Then he registered the liquid patter of the noise, the way it seemed to come from everywhere at once. With a lurch of panic he put his eye to the gap in the shutters. Although the darkness was still almost total, Pazon could make out thin lines of liquid cutting through the air, and slowly pooling on every available surface.

Rain. Pazon backed away into the centre of the stall, staring up in panic. Was the roof of the shack robust enough to withstand the corrosive Endpoint rain? Or would the flood spread from outside, seeping in under the walls to burn his boots away? The last time rain had fallen in Hope dozens had died, caught outside in a shower of acid. Dead in the street, skin burned away. Support chains and other structures had been corroded causing severe damage.

Pazon sat in the centre of the shack, trapped by the rainfall outside. He only hoped his little shack could withstand the rigours of the weather. He dropped his weapon and wrapped his arms around his knees, hugging himself in fear.

Lightning illuminated the orchard, and Anji raised her arm to cover her face, instinctively protecting her eyes against the rain. Then she remembered she was indoors, and looked up. High above her, she could see the sky through the windows on the Palace's roof. Storm clouds were racing, lightning crackling within. The image seemed blurry; rain may have been pooling across the panes, it was too far up for Anji to tell.

She remembered another storm, on the planet Hitchemus. The Doctor, an alien device strapped to his arm, commanding the weather. Lightning and violins. The Doctor had deserted them on the basis of his own principles, risked his life among the tigers and the humans, and proved himself stronger than all of them. The Doctor could look after himself, and tried to do what he considered to be right, no matter what the cost.

Whereas Dave had never made that choice. Accident had brought him into the path of an alien conflict, and he had died for it. And if Anji was to stick to her own principles, then she would have to try to give some version of Dave another shot at life. As for the Doctor… wasn't it him who had always stressed the importance of doing what was right? Anji was certain that whatever damage she did to the Doctor by revealing his secrets, the Doctor would pull through to face the challenge. He was a survivor. Dave hadn't been. Anji would have to worry about the weak, and let the strong look after themselves.

To her surprise, Anji found she had a clear way forward.

Miraso was woken by the bleeping of the communit next to her bed. She fumbled in the dark, trying to find the headset. Finally she slid it over her smooth scalp, ear pieces clicking into place.

'Miraso here,' she said into the mouthpiece. 'I thought the communication channels were still down.'

'They are,' said a deep, familiar voice. Miraso was instantly awake.

'Silver?'

'The same. I'm speaking from outside the normal channels, as you still seem to be having power problems. Meet me on the roof of the Palace in twenty minutes.'

'What for?' asked Miraso, but the line was dead. She swore, rolling out of bed in one catlike motion, grabbing her clothes from a chair.

All the militiamen in Powlin's watchtower had come to the upper gantry, to watch the storm from behind the shielded glass. It made Powlin nervous to be so close to the rain, running down the outside of the windows. Endpoint rains could scorch the skin and poison everything they touched. The watchtower was sealed, but all the same it unnerved him. Normally he wouldn't have been up there for love nor money. None of them would have been, with the possible exception of the more foolhardy men, the ones who lived for this kind of danger.

But without exception they were there, watching a storm like none they had ever seen. Lightning rippling through the clouds was one thing. But from within the sea as well? From the stratosphere to the depths, vast energies were being released.

Powlin could taste it in the air, a new electricity, a tang of static.

Someone swore, while others gasped. At first Powlin thought they were overreacting to another flash of lightning, another spectacular fork slicing through the air. Then he saw it for himself.

Through the mist of fog and rain it was hard to make out, only the outlines of its shape could be clearly defined. A vast, dark shape lifting out of the sea, a broad cigar-shaped object that floated in the mist, just out to sea. As Powlin watched it rose higher, then began to move overhead, towards the centre of Hope.

Someone was pulling at Powlin's shoulder.

'Shouldn't we do something to stop it, Chief?' asked one of the militiamen.

Powlin tracked the craft with his eyes, not turning to look at his colleague.

'What can we do?' he said simply, watching the object glide deeper into Hope.

The environment suit was bulky and inconvenient, but it was the only protection Miraso had against the rains. She stomped out on to the roof in her heavy boots, trying to see where she was going through the cowl's narrow visor. At least Silver wouldn't miss her – the suit was bright yellow, apart from the black, insulated gloves that prevented her from scratching the many itches the damn suit was giving her.

When the spotlight shone down on her, Miraso instinctively dropped to her knees, searching for her gun. Of course the environment suit prevented her from reaching it, but she soon gave up, stunned by the ship hovering above her. It was dark and tubular, like a submarine or missile, but hovering from a series of rotors whirling above it. On its underside was the spotlight that surrounded her. Something fell from the top of this magnificent vehicle, dropping like a stone nearby. She turned to see Silver pulling himself to his feet. Where he had landed there was a crater in the roof a couple of inches deep, the shape of his boots and left knee clearly imprinted where they had hit.

The rain was pouring down Silver's face as he approached. Miraso realised he wasn't wearing his diving equipment, that the toxic fluid was touching his skin, dripping into his human eye.

'Doesn't it sting?' she asked, the only thing she could think to say.

Silver didn't reply. Instead he gripped the cowl of her environment suit in his metal fist and ripped it away, thick material tearing across the shoulders. Miraso instinctively closed her eyes and tried to force her head down, out of the rain, but a steel thumb pushed her face up, gently but firmly. She kept her mouth shut, waiting for the water that pooled in her eye sockets to start stinging. But the pain never came.

'Open your mouth,' said Silver, and Miraso found herself obeying, guts clenching as the rain drops fell on her tongue. But instead of stinging, the water was cool and refreshing. She opened and closed her jaw, tasting the rain water. It was clean, fresher than anything she had tasted before.

Miraso opened her eyes. She had to blink the water out of her eyes to see, but it didn't hurt at all.

She looked at Silver.

'Forget the rain,' said Silver, 'and breathe.'

Miraso breathed, first tentatively, then filling her lungs. The air was as clear as the rain water, oxygenated and invigorating, even more so than the processed air within the Palace.

Clean water, clean air. Miraso, who had spent her entire life fearing the damaging effects of Endpoint's polluted environment, had never experienced anything like it before.

'It's a miracle,' she told Silver, staring up into the sky and feeling the cool rain on her skin, the breeze sweeping the droplets off course.

'My miracle,' said Silver, the metal on his body gleaming wet. His eyes were burning with the immensity of his achievement. He raised his fist to the sky. 'This is my gift to the world!'

Chapter Twelve
Blue Sky Propositions

In the orchard, an apple falls. Red and juicy, it plummets towards Anji's sleeping head, although whether its impact will cause any scientific revolutions is debatable. The point becomes irrelevant as the apple is snatched out of the air before it can hit Anji, then lifted up to eye level for a solemn confrontation.

'Keep the Doctor away, do you? We'll see about that.'

The confrontation ends with the apple being bitten into hungrily, the chomping and appreciative sounds from its consumption finally causing Anji to stir. She stretches out on the grass, back arching, eyes flickering open.

'Doctor,' she says. 'You're alive.'

'Yes, I am,' he replied happily, dropping his apple core and kicking it across the orchard. 'Did you doubt I would be?'

'No,' said Anji sleepily. 'No, I didn't.'

The storm was to get worse before it got better. In Hope, and in all the other communities of Endpoint, the hatches were firmly battened down as the wind and rain hammered the buildings. Clouds raged, fierce lights burning within, as the pollutants in the atmosphere were driven away. Below, the seas bubbled with a harsh fire, a similar process making those hostile waters fresh again. The rains over Hope had been just the beginning – in the end it would take five days of storms across Endpoint for the seeding pods to do their work.

For the people of Endpoint, there was little they could do as the storms raged. In the heart of Hope, in the Silver Palace, people talked and drank and played cards by candlelight. Anji and Fitz both talked to the Doctor upon his arrival, then had to wait for another day before hearing the full story of his ordeal in the bunker; within minutes of talking to Anji he retired to his bed, where he slept a disturbed but healing sleep for almost a full day and night. When he woke again he seemed happy to join in the quiet life of the Palace staff as the storms raged outside.

While the others rested, Miraso couldn't settle. After his meeting with her on the rooftop, Silver had returned to his new ship, sending the occasional communication as he went about remodelling the planet's environment. Miraso absorbed these messages with due diligence, but was left unsatisfied by Silver's absence from the Palace – every palace needed its king, or else what purpose did it have?

On the sixth day after the storms began, dawn rose over Hope, and the people found themselves waking to a new world. They flinched as they left their homes, stung by the brightness of the sunlight coming from a clear blue sky. Where there had been persistent fog, now there was only the occasional wisp of white cloud. Those near the coast were surprised to see the colour of the sea was a deep green, although no one yet had the nerve to see if those waters were still hostile.

The previous week's storm, whipped up through a cluster of terraforming pods, had changed the world of Endpoint for ever. The buildings of Hope, dirt battered away by the rain, now gleamed like silver, as if in tribute to the city's saviour.

The Pier was a different place from the one it had been a week before. The first day after the storms ended proved to be a sunny one, the first sunny day in a very long time, and the Endpointers responded with appropriate wonder. The people of Hope hadn't quite got around to re-inventing ice cream, which Fitz considered a nuisance, but at least the bright sunlight gave him an excuse to wear his shades. Crowds were gathering to look out to sea, no one having seen the horizon before because of the thick fog. Fitz ducked between gleaming bald heads, wondering how many of them would be sunburned by the end of the day.

He found the Doctor and Anji sitting at the Pier's end, feet dangling over the edge. Fitz dropped down to sit with them, arms draping over the railing, looking out to sea.

'Well, we've made some changes to the places we've visited,' said Fitz. 'But this is ridiculous.'

The Doctor tried to look modest. 'I wouldn't take all the credit. Silver was quite capable of working out how to use most of the technology necessary to remodel the environment. It's just a shame the humans down there didn't have the initiative or intelligence to do this years ago.'

'When are we going to meet these humans, anyway?' asked Anji. She seemed to have a greater certainty and poise than Fitz had seen in her for a while.

The Doctor seemed uncertain. 'This is a very delicate situation. In spite of all the change around here, the killings can't be forgotten, reparations will be made. And the humans down there have been isolated for some time, most of them aren't ready to face the outside world yet.'

'All the same, you must be pleased to see them,' said Fitz. 'What with your bonding and all that.'

'It's true, with my ties to the Earth, to humanity, it was disconcerting coming to a time when Earth is gone,' replied the Doctor. 'Ironically, it was only when I discovered there were humans still alive that I realised that the survival of humanity as we knew it is irrelevant.' He gestured to the Endpointers crowded on the Pier. 'These people represent all that was good and bad in humanity. Earth's legacy lives on.'

'And so does its champion,' added Fitz. He looked out across the glittering sea. 'Happy endings all round.'

'Almost,' said the Doctor. 'There's just one piece missing, and I think it's about to arrive.'

Fitz looked across at Anji, who was as puzzled as he was. Then there was a commotion out to sea, and Fitz saw something large and grey emerge from the deep, displacing huge ripples of water in its wake. As the water crashed back down around it, Fitz could see a familiar blue shape tied to the submarine's deck.

'Now we're ready for that happy ending,' said the Doctor, beaming at his beloved ship.

'There will be no reopening,' said Silver.

'What?' said Miraso, head flicking up from the accounts she had been reading through before Silver interrupted. She had come to his office to go through plans to get the Silver Palace up and running again, after the recent closure and disruption. It had never occurred to Miraso that this might not be on the cards.

Silver drummed heavy fingers on the desk. Miraso hadn't even realised he was back in the Palace, never mind about to pay her a visit. His sudden appearance put her off balance.

'There will be no reopening,' he repeated impatiently. 'The business side of my concerns are of no interest to me now. At last, opportunities for an expansion of my interests are emerging, and before then we need to break out of the holding pattern commercial dominance provided, and consolidate all assets. From there we will have a solid foundation from which to expand.'

'Expand?' echoed Miraso. She had no idea what Silver was talking about, and was under the distinct impression that he was talking to himself rather than to her. All she could make out was that most of what she had ever worked on was becoming irrelevant in the face of Silver's new ambitions, whatever they may be. Where did Miraso herself fit into these great plans?

Silver's eyes swivelled towards her, having drifted to stare out of the window. He looked about to speak, when there was a knock on the door. Silver called out for the person to enter.

Anji stuck her head around the door.

'I just thought we might have a little chat,' said the human, with an informality Miraso would never have dared to have with Silver.

In spite of his increasing ambitions, Silver reacted positively to this impertinence. 'Please, come through,' he said, gesturing for Anji to sit in the chair opposite him. The chair Miraso was currently occupying. 'Miraso and I can resume our conversation at a later time.'

Miraso nodded to them both, rising from her chair, and tried to make as dignified a withdrawal as possible. As the door closed behind her, she could hear Anji's first words to Silver, something about an offer he had made. This set Miraso's mind racing. What kind of offer? What position would Anji hold in Silver's organisation? Where did Miraso fit into his brave new world?

Miraso desperately wanted to hear more, but knew full well that Silver would see if she hesitated in the corridor to listen in. So she forced herself to walk away, her frustration at the uncontrollable changes around her growing with every step.

To his own great surprise, Fitz found himself unable to relax, something which had never troubled him in the past. He prided himself on his ability to loaf around, doing very little for days at a time, yet now it was a beautiful, sunny day, and he found himself unable just to lie back and enjoy it. There was an urge to do something worthwhile with his time itching the inside of Fitz's skull, and no matter how hard he tried to suppress it that urge just wouldn't go. The whole situation was frankly embarrassing – 'Fitz Kreiner, driven man' just didn't fit with the laid-back self-image he tried to project – but he seemed to be left with little choice in the matter. So he purchased some noxious-looking food from Pazon's stall, sat at a deserted card table and tried to decide what was bugging him so much. The food was not unlike a rather sweet curry, and Fitz chewed as he thought, the rolling motion of his jaw matching the slow ruminations of his thinking.

It just all seemed too easy, he concluded. The whole of Endpoint had been turned on its head, a new golden age was supposedly dawning. It was all far too easy, too uncomplicated. The Doctor had his TARDIS back, Silver having fulfilled his side of the bargain, without any tricks or subterfuge. The killings had come to an end. Even Anji seemed to have perked up a bit. All's well that ends well.

Way too easy, no doubt about it. There had to be a catch, some dark secret waiting to get them. The Doctor had disappeared into the TARDIS, eager to discover to what extent the ship had recovered from the exertion of pushing this far into the future. Anji was elsewhere. If Fitz was to discover whatever dark secrets were lurking beneath the surface of this supposedly happy ending, he would have to discover them himself.

The blue painted wood of the TARDIS felt warm beneath Anji's hand; whether from the sun beating down on it, or from its own internal heat, she wasn't entirely sure. She pushed gently, and walked into a brightness entirely different from that outside, the clinical whiteness of the TARDIS. Electric hum and conditioned air, a hygienic, alien space only one step and a whole world away from the Pier.

'Anji,' said the Doctor cheerily. 'How are things?' He was examining the controls when she came in, but gave her his full attention as soon as he was aware of her presence. He seemed fully recovered from his ordeal beneath the sea just as, only a short while ago, he had recovered from one of his hearts failing then being gouged out of his chest. The Doctor always survived, always pulled through.

'Fine, fine,' she replied hurriedly, running her fingers around the edge of the console. 'I just wanted to check how the TARDIS was, get a couple of things from my room.'

'Well, the TARDIS seems to have recovered perfectly well from my idiocy. We'll be able to leave soon,' said the Doctor, scraping his fingers through his hair. As a slight frown appeared on his forehead he paused, became so absolutely still that for a second Anji thought there had been some horrible time spillage, that the Doctor would be stuck like that, one hand in his hair, frowning, for the rest of eternity.

But then she noticed his chest rise and fall, and realised that this pause came from within him. He wanted to say something, but was conflicted. So she said it for him.

'We're not leaving quite yet,' she said.

The Doctor came back to life. 'No, I don't think we are. It's an exciting time for the Endpointers, I think we should see them through the next few days at least.' And he smiled, but his forehead creased further as he did so, torn between his desire to get away from Hope and his awareness that their business here wasn't quite finished.

The Doctor smiled an unconvincing smile. 'I offered to help Silver with his researches,' he said, walking towards the outer doors. 'Close the door on your way out.' The Doctor paused, smiling at her, framed by the sunlight from outside. Then he left.

'I will,' said Anji, sliding down the lever that closed the TARDIS doors. There was a faint hum as the double doors clicked back into place. She reached into her coat pocket, and pulled out a thin black rectangle given to her by Silver. One button press released a couple of antennae which flicked out of the side of the scanner, whirring as they absorbed information about everything around them.

'Just let me get what I came for,' said Anji quietly, delicately holding out the instrument of her betrayal.

It hadn't been too hard to find the members of the Brotherhood, as they were out sunbathing on a rooftop near their lair. Sunbathing while wearing full ceremonial robes, admittedly, but sunbathing nonetheless. When Fitz arrived they were engaged in a debate over whether Silver's miracles should upgrade him from 'unholy' to 'most holy', a transition so radical that it made the schism Fitz had caused seem like a minor problem, a fact for which Fitz was eternally grateful.

One quick conversation and a hastily-sketched map later, and Fitz was heading down into the depths of Hope. When the Brotherhood had mentioned, during his aborted initiation ceremony, that there were hideous creatures living in the tunnels beneath the city, Fitz had been intrigued. Miraso's attempts to warn him off only heightened that interest. If there was a dark side to this brave new Hope, then this was the lead to follow. Fitz wondered when a warning of extreme danger had stopped being a threat to him, and become an invitation too good to resist.

The Brotherhood's map had been eccentric, but clear. Fitz headed down a rickety stairwell and into the side door of one of

Hope's large tenement blocks. Inside slits of light crisscrossed the corridors, breaking in through shattered, boarded-up windows. Fitz took a stairwell down into the basement, where he had to find his way with a pocket torch. In the far corner there was a manhole cover, just as the Brotherhood had said. He levered it up, and lowered himself down slimy rungs.

He was now in the real undercity, where pipes and tunnels formed a web between the struts. The Brotherhood had advised Fitz to follow the tunnel until he reached a barrier, but not to approach that barrier. If he stayed at a distance, he would get a good look.

The concrete tunnel was dripping with foul water, and Fitz had to stoop to walk down it, torch piercing the darkness. Mould crawled up the grey walls around him. Eventually he approached a grating that blocked the way ahead. By his reckoning Fitz had to be nearly under the Silver Palace by now. Fitz waved his torch at the grating, but couldn't see anything. He whistled, leaning forward to get a closer look.

'Doctor,' said Silver, standing on the deck of the submarine. 'We'll be ready to leave shortly.'

The Doctor vaulted over the railing along the Pier, landing a few feet below on the deck. 'Excellent,' he said, smiling disconcertingly at Silver.

One of Silver's crimson-uniformed staff came up from the depths of the sub, an environment-suited figure with handcuffed wrists staggering in front of him.

'Mr Stephens,' said the Doctor, peering through the suit's visor. 'Welcome to the world above.' Even with his eyes shielded by the tinted visor, the old man seemed to squint at the bright sunlight.

'Take him to the watchtower,' said Silver. 'Powlin will be waiting for him.'

Stephens said something obscene as he was led away.

'You know,' the Doctor told Silver. 'I don't think our Mr Stephens likes being on the surface.'

'His kind have lived in a hermetically sealed world for a long time,' replied Silver, as if it had been a serious question. 'They have no resistance to disease, their skins are unused to natural light. He is right to feel threatened – the whole environment up here is hostile to him. But it is vital the people of Hope see him stand trial.'

'I couldn't agree more,' said the Doctor, watching as the old scientist shakily ascended a ladder to the Pier.

The sensor finished whirring and withdrew its antennae, the unit settling into a contented hum. Anji had walked around many of the rooms with it in her hand, watching figures and symbols scroll down a little screen in the front of the unit. She had no idea what the information represented but, in spite of her knowledge that the Doctor would so vehemently object to his secrets being taken from him, Anji found herself conscientiously hoping that the information would be of use to Silver.

Sliding the scanner into her pocket, Anji went to her room to retrieve the precious hair of Dave's. As she did so she thought about what she was doing, placing the Doctor's treasured secrets and her most prized possession into Silver's care. Then again, surely Silver had proved himself trustworthy by now? He had rescued the Doctor and was in the process of trying to improve Endpoint for all its people. In spite of his menacing appearance, Silver seemed to be one of the most trustworthy people Anji had ever met.

Something jumped up to the grate, slick fingers clawing through the gaps to try and tear into Fitz. He fell back, scrambling through a few inches of rancid liquid, hands slipping on the wet concrete. The creature ahead of him was hideously mutated, limbs twisted and eyes bloodshot, but it clearly had some features of the Endpointers in its genetic mix. Another creature attacked the first beast, and it too bore Endpointer characteristics, although its own individual features were different from that of the first.

Realising that the grating was solid enough to keep them back, Fitz pointed his torch past them, waving it around the chamber they lived in. The sewer-like space had a high ceiling, and Fitz could just make out a hatch in the roof. Immediately below the hatch was a mess of food, which had clearly been dropped through the hatch. The food had been dropped in canvas bags, now torn to pieces, but as the creatures jostled for position at the grating Fitz caught a glimpse of a shred of material floating in the fetid water. That glimpse, coupled with the metallic sheen to the mutations' skins and his ideas of where they were located, confirmed Fitz's feeling that something was very wrong with Hope's new saviour.

Fitz turned and started to walk back through the tunnel, leaving the creatures to their unhappy state, their pitiful growls echoing after him. In his mind he held the image of a fragment of material bearing a sloping 'S' with a line through it: the mark of Silver.

The Doctor's tongue nervously clicked over his front teeth as he loosened the panel. The laboratory equipment used by Stephens and his associates was some way in advance of that in the Silver Palace, but this was still a delicate operation. They were sealed in a sterile area similar to the one they had kept the Doctor in, and the Doctor was clothed in a protective suit. He held a microscalpel between his fingers, gingerly opening the panel in the back of Silver's skull.

'Well, well,' the Doctor said when the panel was open. A section of Silver's brain was exposed, but it was not the brain itself which was of interest, but the shining, mercury-like fluid that flowed through it, that rose and fell on the very surface of the brain itself. With the brain exposed the fluid danced towards the light, straining towards the tip of the Doctor's scalpel.

'Remarkable,' said the Doctor. 'Quite remarkable. Have you any idea where this substance came from?'

'I believe it was synthesised from alien technology,' replied Silver. 'It may therefore be possible to synthesise it again using the technology in this bunker.'

'It should certainly prove easier to reproduce than Kallisti,' said the Doctor, letting a small amount of the substance stick to the end of the scalpel. He began to lift the scalpel away, letting the shining blob detach itself from the rest of the material. It needed to be done gently, to allow any data in that area to be downloaded to the rest of the brain. The Doctor didn't want to accidentally amputate part of Silver's thoughts.

'Kallisti will prove remarkably easy to reproduce,' said Silver casually. The Doctor almost dropped the scalpel into Silver's head in shock. He had no idea Silver was so far advanced in his researches.

'Doctor?' said Silver.

'Yes?' replied the Doctor.

'Please could you take the sample,' said Silver. 'I find the feeling of air on my brain is disconcerting.'

'Oh, of course,' said the Doctor, taking the sample of liquid intelligence and sliding it into a test tube. He stoppered the tube, then turned to Silver and closed the panel on the back of his head.

'Thank you,' said Silver, rising from his chair. He took the test tube from the Doctor, and tapped on the wall of the containment area. Richard, who had been watching the operation with interest, activated the control and the barriers slid up around them.

'So, you have already worked out how to synthesise Kallisti?' said the Doctor as they walked over to a bank of analytical equipment. Richard got to work running the sample from Silver's brain through the analyser. He was assisted by a member of Silver's staff from the Silver Palace's laboratories. Indeed, the bunker as a whole seemed to be manned partially by Silver's personnel. The Doctor recalled the early days of the Red Army, where officers were shadowed by political commissars to keep them in line; the same principle applied here, Silver's people keeping an eye on the humans while they worked. It was quite a complex set up, one which had been established in less than a week, yet already Silver seemed in complete control.

'The problem needed to be resolved if a repetition of Stephens's experiments was to be avoided,' said Silver. 'Once a search for knowledge has begun, it will continue regardless of laws and impediments. Once I have synthesised Kallisti, there will be no need for any more unpleasant incidents.'

'And how do you intend to do this?' asked the Doctor.

'By applying my mind to the problem,' said Silver. 'Literally. The batch of liquid intelligence contains a programme created while it was part of my brain, a programme to merge with and synthesise Kallisti. All we need to do is let the sample breed, and then introduce it to a vivactic gland. One super-intelligent micro-organism will then take over another, merging with it to create a hybrid substance that can be replicated to order. The possible uses for such a substance are vast.'

'The potential applications could be horrific,' countered the Doctor.

'That is why we must keep it in safe hands, Doctor,' replied Silver. 'Now, shall we return to the surface and leave these people to their work?'

This surface world was a nightmare for Stephens. Wherever he went there were the strange, bald mutations. The quality of the light was unusual, and no one seemed to have control of it. Why else would it be so uncomfortably bright? Then there was the city itself, a mess of recycled garbage built into some form of community. It was disgusting, chaotic and unpleasant in its sprawling disorganisation. There was no order here, only a primitive assertion of dominance. The creature Silver was proof of that – a monster whose position was enforced by brute strength, his power lay not in wisdom or leadership but in his physicality, the gun built into his hand, the speed of his electronically enhanced reflexes. Stephens despised the entire situation, was repulsed by this scrap-metal world and its savage inhabitants. Everything he saw reinforced the rightness of his previous actions – these creatures were better for nothing more than cutting up. They were cattle, nothing else.

He was taken to something called a watchtower, where what passed for the law enforcement officials in this foul place resided. Stephens was taken to a dank room where he was chained to a metal chair, presumably to stop him from harming himself. His skin crawled as he sat there, unable to scratch the many itches he had under the environment suit.

'So,' said a saggy-faced mutation who appeared in the doorway. 'You're the killer we've been looking for. You don't look very threatening now, do you?'

'I'm not a murderer,' replied Stephens indignantly. 'I'm a scientist. Who the hell are you to question me?'

'I'm Powlin, Chief of Militia,' said the creature, sitting down opposite Stephens. 'I've been investigating your handiwork for some time. Or should I take it from your previous statement that you deny any involvement in the killings?'

'Killings?' spat Stephens. 'That was a legitimate experiment, authorised by my predecessors and approved of, participated in most of the time, by every human being in that bunker. You cannot single me out for this treatment.'

'Oh, but we can,' said Powlin, leaning to face Stephens, who found this odd, hairless face disturbing. 'You see, our Mr Silver has use for the rest of your people. Seems to think the last of the human race have potential. So they get off the hook. But someone has to pay for those deaths, and as the big man giving the orders, that person turns out to be you. Silver knows the people want blood, and he's happy to give them yours.'

'So what are you going to do, just kill me?' asked Stephens. 'Put me up against a wall somewhere and shoot me?'

Powlin shook his head slowly. 'No, Mr Stephens, we're not murderers like yourself. You see, the forces of justice are about to expand, taking over several territories previously beyond our reach. Your trial will be a vehicle for this process of unification, showing why Hope's laws should be spread across Endpoint. By sentencing you in full public view we show everyone why they're becoming part of our new order. Congratulations, Mr Stephens, you're going to become poster boy for law and order.'

'I'm honoured,' said Stephens. 'Do I get a fair trial, or will you just lock me up whatever the decision?'

'Oh, it'll be a fair trial. But you better hope we lock you up,' said Powlin. 'You see, there are a lot of people on this planet like those you killed, a lot of people to resent what you did. And once you've been labelled as the one responsible, well... the worst thing that could happen to you might be an acquittal.'

Powlin walked over to the door. 'Have fun, alone with your thoughts,' he told Stephens. 'You can guarantee there are plenty of people out there thinking of you.'

As the door closed, Stephens was left alone to face his future, his defiance wilting in the darkness.

The Silver Palace was closed for business. It was now merely Silver's base of operations, a genuine Palace for the saviour of Endpoint to reside. Anji walked into the main hall and over to the bar. There were no bar staff, as it was no longer a commercial concern. Anji considered this to be reason enough for her to jump on the bar, and lean over to grab a bottle and glass from underneath it. If it wasn't a commercial concern, she didn't need to pay for anything, did she?

She poured herself a drink of a fruity liquid she had become increasingly fond of, and went to sit at her usual table. She could feel the weight of the data-packed scanning unit in her pocket. That weight was both literal and metaphorical, as the strain it exerted on her was mainly due to the nature of what she was about to hand over. Checking that no one was around – she would have hated to have to lie to Fitz or anyone else about what she was up to – Anji slid the unit out of her pocket and placed it on the table. She had a sudden urge to smash the damn thing to pieces, to tell Silver to go stick his deal.

But then she remembered the other thing she had taken from the TARDIS – Dave's precious hair, a reminder of why she was doing this. And she was certain once more that she had made the right decision. All she could do was wait. She slid slightly down in her chair, staring up at the stars emblazoned on the ceiling. She was looking at the early part of the mural, staring at the picture of stars and planets comfortably located, before most of those worlds were destroyed.

'The system as it once was,' said Silver, following her gaze as he entered the room. 'And beyond, showing all the worlds that are still out there but inaccessible. The star on the far left is the Prime Sun, around which the Imperial Throneworld orbits. Once ships from all across the system visited there regularly to pay homage. Now a hypertunnel would be required to make the journey.'

'I have no idea what you are talking about,' replied Anji.

'That,' said Silver, sitting opposite her, 'is why I am telling this to you.'

Anji blinked. She had more important business to attend to than solving Silver's riddles. She placed a finger on the data unit, sliding it across the table. Silver picked it up, flicking a switch casually. Anji could see the twitch of obsession beneath his eye as he began to look over the data, the giveaway signs beneath his attempts to appear disinterested.

'Fascinating,' said Silver, flicking the switch back into place and sliding the unit into a pocket. 'This will prove interesting reading. As the Doctor did before, you have fulfilled your side of our bargain. Now, as I did for him, I will fulfil mine. Do you have the genetic sample?'

Anji patted her pocket to indicate that she did.

Silver raised his eyebrow. 'Don't you think it would be useful to give it to me?'

Anji shook her head. 'I'll only pass it over when the process needs to begin. I need to be there, to make sure you're using the right hair. I just need to be sure, to see it happen.'

'I understand,' said Silver. He stood up. 'Shall we go then? I'm afraid my scientific operations have been moved to the human bunker, but the journey is a brief one.'

'You're going to begin straight away?' asked Anji with a lurch of apprehension.

'Why not?' boomed Silver. He extended his metal hand to her, to help her up. She found herself taking it, allowing him to bring her to her feet once more. She realised her hand was shaking slightly. What she was about to do...

'Don't be nervous,' said Silver, his red eye gleaming at her. 'We are about to embark on the creation of life. What is there to fear?'

Part Four
The Silver Age

Chapter Thirteen
Paranoia

Banners fluttered in the air, there were chants and singing and the smell of smoke. Night had fallen, but the gas torches flared brilliant blue as the parade crossed one of Hope's most central bridges, gathering more people as it went. The people were wearing half-masks over one side of their faces, a single red eye drawn on each mask. The object of their affections, their celebration, was unambiguous. The atmosphere was giddy, unreal, as if they would all wake up the next day to find that the fogs had descended once more, that the air and the sea burned again.

Fitz found Miraso on a higher, smaller bridge that crossed over where the parade was dancing past. He stood by her, leaning over the railing, looking down at the happy crowds with their home-made Silver masks.

'One of yours?' he asked, nodding to the parade.

'No,' said Miraso, voice flat and unreadable. 'This is genuine, a spontaneous show of the people's love for Silver.'

'You don't sound too happy about it,' commented Fitz.

She turned to him. Her eyes flared brighter than Silver's when she was angry, bluer than the clearest sky.

'Have you ever been in love, Fitz?' she asked.

This was rather more intense than Fitz was comfortable with, even from an attractive young woman like Miraso.

'It's not been unknown,' replied Fitz warily.

'Well, in that case you know the state they're in,' said Miraso, pointing down at the parade. 'Blind to reason, they'll do anything for the one they love. Now imagine a whole world like that, dizzy and jubilant, walking on air. Unstable, vulnerable to suggestion.'

'It's like a collective madness,' said Fitz, clarifying for himself apart from anything.

Miraso clicked her fingers. 'Exactly.' She stared at the crowd intently, her voice dropping to a whisper. 'Manipulating public opinion, trying to keep control of people on the edge… we were fighting a losing battle, that was the fun of it. It was a struggle, but we knew with Silver we were maintaining order in a hostile world, introducing stability. Now… I don't know what these people could do.'

'And you don't know what Silver might ask of them,' said Fitz.

Miraso didn't answer, but Fitz suddenly saw a startling vulnerability in her eyes. She needed someone to understand her predicament.

'I went down into those tunnels,' said Fitz. 'I saw the creatures he created.'

'Rejects,' said Miraso. 'The result of his experimental failures. Sometimes I wonder whether it would have been more merciful to kill them, or if we're doing them a favour keeping them alive.'

'Were they people?' asked Fitz in disgust.

'Not really,' said Miraso, shaking her head. 'Although they would have become people if the experiments had succeeded. No, they were embryos manipulated in their early stages and fast grown in the lab. Unfortunately Silver's "modifications" didn't take.'

'Silver certainly puts on a good show,' said Fitz. 'The Doctor and Anji seem to have been convinced.'

'He gives people what they want,' said Miraso. 'That's what makes him so persuasive.'

Fitz snorted. 'That explains it. Silver doesn't have anything I want. Although I still didn't see anything wrong with him until now.'

'He only acts ruthlessly when it suits his purpose,' explained Miraso. 'Silver is pragmatic, he knows to appear righteous whenever possible, no matter what his intent. With Endpoint's isolation, with all the power he wields here, there has rarely been any reason for him to break out of that mould.'

Fitz looked down at the crowds. The last stragglers were

disappearing across the bridge, but their music and cries echoed between the buildings. 'Now everything's changing. The old rules don't apply.'

'No one knows where they fit in,' said Miraso wistfully. 'You, me, Silver. Everything's up for grabs.'

'The question is,' said Fitz. 'On which side do we all land?'

Miraso didn't answer.

'Wow!' said Richard, circling Anji intently. 'Another human being, one who has lived outside the bunker. It's amazing.'

'Can you stop looking at me like that?' said Anji, discomfited. 'It's rude.'

'Sorry,' said Richard, stepping back and addressing her in a more normal manner. 'As you can imagine, it's been a long time since we've had another of our own kind down here.'

Like I'm your kind, thought Anji spitefully. She wasn't too impressed by this first example of the surviving humans. Although he was a young man, his frame was spindly and underdeveloped. His skin looked distinctly unhealthy, and although he was wearing some kind of automatic contact lenses – Anji could see glowing irises adjusting in his eyes, the thick rim of the lens on his eyeball – Richard seemed to be constantly squinting. Presumably this was partially the result of his environment: the bunker was sterile and slightly dank. Endless bare light bulbs burned in the ceiling, while the air tasted over-conditioned, devoid of any texture. Anji was a city girl at heart, she liked to breathe something with a bit more body.

'How many of you – sorry, us – are there down here?' she asked. As Silver's guest, she thought she had better make polite conversation while waiting for the cyborg to emerge from the airlock. He'd sent Anji on ahead to meet Richard, a gesture for which Anji would be eternally ungrateful.

'There are only a few of us active,' said Richard. 'Less of late.'

Anji caught the young scientist glancing nervously at something over Anji's shoulder. She turned to see a couple of bullet holes in the smooth white surface of the wall.

'However,' continued Richard, not allowing her time to ask any awkward questions. 'There are many more of us still in storage, awaiting a suitable time to resume our place in the universe.'

'And what place is that?' asked Anji.

Richard frowned. 'I'm not really sure. Somewhere important, I think.'

'That's good to know,' said Anji. 'It would be depressing to think we were just another group of people, the same as any other.'

Richard didn't seem to notice the sarcasm. Anji was about to lay it on thicker concerning the evils of equality when Silver arrived, cutting short an increasingly torturous conversation.

'Shall we proceed?' he asked, not even bothering to greet Richard.

Powlin returned to his office to find the Doctor sitting behind his desk, reading through one of the recent case files. There was a frown creasing his forehead, as if the Doctor was finding it difficult to concentrate on the words in front of him.

'I'm going to have to close that,' said Powlin, by way of greeting. 'Thanks to you, we have our killer. Case closed, and we couldn't have done it without you.'

The compliment seemed to slip past the Doctor unnoticed. 'Where are you keeping Stephens?' he asked.

'There are holding cells on the ground floor,' replied Powlin. 'One of the men will open it for you if you want to see him.'

'Yes, yes, I'll do that,' said the Doctor, agitated. 'But not quite yet. Now this case has been resolved, Mr Powlin, what next? You've been working on this case for a long time, where do you go from here?'

'That's a big question, Doctor,' replied Powlin, sitting opposite him on a pile of case files. The huge stack of paper wobbled slightly, but stayed upright. 'Thanks to Silver and yourself, we now have a chance to establish law and order here in Hope. The criminals and scum have hidden in the fog and the shadows for too long. They shouldn't be able to cope now that the sun is shining.'

'A new age of prosperity?' said the Doctor, standing up. He didn't seem too convinced. 'I think I'll go and talk to the prisoner now.'

Powlin watched him leave, baffled by the whole conversation.

It all begins with the smallest of things.

Richard carefully took the precious hair from Anji, and placed it on a glass slide. That slide was then placed on a plastic tray sticking out of a squat black machine. The tray slid into the machine, a little door closing behind it with a hollow click. Richard flicked a couple of switches on a bank of controls, and the whole room came to life.

When computers had first been invented, they had filled whole rooms, but by Anji's time they had been miniaturised beyond belief. The set up in the laboratory reminded Anji of those old computers, huge banks of equipment whirring and clicking, processing the genetic data.

'There's a spot of blood on the end of the hair,' said Richard, squinting at a magnified image of the follicle.

'It was his first grey hair,' explained Anji. 'He asked me to pull it out for him, and I kept it. It was a joke, initially. I used the hair to remind Dave he wasn't perfect.'

'Thanks to you having drawn blood, we can extract a working DNA sample,' said Silver. 'From that we can create a clone.'

'Dave II,' said Anji quietly.

'Precisely,' said Richard, beaming. He didn't seem to realise how momentous this was for Anji.

'Begin the cloning process,' said Silver. 'Follow the procedure as I instructed, including the appropriate memory download templates.'

'Memories?' said Anji.

'Basic knowledge,' said Silver. 'The clone will be grown to full adulthood. Memory implants act as a substitute for childhood development – they contain basic survival knowledge of the world the clone is coming into, the skills he will need to live.'

'It's a technique we have perfected when reviving people from cryogenic suspension,' added Richard. 'We can get them from deep freeze to manning a workstation within two hours, if needed. It's a valuable tool for preventing culture shock and increasing efficiency.'

Anji found the whole process too confusing even to alarm her.

'How long will the cloning process take?' she asked.

'Many hours,' said Silver, placing a cold metal hand on her shoulder. 'We'll return for the beginning of the cloning process, but for now I think we should leave these people to their work. Once the sequencing has been completed, then cloning will begin. But for the next hour there will be nothing to see, and there's something else I want to show you in the meantime.'

Reluctantly, looking back at the magnified image of Dave's hair, Anji allowed Silver to lead her away.

'Come to gloat, have you?' spat Stephens, as the Doctor entered his cell. 'All my work, ruined because of you. I hope you're happy.'

'Stephens,' said the Doctor wearily. 'If you were vital to your own experiments, then you wouldn't be here.'

'What? What do you mean?' Stephens was momentarily thrown off balance.

'You really are a very stupid man,' muttered the Doctor. 'And that's the reason you're here. Silver has kept everyone he needs to complete and continue your work in the bunker. He's already cracked the Kallisti problem without you, and your scientists are more motivated than they've ever been. You were dispensable all along, Stephens.'

Stephens sank back into the darkness in the corner of his cell. 'Did you just come here to outline my shortcomings?' he mumbled, pushing up his knees to block his view of the Doctor.

The alien, with his deceptively human appearance, dropped down to squat near Stephens. 'No, I came to ask some questions. I'm genuinely curious.'

'Curious?' replied Stephens, his own curiosity piqued.

'Yes,' said the Doctor, sitting next to Stephens in the dank cell, seemingly untroubled by the damp floor. 'I want to know about the rest of your plan. You intended to merge Kallisti into the human genetic makeup, to make your people stronger, more resistant to environmental threats. But what then? You're isolated here, what could you have done except retake the surface?'

Stephens chuckled, his own hot breath steaming up the visor of his environment suit. 'Oh, Doctor, the surface would have been only the first stage of our assault, a simple cleansing of the planet to secure the area. Once the mutations were all scrubbed off the face of the planet, and our sleeping population remobilised, we could make the first moves to reclaim the rest of space.'

'But how?' asked the Doctor. 'The planet is completely isolated.'

'Psh,' exclaimed Stephens. 'Physical obstructions are no obstacle to a hypertunnel.'

'What's a hypertunnel?' asked Anji. The word was emblazoned in red letters across a pair of impressive double doors. Warning signs and safety logos were dotted around the area. From behind the doors she could hear mechanical noises, the grinding of heavy machinery being operated.

Silver, who had been leading the way, turned back to face her. 'It's an advanced form of garbage disposal,' he said. 'An enclosed system like this cannot afford to leave refuse lying around. Now, shall we see your descendants?'

Anji followed Silver as he led the way down corridor after corridor. They seemed to be zigzagging through the bunker on a slight incline, as if descending into the bowels of the planet. Certainly, the air seemed danker, the atmosphere more pressurised, the further they went. She felt a chill around her, and pulled her coat tight.

Eventually they reached a dark bulkhead with a large wheel set into it. Silver reached out with his metal hand and twirled it like the dial on a washing machine. After a couple of revolutions of the wheel, the bulkhead opened with a hiss, cold air pouring out. Beyond the door was darkness. Silver stepped to one side, indicating that Anji should step inside first. She walked through the door, and found herself on a steel gantry, with a line of caskets to her left, and a drop to her right. Looking over the edge, she saw rows of caskets stretching downwards, disappearing into a mist far below her.

'There are so many of them,' said Anji. It was a banal statement, but an honest one.

'Not that many, for the sole repository of humankind,' said Silver. 'Humanity dominated their home planet, then their solar system, spreading ever outwards to conquer galaxies. Now this is all that is left. Not so many, when put in that context.'

'When you put it like that, it is odd,' said Anji. 'To be in the same room as your entire species.'

'I know,' said Silver, looking over the railing. 'I was human once, myself.'

Anji looked up at him, startled by this sudden admission. She placed her human hand on his metal fist on the railing. It was an involuntary gesture, almost, on her part, a sudden desire to give comfort in the face of something far bigger than both of them. Their entire species, reduced to one refrigerated room.

His hand was hard and cold beneath hers, but she squeezed it anyway.

'Where's Anji?'

The Doctor's question jolted Fitz out of his evening reverie. After watching the parade he had wandered back to the Silver Palace, raided the bar and got a little drunk. Without anyone else around, it had seemed the only solution to his oncoming depression. In fact the booze had just knocked him out, allowing days of exhaustion to crush him. Clearly he had been running on stress too much lately.

'No idea,' he replied to the Doctor's question, pulling himself up on his bed. The Doctor was framed by light, standing in the doorway of Fitz's room. Fitz couldn't see his face, had no way of making out his expression or mood. 'Drink?' asked Fitz, freeing the bottle from where it had become jammed, stuck between the mattress and the wall.

'No thank you,' said the Doctor. 'She isn't in her room,' he added. 'Or the orchard.'

Fitz shrugged. 'Where could she be, then?'

'I don't know,' said the Doctor. 'But I'm not entirely comfortable losing touch with her in Hope. I'm beginning to think this new age isn't going to be quite what it may seem.'

'Funny, I was thinking just the same thing,' replied Fitz, thinking of those odd, twisted mutations in the tunnels beneath the Palace. With a jolt he realised they could be below him right now – albeit several floors below. Fitz needed to tell the Doctor about the creatures, and he needed to tell him now.

'When Anji returns we need to discuss what to do next,' said the Doctor, closing the door as he hurriedly backed into the corridor. 'We need to watch Silver,' he said quietly, the door closing behind him, leaving Fitz in the dark once more.

Fitz realised he hadn't told the Doctor about the creatures in the tunnels. But before he could work up the will to get up and tell him, Fitz had already drifted off to sleep.

After spending some time in the cryogenic chambers, awestruck by the mass of humanity preserved there, Anji had asked Silver whether they could look in on the attempts to clone Dave. Silver had replied that on the surface it would be night by now, and that he should return her to the Silver Palace so that the Doctor and Fitz didn't worry. But Anji had insisted, and so they returned to the laboratory. Richard had gone for his sleep shift, leaving the laboratory in the care of another team headed by a woman with thin blonde hair and an unusually high forehead. The woman had shown Anji what there was of Dave II so far – to her surprise she saw not a small cluster of cells that needed to be viewed through a microscope, but a tiny, tiny embryo floating in a canister of clear fluid. It wasn't at the stage where its human nature was visible, but the vertebrae and eyes of the mammal were clearly visible. Anji looked on in wonder, and could have stayed there all night, watching this small human grow. However, Silver insisted that the project would be threatened if the Doctor became suspicious of Anji's absences, and this was enough to encourage Anji to reluctantly return with him to the surface.

It was midnight when the sub sploshed to the surface by the Pier, and Anji and Silver emerged on to the deck. This was Hope's first full night since the atmospheric storms had subsided, the first night with no mist or fog to obscure their view of the night sky. It was like no sky Anji had ever seen – swirls of many colours intermingled, with a constant pattern of glittering objects shifting and whirling around each other.

'Are those stars?' she asked, the spectacle causing her to stop in the middle of the submarine's deck.

'No,' said Silver, looking up into the sky with her. He stood at her shoulder, his voice barely a whisper as he spoke. 'That is what remains of this star system – debris, a constant field of fragments. In the day, the sun shines straight through this minefield of energy and artefacts. But at night, the sun reflects off every fragment.' As he spoke he raised his metal hand, indicating the sky above them.

'It's like a curtain,' said Anji. 'A barrier, closed between you and the stars.'

'Exactly,' said Silver. 'But imagine parting that curtain, to be able to see the stars, to touch the rest of the universe…'

Silver trailed off. His hand had become a fist, as if he had reached out through that veil to grasp the stars themselves.

Chapter Fourteen
Chaingun Diplomacy

The endless sea rolled below them, great waves heaving up and crashing down. Fitz felt like doing some heaving of his own. Even though the sub wasn't actually sailing on the sea so much as gliding above it, the view over the edge of the railing was nauseatingly vertiginous. Fitz leaned over the railings, closed his eyes and breathed the sea air deeply.

It was far too early in the morning for this kind of thing. He had been woken up at dawn by Miraso, who had barged into his room and shouted at him until she was certain he wouldn't fall asleep again. Once he seemed conscious enough for her to talk to, Miraso told Fitz that they would be accompanying Silver on a diplomatic mission to Persistence, Endpoint's second largest city. Fitz was there to represent the newly rediscovered humanity – although he wasn't actually one of the humans from the bunker, there was no way for the good burghers of Persistence to know that. When they had arrived at the sub Silver had explained all of this, describing the substitution of a bunker human – all too weak and antisocial to be suitable – with Fitz as sleight of hand. Fitz found it hard to imagine Silver performing illusions, producing doves from his sleeves.

If Fitz had any doubts that this trip was as much about showmanship as diplomacy, they had been dispelled as the submarine departed from its now regular docking place by the Pier. Instead of diving beneath the surface, the sub extended two tall, robust metal towers from its deck; these had partially unfurled, rotor blades spreading out above their heads. The blades had begun to whirl, and the sub had lifted up out of the water, Silver and his party still standing on the deck. The sub-copter stayed at a reasonably low altitude, moving at a leisurely speed across the sea. Silver's intention was clearly to glide majestically into view as they approached Persistence, leisurely and regally arriving like royalty at some grand social occasion. Fitz supposed that, by Endpoint standards, Silver probably was royalty.

Miraso joined him at the railing.

'So, have you ever been to Persistence before?' Fitz asked, trying to make polite conversation.

Miraso shook her head. 'Up until today travel between communities has been difficult, long and dangerous. I never had to take the risk. Now we get to travel like this.' She made a sweeping gesture, the feyness of the movement suggesting a difficulty in grasping their surreal situation.

When Persistence appeared over the horizon, it initially didn't seem to be that different from Hope, at least to Fitz's uneducated eyes. But as they got nearer and nearer to this other community Fitz could increasingly see the differences. Persistence was a flatter, smaller community than Hope, consisting of buildings only a few storeys high. Unlike Hope, there were a number of windmill-type constructions jutting above the squat buildings. When they reached the edge of the community the sub-copter didn't stop, but instead flew over the town itself. They passed a number of ornate, almost ecclesiastical, buildings scattered between the shorter buildings and the windmills. Fitz by now had a fairly good idea of what he thought Persistence was like; a small town to Hope's urban sprawl, where tall buildings were a sign of power rather than a necessity, where the people lived off limited power supplies reliant on the weather. It almost seemed idyllic, although Fitz was fully aware that it wouldn't have been all that nice three days before, when the skies still rained acid and the air scorched lungs and eyes. Back then, this simple life would have been a constant struggle. No wonder it was called Persistence.

The sub-copter halted near a domed structure in the centre of town, hovering over an adjacent square. Robed men - presumably the town elders, or the good burghers or whatever, thought Fitz – gathered beneath them at the doors to the domed building, clothes flapping as the ship's rotor blades tore up a storm. While Fitz and Miraso clambered down rope ladders to reach the square, Silver simply jumped over the side, leaving cracks in the panelled floor where he landed. The noise of Silver's impact gave Fitz the shock of his life as he tried to get down the ladder without falling.

Fitz had been right about the robed men – they were some form of council, and as Fitz and Miraso approached the councillors were nervously introducing themselves to Silver, who was nodding thoughtfully at the mention of each name, as if noting them on a mental hit list. Silver stopped one of the councillors, making a great point of introducing Miraso and Fitz as representatives of, respectively, the Endpointers and the newly rediscovered human race. The councillors seemed unusually impressed by Fitz, admiring his straggly hair and wonky eyebrows. Fitz felt strangely touched.

They were led through to the centre of the dome, an amphitheatre-type room where Silver was to address the gathered leaders of Persistence. Fitz and Miraso took seats either side of the podium, which Silver stepped up to.

'People of Persistence,' said Silver, his voice carrying without any external microphone. 'You will no doubt have observed the changes to the environment of Endpoint wrought during the last few days. Via the communications channels, you will, equally, doubtless be aware of my involvement in these changes. The discovery of a human community, and their long lost technologies, has allowed a quantifiable and immediate improvement in the quality of living for every Endpointer. The air is now clear, the seas no longer burn. The sky can now be seen, the fogs have cleared.'

'This is only the beginning.'

'While much has already been done, there is still some way to go to improve the lives of the people of Endpoint. We must resolve the problems of crime and disorder on our world – to that end I am expanding the militia on Hope, spreading their word of law across the entire planet. We must unite the long geographically separate communities – and to this end I am making contacts with other communities, on diplomatic visits like this one. Finally, we must then be able to make contact with the outside universe, to rejoin a wider galactic community.'

'All these things are possible. All these things can be done, and in the immediate future. I can do these things. I can bring you a lawful, clean, safe world. I can take what was once a polluted hell and make of it a heaven. I ask only one thing in return. Your absolute, total obedience to my will.'

Silver's red eye looked out, unflinching, across the gathered leaders, his steady gaze daring them to challenge his authority. But no challenge ever came.

For some unfathomable reason, when the knock on her door came, Anji thought it was Silver. The knocking woke her from a deep sleep – she had arrived back at the Silver Palace quite late, causing her to sleep through until mid-morning – and her semi-conscious mind presumed that it was Silver at the door. She pushed herself up in bed, head bumping lightly on the wall behind her. She still hadn't become used to the cramped accommodation. She rubbed her head, calling for whoever was outside to come in. She was expecting Silver.

Instead, it was the Doctor's head that appeared around the door. His blue eyes danced around the room, as if searching for clues to Anji's life in a generic room she had barely inhabited. His expression was fixed in a permanent half-smile, a sure sign of serious thoughts in progress. 'Breakfast?' he suggested, as if the concept of a morning meal had only just occurred to him.

Anji had been expecting Silver, and the Doctor had arrived instead. His appearance caused her feelings of disappointment, feelings of guilt, feelings of distress at her own confusion.

She forced a grin. 'Breakfast would be great,' she enthused.

So, within twenty minutes she was sitting on the roof of the Palace, eating breakfast in the morning sun. It had the civilised air of a country veranda, although the burnt-out satellite dish stopped things from seeming too Merchant Ivory.

'Beautiful, isn't it?' said the Doctor, blinking in the sunlight.

'Hard to imagine that it's the same Hope where we first arrived,' said Anji, between mouthfuls of the thick, pitta-like bread that was one of the Endpointers' staple foods. 'It almost lives up to its name, now.'

'I know,' said the Doctor. 'When we arrived here, this world seemed without redeeming features, without any possible future. Now the Endpointers are at a crossroads. On one hand, they have the chance to build something wonderful here, where the freedoms and liberties of a frontier existence are preserved, where the scientific discoveries of the humans are shared for the good of all. There's plenty of everything to go around, therefore no one should go without.'

Anji was about to argue that this theory was unworkable, that inequalities and hierarchies would develop as value judgements were made. But she kept quiet, fearful of giving any sign of her betrayal. Instead, she simply asked what the other option was.

'Power becomes consolidated,' said the Doctor. 'Knowledge and technology coalesce around a privileged few, who use their possession of resources to lever obedience from everyone else. Rather than creating one unified Endpoint, the communities could become increasingly feudal.'

Anji didn't have to ask whose authority and power the Doctor was worried would become too great. Her stomach clenched. If the Doctor was considering making a play against Silver, then Anji needed to place herself to protect Dave II. Regardless of the Doctor and Silver's conflict, and the rights and wrongs of the situation, Anji couldn't allow this new Dave to come to harm. She wasn't going to lose him twice.

Silver's 'diplomatic mission' returned to Hope to find theirs was not the only submarine berthed near the Pier. Another of the sleek craft was parked at the other side of the Pier, both crimson-clad staff from the Silver Palace and environment-suited humans wandering its deck.

'I didn't know there were more than one of those,' said Fitz as they ascended to the Pier.

'There are several,' said Silver, clearly reluctant to reveal exactly how many. 'But more will need to be constructed. Miraso.' He turned to his deputy. 'I need you to assist the human scientist, Richard, in locating and dismantling whatever he requires from the Silver Palace. You will load this second sub with all the vital components, and then join me in the Bunker.'

'Aren't we leaving anything in the Palace?' asked Miraso.

'For now, no,' said Silver. 'Our base of operations will be in the Bunker from now on, a place only accessible with our permission. Presently the Palace will be refitted to become the public face of our government.'

Fitz suspected that when Silver said 'our', it was very much the Royal We.

Miraso didn't argue with this, instead giving Silver a tight nod.

Silver nodded towards the second sub. 'You'll find Richard either on or below deck,' he said. Miraso stepped in that direction, visibly smarting from the dismissal.

'I'll just go find the Doctor,' said Fitz, backing away. But neither Miraso nor Silver were listening, too wrapped up in their own power games to notice Fitz.

The Pier had changed rapidly in the previous couple of days. Whereas before it was a foreboding multistorey shantytown, the presence of the submarines, and the attention they drew, had driven the derelicts away. However, evidence of the Pier's previous occupation lay all around – metal cylinders where crude fires had once burned, lean-tos in which the poor wretches who lived there had slept, this and other debris littered the area. It hadn't been too difficult for Anji to find somewhere to hide.

After breakfast Anji had left the Doctor on the roof of the Palace, pleading heatstroke as an excuse to get out of the sun. From there she had gone straight to the Pier, keeping out of sight and waiting for Silver to return. The second submarine had caused some initial confusion, but when Anji saw Richard walking around on deck, unselfconsciously trying to scratch himself within his environment suit, she realised Silver must have had more than one sub making trips between the Bunker and the surface.

So Anji had waited some more, tucking herself into a hidey-hole between a large sheet of metal and a wall. Some derelict had lived here recently, and in the heat the smell was intense, but nonetheless Anji remained out of sight. From where she stooped, she could make out the TARDIS further down the Pier. If the Doctor came to visit his ship, Anji didn't want to be spotted.

Eventually, Silver did return. Anji waited for Fitz to leave – she didn't want to have to explain her presence to him – and then scurried out of her hiding place, running towards Silver. Naturally, his heightened senses registered her presence, and he turned to greet Anji, a quizzical expression on the human side of his face.

'I was wondering when I could next see Dave,' said Anji, slightly out of breath. Her hair had become clogged with sweat in the sun, and she nervously tucked it behind her ears, painfully aware that her request hadn't come across as the casual enquiry it should have been.

Silver, perhaps surprisingly, didn't question her barely concealed urgency.

'Then you have picked the perfect time,' he replied, a smile on his face. 'I was just about to return to the Bunker to inspect my work there. Would you care to accompany me?' He offered his arm to Anji.

Like the reluctant participant in an illicit affair, fearful of who might be watching, Anji nervously took Silver's arm, allowing herself to be walked to the submarine.

Fitz, in far too much of a hurry, ran into the Silver Palace, slipped and nearly fell flat on his arse. He swore as he skidded, trying to regain his balance. He only succeeded in righting himself when a steadying hand clasped around his arm, keeping him upright.

'Where are you going in such a rush?' asked the Doctor, letting

Fitz stand unassisted.

'I was trying to find you,' said Fitz, straightening his sleeve as if tweaking out the folds in his crumpled dignity. 'What is this stuff?' he asked, pointing to the pool of liquid he had slipped in.

'Oh, Silver's staff have been moving equipment out of the labs here all day,' said the Doctor.

'Yeah,' said Fitz. 'He's moving all his operations down to the Bunker.'

The Doctor made a thoughtful sound, pacing the hall. 'I don't like the sound of that. You know, I don't think Silver can be trusted.' He suddenly stopped in his tracks, looking at Fitz eagerly. 'Anyway, you were looking for me. Any particular reason?'

'I wanted to tell you that Silver couldn't be trusted,' said Fitz, aware that his thunder had been stolen. 'I meant to tell you last night, but I never got chance, and this morning... well, I was out of here before I had time to even wake up.' Fitz told the Doctor the whole story of his exploration of the tunnels, about the mutated results of Silver's experiments, and about Silver's dictatorial approach to the people of Persistence.

'How unpleasant,' said the Doctor, once Fitz had finished speaking. 'Clearly we have underestimated the depths to which Silver might sink, and the heights to which he aspires. There's only one honourable thing we can do.' He paused for effect. 'Let's break into his office and rifle through his personal belongings.'

Within minutes of declaring his criminal intentions, the Doctor had led Fitz to the door of Silver's office.

'I'm hoping,' said the Doctor, carefully turning the handle on Silver's door, 'that Silver is arrogant enough to allow fear alone to protect his chambers.' As if to prove this, the door opened at his touch. The Doctor cautiously led the way into Silver's office.

'Don't touch anything,' the Doctor told Fitz. 'Silver may not have put any security devices on the door, but you can bet he will have been more careful with his more precious possessions.'

'OK,' said Fitz. 'I'll just admire the view.' It was a real Bond villain's office, all wood-effect panelling and sleek lines. The highlight of the room was the large desk, with the swivel chair allowing Silver to whirl around and look out over the whole of Hope. A real megalomaniac's set up, allowing him a panoramic view of his domain.

'Locked,' muttered the Doctor, examining the desk drawers. He then looked at the bookshelf, where the heavy leather volumes were locked behind glass. 'Alarm,' he said to himself, running his fingers down the frame of the door that slid over the shelves.

'Keeps things pretty tight, doesn't he?' said Fitz. There was nothing on Silver's desk except some kind of chunky control box, and three slim pens.

'Do you think this unlocks anything?' asked Fitz, peering closely at the control box but, following the Doctor's instructions, not daring to touch.

The Doctor abandoned his attempts to disable the alarm mechanism, and joined Fitz in staring at the control. 'It doesn't appear to have anywhere to enter a code,' said the Doctor. 'Let's see now.' He reached across, his finger hovering over the buttons, tensing like a man forced to choose between cutting the blue wire and the red. 'This one,' he said, prodding a button at random.

Both the Doctor and Fitz backed away as the window behind them turned opaque, plunging them into darkness. In the centre of the room a swirl of light appeared, and Fitz braced himself for some kind of horrendous laser attack.

Instead, the light spiralled out to coalesce into a number of spheres in the centre of the room. Names and numbers floated around in midair, marking out each of the spheres.

'Fascinating,' said the Doctor, casting away caution and walking into the centre of the hologram. 'This is a galactic map noting places of interest. Look, here's Endpoint and its sun, complete with the cloud of debris that isolates it from the rest of the universe.' He pointed to two spheres within a miasma of fragments. 'The level of detail here is really astonishing. The planets are rated on a number of statistical bases. This one has a very high rating on all counts – it's a centre of imperial power, with a healthy ecosphere and good prospects. This poor little world, on the other hand, is completely dead, a graveyard planet.' The Doctor prodded the holographic planet with his finger, and the name A2756 and a string of co-ordinates appeared. The Doctor read them closely before proceeding with his lecture. 'The most notable aspect of this map is that both planets seem only an arm's length apart.' The Doctor sighed. 'Prosperity and devastation, so close together. Some things never change.'

Fitz watched the Doctor as he stood, silent, among the hologram stars. It was as if he were at peace, as if he felt at home standing taller than worlds, able to snuff out suns with his hands.

'You know, I was sent to lock this place up,' said a familiar female voice. 'Guess I'm too late for that.'

'Miraso,' said the Doctor, turning around. Star systems were disrupted briefly as his coat tails flapped through them. 'Have you seen this map before?'

'No,' she said, thoughts of security clearly forgotten. 'This might be new. It's hard to tell.'

'I think this was the most recent thing Silver consulted,' said the Doctor. 'Now, considering his current ambitious state of mind, why do you think that might be?'

'He wants to take it all over,' said Miraso, stepping between the stars. The Doctor backed away to make space for her. 'Silver has never had the chance to expand his influence, now he wants to make up for it. I don't know whether he's mad to want to rule the galaxy, or that I'm mad to think he might be able to pull it off.'

The Doctor sat on the edge of Silver's great desk. 'And where do you stand on this?' he asked politely. 'Do you want to be Deputy Dictator of the Universe?'

Miraso stood amongst the stars for a while, not answering.

'No,' she said eventually. 'Keeping order here was one thing, but now Silver is throwing away everything we built. I don't know what he wants to do next, but I know there isn't room for people like me in his plans. What do we do?'

The Doctor pushed a button on the control, and the starfield disappeared, light flooding back through the window. 'Silver has access to all the technology of the Endpointers and humanity,' said the Doctor. 'He's an expert in genetic experimentation with a penchant for radical, brutal tests, and down in that bunker he has a whole army of frozen humans as test subjects. Whatever he is up to down there, we need to get in and stop him.'

'Well,' said Miraso solemnly, unhappy about the inevitability of betraying her former leader. 'I guess I'll be giving you a lift, then.'

The Bunker seemed like a different place. Not as radical a transition as that which had occurred on the surface – the change was one of mood rather than environment – but a tangible change nonetheless.

As above, so below, thought Anji.

Since her previous visit, which Anji had to remind herself had been less than a day before, the Bunker had gone from being an echoing, empty space, to being more organised, closer to a military base. Boxes of equipment littered every available space.

'I see you've moved in,' she said to Silver, her voice more nervous than she would have liked.

'This will be my base of operations now, yes,' replied Silver. 'The facilities here are more suitable for my purposes than those on the surface.'

And more easy to cover up, thought a rebellious part of Anji's brain. She quickly suppressed the rogue thought. Paranoia would get her nowhere. Silver led the way to the laboratories where she had left Dave II. Anji wandered along in his wake, weaving around crates and stepping over cables. A thick, clear pipe snaked down the corridor, a viscous, shining fluid flowing through it. Anji had to step over the pipe a number of times, worried that the liquid within might be toxic if she punctured the pipe with her heel.

Eventually they reached their destination. Silver paused at the doorway, asking if Anji was ready. She nodded nervously in reply.

Silver opened the door, letting Anji through. As she entered the lab, her attention instantly turned to the tank she had been examining the previous day. Then, Dave II had barely constituted a foetus.

Now, the tank contained a full-grown man. Anji speechlessly stepped forward, the enormity of what she had done sinking in. Eyes closed, suspended in fluid, was the man she had loved and lost.

Fitz had never met anyone as clueless as Richard. The human scientist was so naive, so sheltered that his version of the Nuremberg defence – the fact that he participated in the culling and testing of live subjects because that was what he was told to do and he knew no better – became strangely convincing. Born as humanity was in retreat, confined to its fleet, then frozen for centuries only to be trapped in the Bunker once awoken – perhaps it was no wonder that Richard seemed to lack common sense, to believe whatever he was told. Perhaps it was the only way he could function in a world that made no sense to him, an environment where one day he was performing experiments in an undersea laboratory, the next he was performing errands for a cyborg in a surface world he had never seen before. The orders and the people giving them changed, and the only way to cope was just to follow the most recent order.

For the purposes of Fitz, Miraso and the Doctor this naivety was perfect. Miraso gave Richard a phoney reason for why Fitz and the Doctor were accompanying them down to the Bunker, and Richard accepted it. Miraso gave Richard a reason for why they should go early, abandoning much of the equipment Silver had ordered to be transported, and Richard accepted that too. Fitz feared that when the poor boy finally got around to thinking for himself, the pressure would crack him open.

The Doctor had insisted they leave the surface quickly, find out what Silver was up to in the Bunker and stop it. Fitz had made a brief search for Anji, but had failed to find her before it was time to go. Fitz supposed there was little chance of her coming to harm wherever she was, and so left the sun-kissed surface behind to take his first actual undersea journey in the submarines. Fitz had felt a pressure build in his head as the sub had descended further and further, his stomach feeling increasingly nauseous.

The Doctor and Miraso did nothing to alleviate his discomfort, or even distract him from it. They sat on the hard benches in one of the sub's cramped living areas, absorbed in their own thoughts. Cheery company, guys, thought Fitz. Thanks a lot for your support.

The airlock on their way into the Bunker was more advanced than most – some form of scan occurred, and Fitz felt as if his skin was being picked at on an atomic level as a yellow light swept over him. The Doctor explained that this procedure protected the humans from any viruses or infections in the outside world, their long isolation having crippled their immune systems' capabilities. All the same, the sensation was distinctly unpleasant.

Miraso, as the one member of their party with a legitimate reason to be in the Bunker, led the way as they left the airlock. Their caution was unwarranted; no one seemed to notice their presence, although one human did nip past them to get into the sub, eager to see what goodies Richard had brought from the surface.

'What are we looking for?' asked Fitz.

'Anything unusual,' replied the Doctor.

Fitz and Miraso glanced at each other. They both thought the same thing, but Fitz was the one to point it out to the Doctor.

'But we haven't been here before,' said Fitz. 'How do we know what's unusual?'

The Doctor looked Fitz straight in the eye. 'Fitz, I trust your sense of what is right.' He turned to Miraso. 'And I'm sure that your years of managing security at the Palace have given you good instincts for detecting something wrong, something out of place. We're looking for something bad, some evidence of Silver misusing the technology here. I don't think whatever we find is going to be subtle enough to miss.'

'Well, if this place is ever attacked, Silver is certainly prepared for them,' said Miraso, walking over to a crate, one of many untidily piled around the corridor. She reached into the crate and picked out a small, dark blue disc. 'Low range mines. Extremely focused blast area.'

'Nonetheless, in this environment they can be highly destructive,' said the Doctor tersely, snatching the mine from Miraso and sliding it back into the crate. 'These are not to be played with, especially not when one rupture could bring the sea down on us. Don't forget we're not just dealing with our lives, but those of all the surviving members of the human race.'

'Thank you for the lecture, Doctor,' said Miraso dryly. 'Can we return to what we came here for?'

'No need,' whispered the Doctor. 'I think we've found it.' He pointed down the corridor. Fitz and Miraso followed his finger to a turning, where a thick pipe snaked around the corner. It seemed initially unremarkable, but as they approached they could make out the thick, shining liquid within the transparent pipe. It seemed to pulse with a life of its own – was it being pumped through the pipe, or moving of its own accord?

'What is it?' asked Fitz.

The Doctor ignored him. 'Where does this lead, I wonder?' His eyes followed the pipe down the corridor, and then widened suddenly. 'Oh, no. We need to find the source of this and stop it.' The Doctor started running down the corridor, following the pipe in the reverse direction to the flow. Miraso and Fitz ran to keep up. They passed a few curious Endpointers and humans, and Miraso nodded in their direction, trying to distract from the incongruity of what they were doing. Surely Silver would know they were here by now, anyway?

The Doctor kicked open the door at the end of the pipeline, and Fitz followed him into a room with a mass of equipment in the centre. To Fitz it looked like an advanced form of brewery – pipes, barrels, lots of frothing. The one additional detail was the computer banks manned by a handful of human scientists.

Miraso clapped her hands together as she entered the room. 'This is the Doctor, Mr Silver's Chief Scientist from the surface. Mr Silver wishes him to perform an inspection on the…' – Miraso struggled to find an appropriate word – '…the equipment. He will need time to do this inspection, so you will now be relieved for a rest break. Please return to your work in one hour.'

Looking suspiciously at the Doctor, the humans shuffled out of the room. Miraso closed the door behind them. She leaned back on the door with a sigh of relief.

'Well done,' said the Doctor. 'Now we need to put this out of action. Fitz, pass me –'

He was interrupted by the door Miraso was leaning against being flung open, throwing Miraso across the room. Fitz saw her tumble gracefully, landing back on her feet. He tried to turn around, to see what was happening behind him, but all he saw was a rush of silver as something very fast and very hard hit him in the nose, sending him flying across the room, landing flat on his back. The room swayed giddily. Were there really figures scurrying all around him? He heard the Doctor let out a yelp of pain, protests from Miraso.

'Protect the central supply!' barked an unfamiliar voice, a cold metallic tone to the words. Fitz tried to get up again, but was kicked in the chin so hard and fast that he fell flat on his back before he could even glimpse his attackers. A glutton for punishment, Fitz once more tried to push himself up on to his elbows. Before he could see anything he found himself knocked back as Miraso was thrown on top of him.

'Assailants neutralised. The central supply is protected.' Buried beneath Miraso, who seemed to have been knocked unconscious, Fitz groaned. They had been beaten into the ground by someone he couldn't even see, over a machine the Doctor hadn't even explained the purpose of. Fitz found himself having a slight existential crisis over this as he slipped out of consciousness.

Anji had spent a good couple of hours watching Dave II. Occasionally he twitched in his sleep, a little kick in his artificial womb. The scientists told her that these were reactions to his dreams, the artificially induced thoughts that would allow him to step out into the world with the knowledge to survive in it. Anji half-listened to what the scientists told her, entranced by a vision of a man she had seen die before her. There were differences –

the hair was even, uncut. The muscles were toned where the original Dave had barely exercised at all. But it was recognisably a new version of the same man. A new iteration, version 2.0 of Dave Young. Dave II.

Anji didn't notice when the scientists left the room, or when Silver entered, so entranced was she just watching this new Dave. Even though he was perfectly still, she couldn't take her eyes off him.

'You're perfect,' she said, touching the glass.

'Not quite,' said Silver, startling her. 'But he is a fine specimen of pre-lapsarian humanity, before their gradual decline into an irrelevant species. With this control sample we are hoping to restore some genetic diversity to the human species.'

'He's more than just a sample,' said Anji. She didn't like the turn this conversation was taking.

Silver shook his head. 'He is merely human, in spite of being such a good specimen. We'll keep him here for study purposes, but otherwise the future belongs to others.'

'Others?' asked Anji, backing away at the same pace as Silver advanced on her.

'Others,' echoed Silver, clicking his fingers.

The people who entered the room were of a kind Anji had never seen before. They walked in with mechanical efficiency and great speed, filling the room in seconds. They had human features, human hair, human bodies. But their skin had a silvery, shining quality, their eyes were deep black – although Anji could swear she saw a flare of red deep within those dark eyes. They surrounded Anji, waiting for Silver's instructions.

'I'm afraid there isn't going to be a touching reunion with your lost beloved,' said Silver. 'There will be no more human love affairs, no more humans. Where once there was humanity, where once there were Endpointers, now there will be a new faction.' He made a wide gesture, indicating the room full of almost humans.

'Soon there will be only Silverati. My new race. My followers.' He paused, as if drinking in the presence of the Silverati. 'My children,' he said, with a passion she had never heard in him before.

Anji had been scared by hate before, many times. But she had never before been scared by love.

Chapter Fifteen
Same Old Brand New You

'There's no delicate way to put this,' said Silver. 'Your lover is nothing more than genetic material for my experiments. Your friends have been captured, trying and failing to sabotage my plans. Three dozen of your species have been converted into Silverati, enhanced by Kallisti and my own liquid intelligence into semi-synthetic organisms capable of more than you can possibly imagine. The rest will follow in their footsteps. But before then, you and your friends will undergo a similar conversion. It would be safer to kill you all now, but I cannot allow whatever knowledge lies within you three to go to waste. Soon you will follow me, like all the rest.'

'Why are you telling me this?' asked Anji, shuddering as she backed away from Silver. She could feel the cold of Dave's tank behind her.

'Because I owe you at least that,' said Silver apologetically, stepping slowly towards her. 'You have given me the data to facilitate time travel, once the results have been analysed. And while I have fulfilled my side of our deal and returned your lover to you, I do realise that my current actions may seem less than honourable.'

Anji was now backed into a corner, and could not escape when Silver walked up to her, lifting her chin with his strong hand, looking into her eyes.

'I wish we could still be friends, Anji, but your colleagues have already attempted one attack on my plans.' He let her chin drop, and walked away. 'Take her to the holding room. Lock them up and make sure there are no escape routes.'

Two of the Silverati dragged Anji away, their skin cold on hers.

'And make sure the Doctor is thoroughly searched,' barked Silver. 'Make sure he has nothing on his person to allow his escape.'

Anji could barely hold in the tears. She had betrayed her friend, and all for nothing. She allowed herself to be taken away with little resistance. It was time for her to face the Doctor.

'What the hell were those?' asked Fitz. He and the Doctor had been separated from Miraso, locked in a featureless room behind a very heavy door. Although bare, the room was large, and Fitz paced as he talked.

'They were humans,' said the Doctor. 'At least, they once were. Silver has managed to synthesise Kallisti, the substance which allowed the Endpointers to survive in such extreme conditions for so long. But he hasn't just synthesised that, he has blended it with the liquid intelligence which flows through his own brain. The result is a synthetic, intelligent chemical that permeates every part of the body. And he has clearly been pumping this miracle substance into the bloodstreams of the humans cryogenically preserved here.'

'Turning them into those things,' said Fitz, aghast. There had, he supposed, been something sleek and beautiful about the silver-skinned people who had dragged them to this makeshift cell. But there was also a coldness there, an absence of those gestures that betray human qualities. It was as if they never twitched, or itched, or ached; never shuffled uncertainly, or flinched, or shivered.

'Precisely,' said the Doctor. Fitz had come to a halt, and now the Doctor began to pace. 'Those humans have been changed, their bodies and minds have been resculpted by this substance, turning them into something other than human. You saw how fast they moved, the deadness in their eyes. Those aren't people any more, they're semi-organic machines. Ruthless, efficient.'

'Just like Silver,' said Fitz.

'Yes, just like him. I suppose he thinks of them as his children,' whispered the Doctor, clearly horrified by the thought. 'And after converting humanity, why should he stop there? He's mixed highly advanced alien technologies to create that substance, I'll bet it's smart and adaptable enough to graft itself on to any living thing. The Endpointers will be next. And if he can find a way off world, I'm sure Silver will spread his touch through the galaxy. He could infect water supplies, or spread it through the air. Whole worlds could fall to Silver before they even realise they're under attack.'

'We have to stop him,' said Fitz.

'Quite right,' said the Doctor. 'Well, at least Anji is out and about, but we can't wait for her to free us. Fitz, give me –'

Yet again the Doctor was interrupted as the door opened. But, instead of Silver come to interrogate them, or an execution squad, the Doctor and Fitz were surprised to see Anji being pushed into the room.

They stood in silence for a few stunned seconds.

'I suppose I have some explaining to do,' said Anji.

The silver-skinned men and women had rained blows down on the Doctor, Miraso and Fitz, until they showed no sign of resistance. Then they had been dragged apart, the Doctor and Fitz being taken in the opposite direction to Miraso. She had been carried along by strong hands, too stunned to walk on her own. Carried between these strange humanoids with their shining skin, Miraso had noted the resemblance to those failed experiments of Silver's, the misshapen creatures with their similarly tinted skin. If these were the results of Silver's latest experiment, then clearly he had become more successful in his work. These people were strong, fast, lethal. No wonder the likes of Miraso had become a disposable resource. They guarded over her, impassive, totally still. She had tried to move away a couple of times, and they had blocked her path with startling fluidity and grace, only to become still once more.

Eventually, Silver arrived, and they stepped back to let him through.

'I don't have time to deal with you now,' Silver said, marching towards her. As he approached, his servants backed completely away, leaving Miraso to stand, shakily, on her own two feet. She forced herself to stay upright. It was a wasted effort, as Silver grabbed her by the lapels of her jacket, slamming her up against the wall. She couldn't help noticing that she was being lifted by Silver's human arm, that he wasn't even using his *strong* arm to lift her.

'When there's something that needs to be done later, many people put notes on a pinboard,' Silver said, conversationally. The anger seeped into his voice, a sign of emotion he rarely allowed to become visible. 'The same principle applies here.'

Miraso struggled under Silver's grip as she realised what he had in mind. Her eyes widened as he raised his robotic hand, the hand that held the viciously pointed rod of metal. When the spike went through her shoulder, pinning her to the wall, she had cried out, her scream echoing down the empty corridor. Silver turned and walked away. He didn't look back, and neither did his creatures as they followed their master.

Miraso was left hanging there, a metal rod pinning her to the wall. Left to feel the cost of betraying Silver. She was uncertain whether being left alone was a good or a bad thing, but there was one thing that, even in her current irrational state, she was fully aware of: Silver was going to come back for her. And whatever happened to her then, it would make her current misery seem mild by comparison.

Fitz had listened in growing horror as Anji had explained what had happened. He had gradually retreated into the corner of the room as Anji had described her deal with Silver, and betraying of the Doctor to fulfil her side of the bargain. Fitz looked nervously across at the Doctor, whose expression had darkened considerably. This was going to be a rough one.

'Well, I think you've excelled yourself,' said the Doctor slowly. He was being very careful with every word, twisting each barb. This acidic, imperious side to the Doctor's character was one Fitz was very glad he rarely had to see. 'You've betrayed me, you've given the secrets of time travel to a man who is determined to mutate and corrupt your entire race. Oh, and you've done all this in an attempt to reverse death. In terms of things not to do, that's a pretty clean sweep.'

'I'm sorry, Doctor,' said Anji, slumped and tearful. 'But I had to do it. I had to do it for Dave.'

'Dave is dead,' said the Doctor, more sympathetic now. 'People die, Anji. We can't start reversing death at whim. Some things are not for us to interfere with.'

Fitz noticed the tide turn before the Doctor did, the flare of defiance in Anji's eyes as they sprung up, fixing themselves on the Doctor. When she spoke, the tone of conciliation had gone.

'Since when?' replied Anji bluntly. 'Death isn't a constant, it hasn't been for a while. Those kids on Ceres Alpha, I saw them die and come back. I pretty much died myself there. I've seen you walk through lethal situations dozens of times, and come out with barely a scratch. You were dying for months, but you pulled through. How come you're allowed to cheat death, but everyone else has to play by the rules? You're supposed to have forged a link with Earth, with humanity, yet you still look down from your immortal status and tell us when we can and can't die. Well I'm sick of it.'

'I can die!' exclaimed the Doctor. 'Surely my illness showed that. I risk my life every day, and there are no guarantees I'll survive, certainly not now. All I can do is keep going, try to help people. I have no idea whether I'll live forever, or a normal human lifespan, or whether my remaining heart will fail and I'll drop dead tomorrow. There are no guarantees, Anji, not for any of us. But when we die, we die.'

'Then why save anybody?' snapped Anji, spreading her arms in a wild, exasperated gesture. 'We spend all our time saving others, risking our own lives constantly to try to help people we don't know, but if what you say is true then why should we help them at all? Because Dave is just like them – he didn't die in an accident, or in bed, or in any human, reasonable way I can relate to. He was another victim of alien forces, like all those other

216

people we help. If I can help them, then why can't I save someone I care about for once? Dave was an innocent, more innocent than most of the people we help, and he died because of some *stupid* alien conflict that was nothing to do with him. It was wrong that he died, and I was given a chance to put that right. I took that chance, and I don't see why the hell I should apologise for it.'

'You really did think this all through, didn't you?' said the Doctor quietly.

'Of course,' said Anji. 'That's who I am. Did you think I would betray your trust lightly?'

The Doctor shook his head. 'No, I should have realised you had good reasons.' He smiled sadly. 'All we can do is act on what we think is right. That's what you do, that's what I do. The fact that we've made different decisions shouldn't be an issue.'

'I'm sorry I betrayed you,' said Anji. 'But my first loyalty had to be to Dave. It was a risk trusting Silver, and it's all gone wrong. But I did what I had to do.'

'I know,' said the Doctor. 'I would probably have done much the same in your position.' He suddenly clapped his hands together, shocking his human friends. 'Now, we need to stop Silver from using the secrets of the TARDIS, protect this new Dave and save humanity from becoming these... things.'

'Silver calls them the Silverati,' said Anji. 'Presumably to indicate they follow after him. I think he's sick of being the only one like him.'

'A common enough urge,' said the Doctor. 'But Silverati? How pretentious.' The Doctor shook his head wearily. 'Anyway, whatever they're called they need to be stopped. Where do we start?'

Fitz jumped to his feet. 'By getting out of here?' he suggested with a grin.

The Doctor beamed back. 'Exactly.'

Anji found herself grinning in spite of herself. 'And you have a devious and subtle plan, of course?'

'Of course,' said the Doctor. 'Fitz, could you carefully reach into your right-hand coat pocket. And don't press any buttons you find.'

Fitz, confused, reached into his pocket. With a startled expression he pulled out a dark blue disc.

'It's that mine thingy,' said Fitz, carefully passing it to the Doctor. 'I thought you...'

'Put it back in the box?' finished the Doctor. 'Yes, well, I didn't want Miraso throwing them around but I wanted one handy. And I knew Silver was more likely to check myself and Miraso for weapons, so where better to hide it than your pocket?'

'Explosives? It's not very subtle, is it?' said Anji.

'No,' admitted the Doctor. 'I lied about the plan being subtle. Oh, and about it being devious.' He ran his finger around the top edge of the mine, and it lit up. 'But sometimes, you just have to take the direct approach.' He squeezed a button on the top of the mine and threw it at the door where it clamped itself in place with a faint sucking sound.

'Now,' said the Doctor, putting his arms around Fitz and Anji's shoulders and dragging them away from the door. 'This might be quite loud...'

For the vastly ambitious, even a whole world can seem like a cage.

For Silver, control of Endpoint was nothing. He had manipulated and dominated the planet's economy, its politics, its society for so long that the official seizure of power was nothing but an acknowledgement of the inevitable. Controlling by stealth had been a game, one which had occupied his time when he was without wider options. Now his options had expanded, and the time for games was over. Endpoint was his. The last dregs of humanity were becoming the first generation of a new species, the progeny his unique nature had denied him. The Silverati. Although there were only three dozen of them so far, a prototype batch, Silver was pleased with his creations so far.

He had blessed these offspring of his with all his finest qualities. They closely resembled humans, but all their physical attributes were artificially enhanced. They were fast, strong, with mathematically precise reaction times. While they could still feel

218

pain, their resistance was stronger than any human. But most importantly of all, while their bodies were still predominantly human, their minds were dominated by the liquid machinery that permeated their brains. The Silverati's planning and reasoning were way beyond human capabilities. They were children after his own artificial heart, one foot in their own internal worlds of data. While they were not telepathic, they could communicate through the smallest gesture, with the familiarity of brothers. And they would be a family loyal to their father, subservience hard-wired into their programming. They would be an army that would never falter, servants who would never hesitate.

With the Silverati at his side, and Endpoint under his control, now was the time to expand, to step beyond his comfortable home and into the wider universe.

'How long until full power?' Silver asked impatiently. He paced the Hypertunnel chamber like a caged beast waiting for an opportunity to escape. Rich opportunities for conquest lay just out of his reach. The freedom he had been denied for so long. No more easy victories, no more casual manipulations. The Hypertunnel was his door to a universe of challenges and enemies. Out there, conquests would be hard won, power would have to be seized through strength and strategy.

'The Hypertunnel should be operational within the hour,' said one of his Silverati. Silver nodded for him to proceed with his work.

The Hypertunnel equipment was ugly – concentric rings of blocky nodes and transmitters protruding from one wall of the chamber. Together they produced the interlocking energy fields that allowed the Hypertunnel to form and be contained. On the opposite side of the room were the banks of computers and generators necessary to power the device. Silverati moved across this area, checking and rechecking the equipment, performing maintenance where necessary. They were swift and efficient in their work, as their creator intended them to be.

Ironically, their creator was not currently capable of that kind of focus. He paced the wide area between the inactive Hypertunnel and the control area, hungry for his freedom.

* * *

Two Silverati guarded the rogue humans. They stood in front of the heavily-bolted door, weapons raised. If there was any sign of a break-out, they were instructed to shoot on sight. One of these Silverati was called Joshua Kent.

Kent had been a computer technician in his previous life, before he had been put into suspension. He had been caring and considerate, an inoffensive person who meant no harm. A warm man among the cold machines. He had loved, but had never really been loved back. On some level he had known that his failure in such personal matters had been due to his sheer lack of will – he had never pushed himself forward, never held himself high, never shown the confidence himself that inspired confidence in others.

Now Kent was Silverati, and he had that confidence. His weak body had been made strong – there was a tension beneath his skin, muscles straining and capable of anything. Whereas before the world had swept passed him, now it registered as painfully slow to his enhanced senses. Whereas before he had stuttered and shuddered through life, now he could stand in perfect stillness, absorbed in his own internal thought processes yet having a complete overview of the world around him.

All the qualities his human self wished for, Kent now had. Ironically, though, his human ambitions, his desires for recognition and affection, were gone now. He wanted nothing more than to be. To exist, to be a Silverati, to follow Silver; these were enough to fulfil his life. To be a Silverati was far greater than being human. Where humans crawled, Silverati walked confidently. There was nothing beyond their capability. They knew this with the confidence and certainty that comes from hard-wired programming.

But programming can lie, and absolute certainty is the biggest lie of all.

Kent and the fellow Silverati beside him were prepared for any human attack. They were strong, they were fast. But they were not stronger than fragments of torn metal. They were not faster than shrapnel propelled by high explosive. And their instructions, to stay close to the chamber where the prisoners were kept, to remain ever vigilant, left them vulnerable.

The explosion ripped the bolted steel door to pieces, digging chunks out of the wall around it as its limited but powerful impact blasted outwards, shredding metal like tissue paper. The Silverati, who were only a couple of feet away from the door, only caught the edge of the blast, enough to knock them off their feet. But it wasn't the explosives that did the damage – it was the debris. Razor-sharp pieces of red-hot metal flew through the air, cutting and burning everything they touched. They didn't stand a chance.

Kent lay on his back, a fragment of the destroyed door embedded in his eye socket. A sheet of splintered metal had embedded itself in his gut. He couldn't feel his legs, and from the waist up all he could feel was pain. Smoke billowed out over him, and his surviving eye watered, blurring what was left of his vision. He had been a man once. Since waking as a Silverati, these things had been forgotten, but now they came flooding back. It was the sensory overload, the pain interfering and conflicting with his programming, causing logic errors and failures, allowing him to have thoughts he should never have had. The walls of certainty had fallen, and all Kent could think of was chaos. Confusion crippled him as much as his wounds. Human being or Silverati? The certainty of invulnerability versus the cold reality of the pain in his guts. He looked into the smoke, trying to discern meaning in the haze. He tried to pull himself on to his elbows, saw shapes moving in the smoke. Maybe it was his loss of vision, but these dark figures seemed to tower over him, gods drifting through the wreckage, untouched by the carnage.

The shapes coalesced into three human figures, two men and a woman. They walked out of the smoke with purpose, side by side, without fear. Kent, or whoever he was now, was in awe. He had thought himself invulnerable, but he had been wrong. These towering people had shown him different. He was at their feet, where he belonged.

The man with the longer, curlier hair turned to Kent, and in his eyes there was a sense of purpose. Where he went there would be more explosions. Nothing would stand in his way.

'Where's Silver?' asked the Doctor.

Chapter Sixteen
Closure

'"The heart of the empire lay in the great furnace cities of the southern region",' read Silver, a history book open in his steel palm. His audience was the Silverati working on the Hypertunnel. They showed no visible signs of listening, but he knew their multi-tasked sensors would be absorbing his words. '"The great smoke stacks of these cities were visible from hundreds of miles away, and the factories in the cities produced weaponry and vital supplies not just for the Imperial Throneworld, but for all the colonies and outposts touched by the empire's lash."'

Silver closed the book, and began to pace in front of the Hypertunnel.

'The largest of these furnace cities must be the first point of our attack,' he said, as much to himself as to the Silverati. 'With all those industrial resources converted by Kallisti...'

Silver trailed off in mid-sentence, absorbed in visions of his own power. He stood, still and silent, the work progressing around him, enraptured in his own ambition.

'Hypertunnel,' said the wounded Silverati through blood-flecked lips. Fitz felt ill watching the dying man struggle with his words.

The Doctor was aghast. 'Silver has a Hypertunnel?'

The one eyed Silverati nodded.

'Thank you,' said the Doctor grimly. He reached down, and with one swift tug, extracted the fragment of metal from the Silverati's eye socket. The Silverati wailed in agony.

'You'll heal,' said the Doctor firmly, stepping away. 'You'll be back to normal within the hour. When you're back on your feet, start running. I don't want to see you again.'

'Are you certain they'll be OK?' asked Anji as she followed in the Doctor's wake. She was flicking glances back at the two Silverati, sprawled among the wreckage. To her untrained eye they seemed severely injured.

'Absolutely certain,' said the Doctor. 'They have machine colonies in their blood which will rebuild their bodies. And we have more pressing concerns to worry about.' He stopped in his tracks, spinning around to face Fitz and Anji. 'It will take all of our wits to avert total disaster. If any one of us fails, we all fail. I need you to follow my instructions carefully, and stay alert.'

Fitz and Anji nodded, and the Doctor continued to lead the way. They soon found Miraso. She had been pinned to the wall by a metal bolt through the shoulder. The Doctor didn't hesitate – he pulled the bar clean out of the wall, catching Miraso before she could hit the ground. He indicated for Fitz to help him with the woman. Miraso mumbled to herself.

'Pass me that medical pack,' the Doctor instructed Fitz, pointing to a metal box attached to the wall.

Fitz took the box off its hook and passed it to the Doctor, who clicked it open. Inside were slightly more sophisticated versions of what Anji would expect from a first aid kit.

'Perfect,' said the Doctor, spraying foam over Miraso's wounds. The fluffy substance seemed to sink into the flesh, virtually disappearing. The Doctor lifted Miraso up, sliding his hand under her back to place a round pad over the exit wound, then pressed another of the pads on the wound on her chest. 'That should seal it up and prevent any infection. Now, if I just give her a little shot to bring her round.'

The Doctor removed a black cylinder from the medical pack, and tapped it against his sleeve a couple of times. He then pressed it to Miraso's neck, and there was a slight pneumatic hiss as it injected something into her vein.

'Stimulant injection,' explained the Doctor, diligently returning the medical pack to its place on the wall, while Fitz took hold of Miraso, supporting her head. She stirred in Fitz's arms, eyes flickering open.

'In a few minutes she should be ready to walk,' said the Doctor. 'As soon as she's up and about, I want the two of you to secure one of the submarines. We may need a very quick exit if the Hypertunnel collapses.'

Fitz nodded.

'And what are you and I going to do?' asked Anji.

'We are going to wake the dead!' said the Doctor, already halfway down the corridor. Anji had to break into a run to keep up.

'This time we bolt the door,' said the Doctor as Anji followed him into a room full of laboratory equipment, with a large cluster of casks and pipes in the centre. 'Looks like no one got around to telling the scientists to come back,' he added, picking up a spare length of pipe from a stack in the corner and jamming it through the door handles.

'What are we doing here?' asked Anji. 'And what's all this crap?' She nodded to the mass of pipes and barrels in the centre of the room. A thick pipe full of silvery liquid came out of the mass of the equipment, and disappeared through a hole in the wall.

'This is where Silver produces his synthesised version of Kallisti,' said the Doctor, sitting down at a computer console on the far side of the room. 'He's recreated this remarkable substance by merging it with a self-replicating liquid intelligence. The result is those – what did you call them? – those Silverati who captured us earlier.'

'Shouldn't we cut off the pipeline?' said Anji.

'Well, I tried to do that earlier,' said the Doctor. 'And this time I intend to succeed. But first I need a sample, with a few little amendments.' He was frantically typing, and incomprehensible strings of digits sped across the screens in front of him. 'I'm going to reprogram this liquid intelligence so that it degrades within a day, and just to be on the safe side I'm going to alter the command subroutines. Silver has knocked this set up together, by stealth, in a couple of days. The command structure must be relatively simple. Aha!' The Doctor made a few more delighted noises as he typed, editing the information on screen. 'Gotcha,' he said triumphantly, jumping to his feet.

'There, that should do the trick,' said the Doctor. 'Anyone injected with this Kallisti will bear all the physical hallmarks of a Silverati, but retain human personality traits. What's more, I've added a degrading element to the substance, which will cause anyone infected to revert to human normal within a day. Oh, and just to be on the safe side, there's a short term protocol to help the both of us with any requests.'

'Wonderful,' said Anji. 'But what's the point if we're blowing this place up anyway?'

'Well, this sample is for the next stage in my plan,' said the Doctor with a sigh. 'Which, I'm afraid, you may not like very much.'

As the Doctor spoke, he extracted a sample of the new Kallisti from the machine. He trapped the sample in a test tube, and waggled it under the light as if he could read the code he had programmed into it.

'Why won't I like this?' asked Anji apprehensively. 'What are you up to now?'

'We need someone to "go Silver", so to speak, to go undercover as a Silverati and sabotage Silver's plans,' said the Doctor, sliding the test tube into his pocket. 'And unfortunately there's only one obvious candidate.'

The Doctor picked up a microblade, and waggled it around in a couple of sockets. He then spun the blade between his fingers and slipped it into his pocket.

'What candidate?' asked Anji. She had a horrible feeling where this conversation was going, and was about to protest when the Doctor put a finger to her lips.

'Not just now,' cautioned the Doctor. 'I've just shorted the power relays. This whole room is about to explode into a fireball.' He walked across to the door, pulling the bar out from between the handles. 'I suggest we retire to a safe distance before having any arguments.'

* * *

Richard was walking back to one of his old labs – which felt like a nostalgia trip, even though he had barely been away for a day – when two figures jumped out of the shadows, grabbing him and bundling him into a cupboard. He tried to squeal, but a hand was clamped over his mouth. The cupboard was dark, and whoever had seized him was close – he could feel himself pressed between two warm bodies. It wasn't an experience he was used to.

'Shhh!' hissed a familiar male voice. 'It's me, Fitz. Be quiet, we only want your help.'

Richard calmed down, and found the hand had gone from his mouth. It was still terribly dark, though.

'What do you want?' asked Richard.

'We need to secure one of the submarines,' said another voice that Richard recognised as Miraso. 'It may be necessary for us to make a quick exit. Can you help us?'

Richard sighed. He could feel himself about to agree, without the slightest idea why. He had a funny feeling that any attempt by him to understand what was going on would only confuse him further. Better just to get on with doing what he was told.

His resolve was cemented when he heard the explosion nearby. The Bunker didn't seem to be a safe place to stay.

The sound of the explosion reached the Hypertunnel chamber. The lights flickered, power threatening to cut out altogether.

'What was that?' Silver asked one of his Silverati, who calmly walked across to a control panel in the wall.

'Internal systems indicate power loss and a conflagration in one of the main laboratories,' said the Silverati.

'Which laboratory?' Silver asked.

'G,' came the reply.

Silver resisted a sudden urge to bite into his knuckle. Laboratory G was where the Kallisti synthesis was taking place. There could only be one person responsible for the disruption – the same man who had previously been caught trying to damage the equipment.

'The Doctor is free,' said Silver. 'And no doubt intent on

wreaking havoc here. No matter, this bunker is dispensable. Let the Doctor have his fun.'

Silver turned to the Silverati, who was waiting patiently for further instructions.

'Put out a general order,' snapped Silver. 'Have all Silverati report here. Let the Doctor have this bunker, let him have the laboratories and supplies. By the time he gains full control, we will be long gone.'

The Doctor held the test tube containing the sample – colony? – of his personalised Kallisti up to Anji's eye level. The silver liquid writhed in its confinement.

'I'll only do this if you let me,' he said quickly. 'I can't underestimate the importance of stopping Silver, but neither can I play down the dangers we're exposing Dave to. You're responsible for his welfare, Anji. The decision is yours.'

'If you say it's necessary, it's necessary,' said Anji, placing her hand on the Doctor's. 'I trust you. Do it.'

The Doctor smiled briefly, then rushed across the room to where Dave was suspended in liquid. The Doctor levered open a panel next to the cylinder containing Dave, and clicked the tube of Kallisti into place next to a row of similar tubes, all containing different coloured liquids. The Doctor then jumped across to the other side of the room, manipulating a set of controls and observing the results on a monitor screen.

'Right,' he said. 'Let's give this Dave a kick-start.' He suddenly paused, his finger raised above a button on the keyboard. 'Would you like to do the honours?' he asked Anji.

'OK,' she said nervously.

'Just press that button,' said the Doctor. 'That will trigger the revival process. The new Kallisti will be pumped through his body along with the other stimulants.'

'Here goes nothing,' said Anji, and pressed the button.

The process was a lot quicker than Anji expected. The liquid began to drain from Dave's tank at almost exactly the same time as he convulsed, stirring and twisting. When the liquid had fully drained, the front of the casing opened. The Doctor and Anji rushed forward to catch the naked man as he fell out of his artificial womb, newborn yet fully grown.

Anji shuddered as she held him, helping the Doctor to wrap a blanket around Dave's wet body. It was him, it really was. And he was here, breathing raggedly, blood pumping, alive in her arms.

'Anji,' the Doctor said firmly. 'I need you to keep yourself together. This must be very emotional for you, but we don't have time to crack up now.'

Anji nodded shakily. Dave rolled over on to his back, his eyes twitching under the lids. It was Dave, her Dave. She had brought him back to life.

She jumped as Dave convulsed, taking in a deep breath and arching his back. His eyes opened wide, his expression one of shock, as his eyes turned deep black. His skin took on an unnatural, silvery sheen. His muscles tensed. He exhaled, and the breath was cold like a gust of icy wind.

Anji backed away slightly. The Doctor put a finger to his lips, indicating she should keep quiet.

'Who are you?' the Doctor asked.

Dave croaked slightly, then spoke. The voice was that of the Dave that Anji knew, but the accent was completely different, closer to the people of Endpoint than anything from her time.

'My name's Dave II,' said Dave, pinching his nose.

'And who do you serve?' said the Doctor, tensing.

'I serve no one,' said Dave II. 'But I am to help the Doctor and Anji. My mission is to help them defeat Silver.'

The Doctor visibly relaxed. 'Excellent. Dave, you know your way around this bunker.'

'I have the knowledge you need,' said Dave II. He pulled himself into a squatting position, blinking. He looked at the Doctor. 'You're the Doctor. I'm supposed to help you.'

'Yes,' said the Doctor, smiling widely. 'Yes, you are. This is Anji.'

Dave turned to look at Anji. There was no recognition in his eyes.

'Hello Anji,' he said with clipped formality. 'I'm here to help.'

* * *

All but a handful of Silverati had gathered in the Hypertunnel chamber. Silver looked at them as they stood silently, waiting for his command – perfect sons and daughters, every one of them. Their pitch-black eyes looked to Silver and Silver alone for leadership, for inspiration. Their skins glimmered in the electric lighting of the cold chamber. They were creatures of myth, half gods, half men. Yet it was they who worshipped him.

Silver tried to think of something appropriate to say, over thirty pairs of eyes looking in his direction. For the first time, he found himself lost for words.

'If you think I'm letting you go in there alone…' Anji was almost speechless with fury. On some level she knew that her anger was a release valve, that she was redirecting the pent-up emotions caused by Dave's resurrection. Emotional confusion, boiled up and fired out as a simple, direct outburst against some poor third party. In this case, the Doctor, who was insisting she find Fitz and Miraso rather than go in with him and Dave.

'Anji,' said the Doctor. 'Listen to what you are saying, how you are saying it. That's anger, an emotion you're barely in control of right now. Silver has you riled. If you come in with us you'll be a danger to yourself, to me, and to Dave here. Feel that anger – that's why you can't come in with us. I need to stop Silver, and I need someone with Dave's in-built training to back me up.' He put his hand on her shoulder. 'You would be a passenger at your best, and I'm afraid you're not at your best. I need to know you're safe if something goes wrong.'

Anji shrugged his hand away from her shoulder but knew he was right. She looked at Dave II, who was standing back from the situation, muscular arms crossed over his chest. He was wearing a set of military fatigues they had found in a nearby locker, which only emphasised the differences between him and Dave I, her Dave. Dave II was a different man, a born fighter. There was a certainty in his stance that displayed confidence in himself, even though he had only emerged into the world twenty minutes before. In twenty-odd years her Dave had never gained that kind of confidence.

Different man, but with the same face. Her stomach fizzed at the thought of it, emotions churning through mind and body. How could she face Silver in this state? The Doctor needed someone to stay cool in the face of extreme danger. Anji could barely think straight with this walking anomaly nearby.

'OK,' she said to the Doctor. 'I'll go.'

'Thank you,' said the Doctor. 'I need you to look after something for me.' He took her hand, and pressed something into it. Anji looked down at her palm – it was the TARDIS key.

'You're trusting me with this?' she said, her voice sticking in her throat with emotion. 'Even after what I did?'

'We should never let betrayal destroy our capacity to trust,' said the Doctor, his blue eyes gleaming. 'If we do, then we're all lost. Take the key. Get Fitz away from here if something goes wrong.'

'I will. Thank you for trusting me again,' Anji said, before turning and walking away, trying not to look back.

At the end of the corridor she gave in, and turned around. But the Doctor and Dave had already gone. Keeping an eye open for Silverati, Anji began to make her way to the airlocks.

Dave knew what he had to do. Although his life had begun less than an hour ago, the knowledge installed in his brain gave him the abilities of a trained soldier. He adopted the confident gait of a Silverati and walked straight into the Hypertunnel room, proceeding to the nearest console. As he went he tried not to lose his nerve while surrounded by Silverati – they were everywhere, either working on the equipment, or standing perfectly still while looking to Silver for guidance. Dave looked at the console in front of him, trying to act like the enemy all around him. He examined the layout of the controls, then turned to the nearest Silverati.

'Have the navigation settings been entered correctly?' Dave asked. The Silverati had to turn to answer, allowing the Doctor to dart into the room unnoticed, ducking behind a crate. Dave tried not to look at the Doctor, and focused his attention on the Silverati.

The Silverati indicated a panel of controls manned by one of his fellows in the far corner of the room. 'They are being prepared now,' he said, then returned his attention to his work. Dave ticked a couple of things off his mental list: passed successfully for a Silverati, check; Doctor in chamber safely, check.

Dave was walking towards the navigation console when Silver strode up to it, brushing the Silverati aside and tapping in co-ordinates of his own. Dave instantly changed course, avoiding the cyborg and inspecting a different set of machinery. Not only was Silver an intimidating presence, but he had been involved in Dave's gestation. If he recognised Dave, then the mission was done for.

Richard gained them entry to the submarine. The rest was just a matter of brute force. The captain had protested initially, but once Miraso had kicked him in the throat, causing him to collapse to the ground with a red, bloated face, he became more agreeable to them taking command.

They locked themselves in, keeping one eye on the airlock for the Doctor, Dave and Anji. When they spotted Anji in the corridor outside the airlock, Miraso had gone outside to bring her in.

The human crew seemed amiable enough, and Fitz chatted to them while Miraso kept an eye on the command crew. Anji, for her part, paced up and down.

'We need to stay put,' insisted Fitz, noticing her unrest. 'The Doctor and this new Dave need to deal with Silver alone. We need to provide the escape route if anything goes wrong.'

'But that place is full of Silverati!' Anji said impatiently.

'Yes,' said Fitz. 'Silverati who will tear us apart on sight. You said yourself that this Dave looks just like one. And as for the Doctor... y'know, he's the Doctor, he can look after himself. They'll be safer without us, trust me on this.'

Anji nodded, as if taking it all in. She seemed resigned to staying where she was.

'Miraso,' said Anji innocently. 'Are there any guns here?'

Fitz put his head in his hands.

The Hypertunnel was opening up. The air rippled, a taste of ozone tainting the atmosphere. The wall with the Hypertunnel rippled, warping as the fabric of space was torn asunder. The straight lines and three dimensions of the physical world folded in on themselves, unseen colours and impossible shapes flexing into existence, pushing themselves out of the void. Contained with an aurora of violet-flecked light, the chaos writhed as the Hypertunnel calibrated itself. An image was beginning to form in the distance, a solid point within unthinkable distances. A small circle of landscape, far away but getting closer.

'It is time for us to leave,' said Silver, addressing his Silverati. 'Are you going to come out from your hiding place to see us off, Doctor, or are you going to cower behind that crate all day?'

The Doctor stood up, stepping forward to face Silver. The Silverati stood aside to let him pass, their black eyes impassive to his existence.

'I see more than others do, Doctor,' said Silver, tapping a finger against the rim of his red, artificial eye. 'Did you really think I wouldn't see you there? I can see so much, I know more about you from one glance than you could imagine.' He pointed to the Doctor's chest. 'I could see the cavity there the first time we met. Was it a heart that you lost, Doctor? Your vital signs certainly seem erratic. Whatever you may have been, Doctor, you're less than that now. No longer some magical alien presence, walking among men like a God. You are just one of them now, a fallen angel with your wings clipped. Give up before I break you entirely.' Silver extended his robot fist, clenching it. The colours of the Hypertunnel reflected in the polished metal, flickering along the curve of each finger. The fingertips ground against his palm, metal screeching against metal. 'You know you cannot stop me. I am too strong.'

To Silver's obvious surprise, the Doctor laughed, walking between the Silverati as if they were harmless statues. 'How vulgar of you, Silver, to think that we are defined by our physical

233

presence. How painfully literal, how pathetic. All the cybernetic attachments in the world won't elevate you beyond the level of a pitiful backworlds dictator. And if you think that it was my second heart that made me who I am, then you're an even bigger fool. I can lose a heart, or an arm or a leg, and I would still be capable of dealing with the likes of you. It's not biology that makes us who we are. It's character. Something in which you are sorely lacking.'

Silver shrugged. 'You may have something when you say I overrate physical prowess, Doctor. Let's see how far that overreliance on physical strength gets me, shall we?'

The Doctor rolled out of the way as a shot from the back of Silver's hand fired past him, obliterating the crate he had been hiding behind. Splinters flew across the room.

The Silverati near the Doctor scurried out of the way of the blast. Some ran straight up the wall, strong fingers tearing through metal and rock to give them handholds. They hung back, observing. The Silverati working on the Hypertunnel also paused, observing the action.

'Get back to your work!' bellowed Silver. 'I want that Hypertunnel operational.'

As soon as Silver's back was turned, Dave walked up to one of the Silverati guarding the navigation console and punched him hard in the jaw. The Kallisti injection the Doctor had administered to Dave had given him the strength of a Silverati, and the punch he threw was like a jackhammer, the impact reverberating all the way to his elbow.

The Silverati jerked back, the blow knocking him slightly off balance. But he stayed standing. He touched his mouth, then looked blankly at the metallic blood on his fingertips. Only then did he react to the assault.

Dave's eyes widened in panic as the Silverati went for his throat.

The Doctor ducked as a large robot arm swung a silver fist at his head. Silver's punch missed, and tore a hole in the wall behind the Doctor. Fragments of rock scattered across the floor, dust billowing. Ignoring his sudden sense of déjà vu, the Doctor threw himself to the side, hitting the ground with his shoulder and rolling on to one knee. Ignoring the aches in his legs and arms the Doctor pushed himself on to his feet. He needed to keep Silver occupied, to give Dave the time to do his work.

Silver pulled his arm out of the wall, rubble falling away from the crater his fist had left. He turned and began to advance on the Doctor. His red eye glowed fiercely. The Doctor paced backwards, ready for the next attempted blow. Only when his back bumped into something solid did the Doctor realise he was backed up against a wall. Luckily there was a pipe running up that wall, and with his hands on the pipe and his feet against the wall he began to climb. Silver's hand grabbed at thin air as the Doctor shimmied upwards.

'Very well, Doctor,' said Silver. 'Crawl out of reach if you wish. I'll just have to knock you off your perch like the easy target you are.'

The Doctor's eyes widened as Silver raised his fist, firing an explosive charge straight at him. The Doctor weaved out of the way, and the explosive detonated in the wall behind him, the explosion causing the Doctor to lose his grip on the pipe. In a cloud of smoke he fell, the blast throwing him over Silver's head to land ten feet away. His ankle nearly cracked as he landed on his feet, staggering back as Silver advanced on him once more. Silver unleashed a volley of punches and kicks, and it was all the Doctor could do to block and dodge each blow, his own limbs failing to match Silver's fluid combat. Every time the Doctor diverted a blow it was like physically pushing aside a speeding train. His forearm ached where he had knocked Silver's arm aside, his shin was bleeding from where he had swept aside a roundhouse kick and made contact with Silver's heel. The Doctor was a wreck, while Silver just kept coming. Desperately, the Doctor swung his fist at the human side of Silver's face, making contact with the jawline. The Doctor's knuckles cracked and he cried out, while Silver merely rocked back slightly on his heels.

'Not got anything smart to say for yourself now, Doctor?' spat Silver. A trickle of blood slid down from the corner of his mouth, but his energies were undimmed. Nothing the Doctor could do would stop him.

The Doctor was searching for a witty retort, when Silver's steel hand locked around his throat, lifting him up into the air. He wouldn't even get to have any memorable last words.

Dave had blown his own cover. Once one Silverati had attacked him, the others had soon joined in. One held his arms while another punched him repeatedly in the gut. Dave had the same enhanced strengths as they did, the strategic mind to keep his cool and think his way out of the situation. All the same, he wasn't sure how much of this relentless punishment he could take.

Something cracked, and Dave spat blood, straight into the face of his assailant. This only encouraged his attacker to increase the power of each blow.

Across the far side of the room, the Hypertunnel was solidifying, the image at its end coming closer and closer.

The image on the other side of the Hypertunnel began to coalesce. There was a city, an industrial landscape of vast concrete towers belching smoke into a sky darkened by pollution. Smelting pits licked the air with flame, armies of pistons pumping up and down through the rooftops of vast factory complexes.

'Look Doctor,' Silver sneered. 'A forgecity on the Imperial Throneworld, the great furnace that powers the machinery of galactic government, if my records are correct. I'm going to go there and spread my new Kallisti, until the entire government, including the Empress and all her royal kind, bow down to me. Then these furnace cities will build me a fleet of ships.' Silver produced a datapad from his belt, and flicked a switch. He waved it in the Doctor's face, numbers scrambling up the pad's small screen. 'Ships based on your ship, Doctor. I'll take the data your little friend gave me, and build a fleet of time ships.' Silver slid the datapad back into the pocket on his belt. 'Then there will be no limit to my power.'

The Doctor's eyes bulged, although whether that was because of what Silver was suggesting, or simply the vicelike grip around his throat cutting off the air to his brain, no one could tell.

'I am going to kill you, Doctor, and then I'm going to create a universe in my image. There will no longer be men or women, Endpointers or humans, or any other form of individuality. There will be only Silver, and those who follow him.'

The Doctor's bloodshot eyes began to flutter. A drop of blood rolled out of one nostril, down his cheek.

'I am strong, Doctor,' said Silver quietly, almost whispering into the Doctor's ear. 'You are weak. I am a killer, a conqueror, while you are about to die, defeated, alone, crushed.'

For reasons Dave couldn't quite understand, a dart had appeared in the forehead of the Silverati who was attacking him. That Silverati was looking over Dave's shoulder, and Dave used this as an ideal opportunity to kick him hard in the balls. As he went down, Dave kneed him in the face. The Silverati holding his arms then decided to drag him back, away from the man who had been pulping Dave's innards. This was fine by Dave, who used the momentum to push himself further back, causing both him and his captor to topple backwards. He landed on the Silverati with a crunch, and was free. Another Silverati ran at Dave, and he punched him in the face, following it up with a kick to the shins. By the time the next two came for him, Dave was in full swing, putting every byte of combat information programmed into him to use, stretching the capabilities of his enhanced body as far as they would go. He almost forgot his mission, so entranced was he by the rhythm and beauty of violence, the ecstasy of fighting and winning.

'Let him go,' said Anji. She aimed the gun at Silver, advancing across the space between them. The Doctor seemed on the verge of choking his last.

Silver turned, confused. When he saw Anji, he began to laugh. His hilarity echoed around the room, each peal of laughter folding in and repeating over the next, in a way that seemed to echo around Anji's skull.

In spite of Silver's dismissive reaction, Anji kept the gun level. 'I said let him go.' She nodded to the Silverati. 'And tell your freaks to stay back.'

'Dear me, and I thought we were friends,' said Silver, maintaining his grip on the Doctor's throat.

It was Anji's turn to laugh. 'You make a deal with me then try to zombify my entire race, then have me locked up while you try to conquer the universe. Funny friendship.'

'Anji,' said Silver firmly. 'You are holding a tranquilliser dart gun. That will have no effect on me, my body will be unaffected by the drug in those capsules. He extended his human hand. 'Now, you have a choice. I can either tear your head off with my free hand, or you can give me the gun and let me kill the Doctor here in peace.'

Anji looked at the dart gun sadly. 'I doubt it would even break the skin, would it?' she asked.

Silver shook his head slowly, almost mournfully. In his eyes victory gleamed, a certainty that his logic would prevail. He knew there was no way Anji could harm him. His certainty was absolute.

Anji held out the gun, limply holding it like an offering as she walked closer to Silver. He reached out to take it from her hand.

Dave pulled the piece of scribbled-on paper out of his pocket. The Doctor had written a series of co-ordinates there, and Dave rapidly typed them into the navigation console. The girl Anji seemed to be stalling Silver – it was her who had shot that dart into the Silverati, he presumed – but that wouldn't work for long.

One of the Silverati tried to push himself up from where he lay. Dave kicked him hard in the face, then resumed entering the co-ordinates.

* * *

As Silver was about to take the gun out of Anji's hand, she quickly flicked it up. There was only a few inches between them, and Anji could almost taste his breath on her. As if in slow motion, she lifted the gun away from Silver's grasping hand, and pointed it straight at his human eye. She squeezed the trigger.

Silver's scream nearly deafened Anji. Silver was far more than human, but even he didn't have armour-plated retinas. The high-pressure dart, fired at nearly point blank range, went straight into the soft material of his eye, lodging there. Silver lashed out in agony, and Anji was dashed across the room. Instinctively Silver let go of the Doctor so he could clutch his face with both hands.

The Doctor landed on his knees, taking in a ragged breath. He slid his hand into his coat pocket, and it closed around the microblade. As Silver flailed around, half blind, his robot arm was swinging back and forth. On one pass the Doctor jammed the microblade into the elbow joint, and the leads within exploded with a shower of sparks. The arm fell limply by his side, servos cut and power to his forearm gone. He wouldn't be firing that in a hurry. With one fluid motion the Doctor seized the datapad from where Silver had re-attached it to his belt.

The Doctor collapsed to the floor, clutching the precious secrets of his TARDIS to his chest. His head swam as he tried to breathe properly. He bowed down, eyes closed, trying to pull himself together. He didn't seem to be paying attention to anything.

Silver staggered back, one hand pressed over his bleeding eye. The Hypertunnel had stabilised. The day could still be his. Any injury could be repaired, in time.

'Silverati!' he bellowed. 'All of you, through the tunnel. Now.'

Silver's single, artificial eye looked at the Doctor, lying on the floor, nearly broken. He had, of course, felt the Doctor snatching the datapad. Even with his mind overloaded with pain, his other senses still functioned, monitoring any alteration to his environment. Silver wasn't leaving without that pad.

One arm hanging slack and useless, Silver stepped closer to the

Doctor, and kicked him brutally in the stomach. The Doctor yelled in pain as he was thrown into the air by the force of Silver's blow, and landed on his back, the datapad clutched limply to his chest. Silver leaned over, plucking the pad out of the Doctor's grip with his human hand.

Silver looked around him, his last view of the planet Endpoint, his home for so long. All his Silverati had gone through the tunnel, with the exception of one who was walking towards him with a furious expression.

Time slowed to a near-halt, Silver's brain working way beyond the speed of human thought. He recognised the remaining Silverati; it was the human he had cloned for Anji. The Doctor must have personally converted him. Across the room, Anji was stirring. Silver stood for a second, torn between his desire to kill the Doctor, and the knowledge that in his injured state even one Silverati and a human girl would have a good chance of doing him harm.

Vowing to return at the head of an army, Silver turned and jumped headfirst into the Hypertunnel, leaving his home and his enemies behind.

Dave watched Silver disappear into the Hypertunnel, the air rippling on impact. He looked down at the Doctor, who seemed on the verge of death, battered and bloodied.

One of the Doctor's eyes flicked open, searching the room eagerly. It rested on Dave.

'Has he gone?' asked the Doctor chirpily. Dave nodded.

'Good!' said the Doctor, jumping to his feet as if his fight with Silver had barely left him with a scratch. Only a wince of pain gave away the agony he was trying to conceal. 'Help Anji up,' he said, holding a hand to his bruised ribs. 'We haven't got much time.'

There was dislocation – Silver floated through the void, briefly without substance or place. His consciousness stretched, his atoms spiralling through the emptiness. It felt like death, or something very similar. Then Silver reached the end of the

Hypertunnel, and his existential moment ended, consciousness snapping back into his physical form as he tumbled out of the other end, rolling on the dusty ground.

It took a few moments for his enhanced senses to recalibrate themselves, and he was left lying face down in the dirt. That was the problem with sensitivity – it was all too easy for senses to be overloaded with unfamiliar information. Typically, it was Silver's basic, human senses that returned to him first. A chill on his skin. The taste of ash in his mouth. Although there were logical reasons for these sensations – the city's furnaces doubtless spewed out tons of ash, which probably blocked out the sun, causing the cold atmosphere – together they had the aura of premonition about them.

Silver's senses returned to him, his internal systems scanning the area around him. His robotic arm – damaged at the elbow where the Doctor's microblade had sliced through cables and circuitry – hung useless at his side, so Silver had to push himself to his feet with only his human arm to steady himself. He rose to find his Silverati around him, waiting for instructions, their metallic skins reflecting the pure moonlight.

He looked beyond the Silverati, at the city. It wasn't the hectic industrial city he had seen through the Hypertunnel before, with its pistons and furnaces. It was a silent city of ruined buildings, gutted and crumbling structures piercing the star-strewn sky. Around him was nothing but a desolate grey wasteland. No life, only ruins. His memory instantly compared his surroundings to all his records. He wasn't on the Throneworld at all, but on A2756, a planet without any surviving civilisation. A graveyard of a planet, without usable resources of any kind, sapped of energy and life.

Silver turned to the Hypertunnel, but it was too late. It was receding into itself, and although he grasped at the room behind it, his hand simply went through the tunnel's entrance as if it were a hologram.

'Come back here, Doctor,' he screamed into the Hypertunnel. 'Come back and fight like a man!'

* * *

'Tsk,' said the Doctor, leaning his aching body against a bank of controls as he slid the power gauge down to 'OFF'. The Hypertunnel receded, Silver's furious image reduced to a shadow, until there was nothing there but a wall.

'Dave,' said the Doctor. 'Do you have that piece of paper I gave you?'

Dave nodded, lifting up the note.

'Tear it up,' said the Doctor. 'Then burn it.' He walked over to the navigation controls, and pressed the reset button. 'We don't want anyone getting Silver back, do we?'

Anji staggered over. She had bruised her head slightly when Silver threw her.

'Where did you send him, anyway?' she asked.

'A little place I spotted on his starcharts, some way away from his desired destination,' said the Doctor smugly. He winced as he tried to smile, and rubbed his throat ruefully. 'A desolate rock with no life for him to conquer, dominate or convert. I hope he likes it there.'

'But what about the data from the TARDIS?' asked Anji. 'Won't he be able to build some kind of ship to get him off that world?'

'A ship?' said the Doctor, shrugging. 'Perhaps. I should imagine he has the skill to build a rudimentary spacecraft, providing he can find the resources on his new home. But a time ship? Not without this.' He held up a sliver of circuitry. 'The memory wafer from his datapad. All the data you collected from the TARDIS. Without this, he might as well be holding a pocket calculator. I slipped it out of the datapad when I was ostensibly dying on the floor there. I knew Silver wouldn't leave without the data, so I let him think he had what he wanted.' The Doctor spun the memory wafer between his fingers, staring at it as if he could see the secrets hidden within. 'I think I'll look after this,' he said, sliding the wafer into his top pocket.

There was a moment's silence, except for a slight crackle from some of the machinery. The room seemed much smaller without Silver there, and they could all feel the echo of his presence.

'Come on,' said Anji quietly. 'Let's get out of this place.'

* * *

Time passed, and the impact of events began to sink in. Endpoint had changed immeasurably in a short period of time. The environment had altered, humans and Endpointers had made contact, Silver was gone. Everything had changed, and change brought questions.

The Doctor didn't have answers, at least not to anything other than technical and scientific queries, and soon faded into the background. It was clear to Fitz and Anji that he would have preferred just to leave there and then, but he had loose ends to try to tie up first. The Doctor wasn't inclined to let either Stephens's or Silver's inhuman projects be revived. The co-ordinates of Silver's new home were deleted from all databanks, in case anyone should try to rescue him. The altered Kallisti that created the Silverati had been destroyed, and to replace it the Doctor created a benign, purely organic Kallisti serum that provided the physiological benefits without turning the recipient into one of Silver's 'children'.

One mystery remained. The two Silverati wounded when the Doctor, Fitz and Anji escaped from captivity had not recovered in time to follow their brethren through the Hypertunnel. A search of the Bunker revealed no sign of them, and security cameras showed them exiting via the airlock. Opinion was divided as to whether Silverati would be able to survive the pressure and absence of oxygen at that level.

When told of these two Silverati by Powlin, Anji imagined them down there, walking on the ocean floor, consumed by the darkness. If they lived, who could tell how long their lives would be? They could be walking the sea bed forever, the ice cold water their only companion in the dark.

When the Doctor met Miraso on the roof of the Silver Palace, there were fires burning in the distance, thick smoke hanging in the heat-hazed air, no wind to blow it away.

'It all seems to be falling apart,' said Miraso. 'There are riots breaking out in some of the poorer sections of the city. I keep getting calls from across Endpoint, members of Silver's satellite organisations who want their independence. I've put all of Silver's old guards at the disposal of Powlin and the militia, and they're keeping on top of it, but… it all seems different now. What we had is gone.'

'That's true,' said the Doctor, squinting in the midday sun. 'Part of what Endpoint was about – the struggles against a hostile environment, order imposed through tyranny in a cruel world – that's gone. And for a while there'll be chaos, and disorder, and other teething problems. But that Endpoint spirit, that spirit of Hope and Persistence and all those other places where Endpointers have survived against all the odds, that spirit will see you through, help you survive.'

Miraso smiled thinly. 'And what then?'

'Then… well, that's up to you,' said the Doctor. 'You have immense opportunities to make up for what you have lost. Whereas before you had a fragile order, now you have the chance to build a lasting peace, not the kind of stability necessary just to preserve life, but the kind of environment where people can co-operate, and live safely and happily. This could become a very special place. You have the human science at your disposal. And then there's the humans themselves, you need to decide whether to revive the rest of them, or leave them to their sleep. Then there's the Hypertunnel, of course.'

'That's a decision for another day,' said Miraso. 'To go out into the universe, or build a better world on our own.'

'It's a big decision,' said the Doctor. 'Which only proves my point – it's not the options available that make you who you are. It's the quality of the decision you make.'

'So what you're saying is, it's not what you've got, it's what you do with it?' said Miraso.

'Well, something like that,' said the Doctor. 'We all have our potentials, our opportunities, our limitations and our failings. It's who we are and what we choose to do that matters in the end.'

'You know,' said Miraso, looking out across the city, 'I think you might be right.'

'I very well may be,' said the Doctor, as if he'd surprised

himself. As he followed Miraso's gaze, drinking in the scene, he unconsciously rubbed his chest, following a line with his finger.

And out across the rooftops, a wind began to rise, and these gusts of wind began to blow the smoke away, dispersing it far out to sea.

They met for the last time on the Pier, as the sun went down over Hope. The Doctor and Fitz were already in the TARDIS, waiting to leave. Hasty goodbyes had been said to Miraso, Powlin and the others, all of whom had been frankly far too busy to pay any attention. There was only one more farewell to go.

Anji sat on the railing, watching the red sky reflected in the sea, and worried that she would be stood up. It was a stupid feeling, she knew – this wasn't a date. A date signified a potential beginning, while she was waiting for an ending.

When he arrived, the only thing she could think of was that he was perfect, just how she imagined he would be. But that would have been an inappropriate thing to say, so she said the second thing to come into her head instead.

'Your skin's turning back to normal,' Anji told Dave II awkwardly.

Whereas the original Dave would have attempted some kind of witty comeback, this one just frowned at her. He leaned against the railing, and Anji was struck by how different he was from her Dave, his unselfconscious and confident manner, his tendency to lapse into thoughtful pauses. Not like her Dave at all.

This wasn't her Dave. This was a new Dave.

'You wanted to see me,' Dave II said eventually. It was a statement, and he didn't seem reluctant to be there, but neither did he seem affected by her presence. He just seemed curious as to why he was there, what she wanted him for.

'I'm leaving today,' said Anji, choosing her words carefully. 'And I wanted to speak to you before I left. I wanted to tell you a few things about Dave Young, who you might call Dave I. You're a clone of that Dave, and I wanted you to know why I wanted there to be another Dave out there.'

245

And so Anji told the new Dave about the old Dave. She talked about getting together, and occasionally breaking up, and how she had loved Dave even when he had constantly frustrated her, about their life together, and finally about how Dave had died, leaving her alone and with his own life cut short far too soon. Throughout everything she said, Dave II listened, not interrupting but fascinated by what she said.

'Dave deserved a second chance,' she concluded. 'And so here you are. A second Dave. A second chance.'

'Anji,' said Dave, and for a second it was like her Dave talking to her, the same insistent tone. Then the moment passed. 'I'm not him. I won't be able to live the life he would have lived.'

'I know that,' said Anji. 'Just live the life you want to have. And let it be a long one. That's all I want, is to give you a chance to live.'

Dave smiled. 'That's exactly what you've done. You've given me life.' He seemed thoughtful for a second. 'It's strange, you must be the nearest thing I have to a mo–'

'Woah!' said Anji, putting a finger to his lips to stop him. 'Don't say anything else, or you'll be leaving me with deep, deep psychological issues. I want us to part as friends, and if you get to the end of that sentence that might not be possible.'

'Anji,' said Dave after she'd taken her finger away. 'I was joking.' He grinned briefly at her obvious discomfort, and she couldn't help but smile back at him. There was something there, certainly, some essential Dave-ness. Her Dave, Dave I, would have made a sick little joke like that, she just knew it. This Dave wasn't the same man, but oddly Anji was certain that he had many of the same qualities, that this Dave would be kind, and gentle, and giving, just as her Dave had been. The temptation to stick around, to find out whether her instincts were correct, was strong.

'I'm going to go now,' said Anji quickly, words tripping out of her mouth. 'I need to leave before things get complicated.'

Dave nodded slowly. 'Goodbye then, Anji. It has been a pleasure to know you for this short time.' It was a strangely formal thing to say, but Anji knew he meant it.

She stood on tiptoe, and kissed his cheek. For a second she stood there, her hands on his shoulders, cheek to cheek. And for that second she was somewhere else entirely, on a warm London day with a different Dave, long long ago.

Then the moment ended, and she stepped away.

'Goodbye Dave,' she said, backing away towards the TARDIS. He stood there watching her go, his arm lifted in a half-wave.

As she walked into the TARDIS, leaving Dave behind, Anji felt giddy. Tears pricked at her eyes, but she didn't feel heavy with sadness. She felt light, released, slightly delirious. Part of her life with Dave was finally, irrevocably over, and she was leaving the emotional baggage of that time behind her. But, although those were good times she was leaving behind, Anji felt the lightness of letting them go, the giddy sensation of moving on.

The TARDIS doors closed behind her. Goodbye Dave, thought Anji, certain that she would never think those words again.

Epilogue
Tonight We Fly

They had retreated into the cinema as the evening had become increasingly muggy – a typical summer's day in the heart of London, with the pollution curdling the air until it felt like you were breathing lead soup. The air-conditioned cinema had been a respite from the heat and the bad air, the temperature and the pollen count. By the time they came out it was dark, and pleasantly cool. Crowds flooded the streets, wandering happily between pubs and clubs and other places of entertainment.

'So, what did you think?' asked Anji as they walked arm in arm down the Charing Cross Road, weaving around the tramps and the tourists without even noticing them.

'Well,' said Dave, thoughtfully. 'I think they could have made a better film from that premise.'

Anji was suspicious of this sudden threat of mature insight – she had watched the film with the sinking suspicion that Dave was hating every moment of it.

'In what way?' she asked.

'W-e-ll,' said Dave, stretching the vowel. Now Anji knew something was up, this was too dramatic a pause to be normal. 'For a start, the "Whisperer" of the title should have been something more than a guy who talks to horses.'

'Like what?' asked Anji.

'Like the name of the spaceship,' said Dave, smirking. He slid his arm out from hers, backing away as she threatened to hit him. 'A spaceship carrying a cargo of raptors!'

He dodged as she took a swing at him.

'And then the raptors could free themselves, and start rampaging around the ship, eating the crew of the Hors-'

Anji cut him off, grabbing him around the waist and demanding that he stop. He relented, and they both collapsed into giggles, leaning on each other as they walked up the street.

'Some day,' said Anji, squeezing Dave's arm affectionately. 'I'm going to drag you out of that Sci-Fi world of yours and into the real world, where the rest of us live.'

'Some day, maybe,' said Dave, smiling back at her. 'But not in this lifetime.'

Acknowledgements

Firstly, chunky but well-proportioned thanks go to all the people who read through the book, commented, suggested, and advised, not to mention all those fellow authors who provided manuscripts of their own books, tipped me off on continuity points and otherwise contributed to the process. These two categories heavily overlap, so I've lumped them all in together, authors and readers alike. In no particular order, they are: Susan Clapham (hello Mum!), Lance Parkin, Lawrence Miles, Jonathan Morris, Sarah Archibald, Jim Smith, Lloyd Rose, Paul Ebbs, Jonathan de Burgh Miller, Paul Magrs, Dave Whittam, Steve Emmerson, Simon Bucher-Jones, Eddie Robson and Kelly Hale.

Huge thanks to Allan Bednar for his fantastic work on making Silver seem more real than my feeble words can manage.

Thanks to all my colleagues at the office for allowing me time off to work on the book, and for tolerating the side effects of too many late nights writing.

Finally, writing a book like this involves a lot of sitting around, drinking coffee, thinking and generally doing things that don't actually look a lot like work. It takes a very special person to understand that these periods of seemingly lazy and work-shy behaviour are a part of the writing process, and that a writer's free time can be limited even when he doesn't seem to be doing very much. Davina Malcolm is just that kind of special person, and has always been there for me, even when writing this book kept me from being there for her. For that patience and kindness, I am endlessly grateful.

About the Author

Mark Clapham was born in the dark days of the nineteen-seventies in Harrogate, North Yorkshire, where he had a relatively uneventful childhood. Upon coming of age he showed his gratitude to the home town that nurtured him by moving straight to London, where he studied East European history for longer than anyone should rightfully think about such things.

Having singularly failed to get into publishing on his own merits, he was recruited by Lance Parkin to write the dull bits of the Virgin 'New Adventures' novel *Beige Planet Mars*. This led to Simon Bucher-Jones bringing him in to co-write the highly popular *Doctor Who* novel *The Taking of Planet 5*. Having built a career on nepotism, he continued the tradition by recruiting talented newcomer Jon de Burgh Miller to co-write *Twilight of the Gods*, a 'New Adventures' novel that succeeded in killing that much loved and long running range stone dead. Since then he has written for the *Official Xena: Warrior Princess Magazine*, contributed the second part of a western story to the BBC's *Short Trips and Side Steps Doctor Who* short story collection, and co-written an episode guide to hit TV show *Ally McBeal*.

He lives in Highgate, London, and works for a major regulatory body. This is his first solo novel.